PROTECT MY HEART

CHERRY
BLOSSOM
ROMANCE

JUDY CORRY

Also By Judy Corry

Eden Falls Academy Series:

The Charade (Ava and Carter)

The Facade (Cambrielle and Mack)

The Ruse — (Elyse and Asher)

The Confidant — (Scarlett and Hunter)

The Confession — (Kiara and Nash)

Ridgewater High Series:

When We Began (Cassie and Liam)

Meet Me There (Ashlyn and Luke)

Don't Forget Me (Eliana and Jess)

It Was Always You (Lexi and Noah)

My Second Chance (Juliette and Easton)

My Mistletoe Mix-Up (Raven and Logan)

Forever Yours (Alyssa and Jace)

Standalone YA

Protect My Heart (Emma and Arie)

Kissing The Boy Next Door (Lauren and Wes)

Rich and Famous Series:

Assisting My Brother's Best Friend (Kate and Drew)

Hollywood and Ivy (Ivy and Justin)

Her Football Star Ex (Emerson and Vincent)

Friend Zone to End Zone (Arianna and Cole)

Stolen Kisses from a Rock Star (Maya and Landon)

For my husband, Jared.
You are the reason
I can write love stories in the first place.

PLAYLIST

"Crush" - Mandy Moore
"Send Me A Song" - Celtic Woman
"Last First Kiss" - One Direction
"Measure Of A Man" - Clay Aiken
"I Still" - Backstreet Boys
"Gotta Be You" - One Direction

1

EMMA

TODAY MARKED day nine of my boy-cleanse. That's right—
I'd made it more than a week without drooling over any of the
hot guys at school. I should have won an award for having such
amazing self-control, considering cute guys had once been my
biggest weakness—addiction, really.

After my horrible summer, I had to come up with a plan.
My first step was to wean myself off all thoughts of boys and
dating them. Where daydreaming about guys during German
class used to be my favorite pastime, it was now strictly off-
limits, even if those foreign guys in the textbook did look like
male models. Nope, no big blue eyes or knee-weakening smile
would enchant me this school year. And as for getting butterflies in my stomach, they were definitely not a good sign—
merely a warning that my defenses were low and that I needed
to run in the opposite direction.

My best friend, Maya, thought my boy-cleanse was stupid,
but that's only because she'd never caught her boyfriend
making out with the girl he'd always said was just his *good
friend*. I should have known things were too good to be true.

Popular guys like Nick Bergstrom didn't go for regular choir nerds like me.

I'd thought since Nick graduated last year, I wouldn't have to see him again. But it appeared that even college freshmen needed food every once in a while. That was why I was ducking down behind the chest freezer in Lana's Supermarket on a Friday afternoon, peeking over the top as I waited for Nick to push his cart down another aisle.

I watched him carefully as he moved farther from my hiding place, hoping the whole stack of cereal boxes would land on his head. When Nick finally turned down the chip aisle, I dashed toward the bakery to grab a loaf of French bread, wishing for the thousandth time that I didn't have to run errands for my mom in order to use her car. I mean, shouldn't being the youngest child have some perks? But no, not with my parents anyway.

I was dropping the bread in my cart when I caught sight of a guy walking toward me. He was probably a year or two older and tall, with hair so dark it was almost black and arms that were sculpted to perfection. This guy wasn't just cute. He had "World's Most Beautiful Man" written all over him. Seriously, he put poor Hans from my German textbook to shame.

I straightened as he sauntered closer, and I finally came to my senses when he smiled at me. *Be cool,* I thought as I smiled back. He pulled a bag of whole-wheat English muffins off the shelf and studied the ingredient list.

Realizing I was dangerously close to breaking my nine-day streak of not ogling guys, I maneuvered around him and shuffled out of the bakery, whispering my mantra: *boy-cleanse, boy-cleanse, boy-cleanse.* With a safe distance between us, I peeked back for one last glimpse. I must have stared at his broad shoulders a moment too long, because my cart collided with something. I snapped out of my trance and watched in horror as bagels and muffins toppled to the ground, landing in a heap.

For one tempting moment, I considered leaving the mess and bolting. But my conscience kicked in at the last minute, and I scrambled to pick up the mess, hoping the guy wouldn't notice...somehow. I had just finished stuffing a few boxes of poppy-seed muffins on the shelf when I turned around to find the gorgeous stranger crouched down with five bags of blueberry bagels in his arms.

You have to be kidding me! My face burned hotter than a curling iron.

"Looks like the bagels decided to attack you today." He chuckled as he placed them on the bakery cart.

"Yeah, they just jumped out at me. I think they wanted to scare me or something." I laughed uncomfortably, wishing I could turn invisible. I should have run from the mess when I had the chance.

"Usually it's the paper towels that come at me, but I'll watch out for the baked goods from now on." He winked and bent over to pick up the last box of muffins. He was both funny *and* cute—a deadly combination. Thankfully, the butterflies in my stomach were sounding the alarm to retreat. I needed to get away before I did something stupid like ask for his number—or ask whether he'd marry me. I never dared do things like that normally, but in my weakened state I could already feel my crazy side coming out.

Before I lost my inhibitions, I simply said, "Thanks for your help..." and waited for him to give me his name.

"Arie." He cleared his throat and held his hand out. "My name is Arie."

Ar-ee. Ar-ee drives a Ferrari. The rhyme zipped through my head out of habit. I shook his outstretched hand, noticing his firm handshake. "Nice to meet you, Arie. I'm Emma." I hoped my palm wasn't noticeably sweaty.

He nodded, let my hand drop, and stuffed his hand in his pockets. "I just have to ask..." He squinted and tilted his head to the side, a half smile on his lips. "Were you hiding from someone earlier? I'm new in town and need to know if there are certain people I should avoid."

I cringed. "You saw that?"

He nodded.

How much more embarrassing could this afternoon get? Maybe I should run into the paper-towel display and let it bury me.

"I saw my ex-boyfriend and panicked." I shrugged.

"Oh." Arie nodded, then lowered his voice. "I'm guessing it wasn't a better-off-as-friends thing, then?"

"Not quite. It's hard to stay friends after being cheated on." Why was I telling him all this?

He looked over my shoulder, pointed a finger, and whispered, "Is that him?"

"What? Where?" I snapped my head around. When I didn't spot Nick anywhere close, I glanced back at Arie, only to find him chuckling.

That was just what a super hot guy would do—make a joke at someone else's expense. Nick had done that, too. I may have thought this guy, Arie, was good-looking at first glance, but now I had come to my senses. I could totally tell he must've had plastic surgery or something. His face was a little too perfect. And those muscles...he must spend half the day at the gym to get them that way—just big enough to seduce unassuming girls but not too beefy. Some guys were so in love with themselves.

I huffed and gripped my cart full of groceries. "Good one," I said. "But just so you know, it wasn't because of my ex that I lost control of my cart. It was purely accidental." I squared my shoulders, trying to appear unfazed—difficult considering I was having one of those hot flashes my mom always complained about. "Anyway, I better get going. My ice cream is melting." I actually couldn't even remember whether I'd picked up the ice cream yet, but I needed to get out of there before I did something else stupid.

"It was nice to meet you, Emma." He smiled. "I hope we'll run into each other again sometime." His eyes twinkled like he had some secret delight.

I nodded and angled toward the produce section. "I'll try to keep my cart under control next time."

Arie grinned. It would be a shame if I *accidentally* ran over his foot as I left.

2

ARIE

"HEY, rookie. How's your first day on the job?" The voice of my new supervisor, Jason, boomed through my phone's earpiece. I sat in my truck and waited for my new assignment, Emma Howard, to finish putting her groceries in the trunk of her silver Toyota Camry.

"This internship will be more entertaining than I thought. Are supermarket accidents a regular occurrence for her?"

"Not usually." Jason laughed.

"What about mood swings? You guys told me she's an easy-going girl, but she seemed like she couldn't make up her mind whether to be nice to me or annoyed."

"Well," Jason said. "From what we've observed from a distance, she seemed fine. But we're not the ones right there up close."

"Looks like I get to be the one to discover the answer to my question, then," I mumbled into my phone as I watched Emma put her grocery cart away. I hadn't figured teenage girls out when I was in high school; why had I expected it would be easier a few years later?

Once Emma had backed out of her parking spot, I put my truck in gear. "She's on the move again," I said. "I'll check in soon."

"Let me know if you need anything," Jason said. "And try not to attract too many high school girls with that baby face of yours. Emma is our focus and the only one we need you to befriend."

"That shouldn't be an issue," I said. That's the last thing I needed—hormonal girls trying to distract me from doing my job. If I kept to the shadows this weekend, I could avoid any attention until I officially started school on Monday.

It was hard to imagine one girl would need this much surveillance. She was harmless. I almost felt bad, deceiving her the way I had.

But that was the nature of my work.

Secrecy was everything.

Being an undercover bodyguard for a teenage girl definitely wasn't my dream job, but it would look good on my résumé. And I needed all the experience I could get if I wanted a shot at the Secret Service someday. My being here had been carefully orchestrated in preparation for the expected danger. If someone found out who I really was, it could ruin years of planning...and a lot of document forging to get me into the school in the first place. Not even the principal or teachers could know I was undercover. There could be absolutely no slip-ups.

I followed Emma back to her house and parked across the street at one of the houses Jason and Sophie owned. The night agent, Bruce, had just moved in a couple of months ago, which made it easy for him to keep an eye on her place all night.

Emma got out of her car, popped the trunk, and grabbed several grocery bags before walking into the two-story brick house. The homes here in Utah were a lot newer than the ones in my neighborhood back in Cortland, New York.

From what I'd been told, her house seemed like a calm and loving place. She lived there with two happily married parents. Her dad owned his CPA firm, and her mom was a homemaker who volunteered for a lot of community things. Her older brother and sister were out of the house, leading productive lives. Yep, everyone and everything in her life seemed to be perfect.

Just like everything in mine had *seemed* normal from the outside. But just like my family, hers had dangerous secrets of their own. And unlike her, I'd been able to get away from mine.

Even if I was about to pretend to be in high school again, I'd take it over the pitying looks of the well-meaning citizens of Cortland. Anything would be better than staying in a town where my dad was still considered the local hero.

3

EMMA

I TEXTED MAYA AND KATHRYN: **Running late. Still cleaning the office. Be there in ten min.**

It was Saturday night, and I was stuck at work a lot later than usual. My mom had taken me shopping in St. George all day, so I hadn't had a chance to clean the office until six. That would be fine normally, since my neighbor really didn't care what time I cleaned his office building on Saturdays, but today I wanted to hurry. Landon's beginning-of-the-school-year bash was pretty much the only time the whole senior class would hang out. Everybody would be there, since Landon was the student-body president and everyone's friend.

I rushed through my dusting and vacuuming as fast as I could so my friends wouldn't leave without me.

My phone beeped.

Maya: **Hurry up before Kathryn loses her nerve to talk to Conner tonight.**

A second later, my phone dinged, announcing another message sent to our group.

Kathryn: **Feel free to take your time. I'll talk to him next week instead.**

I laughed and shook my head as I started grabbing the sacks from the trash bins. Kathryn would take any way out she could. She'd been crushing on Conner for months and had still barely said more than two words to him. Maya was right—we needed to get to that party fast.

I locked the building up. Fifteen minutes later, Maya, Kathryn, and I stood on Landon's front porch, listening to the Chainsmokers blasting from his backyard. As usual, my two best friends were already arguing about Landon's taste in music. They were yin and yang, while I was stuck in the middle, ever the referee.

But the funny thing was, they were dressed almost exactly alike—skinny jeans and black tops.

We waited at the door for a few more minutes before realizing we should probably just go through the gate at the side of the house.

As we were stepping off the porch, Maya grabbed my arm and pointed toward the sidewalk.

"Look! It's Mr. Lund," she squealed.

"What? He's at Landon's party?" I squinted into the fading light.

Mr. Lund was the new psychology teacher this year. He was fresh out of college, and Maya seemed all too aware that he was only five years older than us.

"Of course he's not at the party. He's walking down the sidewalk. Maybe he lives nearby." Maya sounded way too excited that her teacher might live in her neighborhood. She ran a hand through her short brown hair and said, "I need to talk to him for a minute...about an assignment he gave us."

"Go ahead." I nodded in his direction, not wanting to be an

accomplice to her flirting with a teacher. "Kathryn and I will wait here."

"Yeah, go ahead," Kathryn agreed.

Maya turned to us. "Come on, he has another guy with him who's really cute." She looked at me, pleading with her eyes. "Pretty please."

Kathryn and I glanced at each other. "Fine," I said. "Let the humiliation begin."

"Thanks," Maya said as she hurried us toward the two men.

The girls at school referred to Mr. Lund by his first name, Shane, as they gossiped about him in the girl's locker room before PE. I didn't have any classes with him, so I'd never had the chance to notice whether his eyes were turquoise green or not. Maya had, of course, confirmed that his eyes were the dreamiest color of green she'd ever seen and he smelled even better than he looked. All I noticed was that Mr. Lund was tall, with light hair, and wore clothes that looked way too expensive for his teacher's salary.

"Hi, Mr. Lund!" Maya waved as we came to stand on the grass at the edge of the sidewalk. "Coming to crash the party?"

"Sadly, I wasn't invited." He smiled. With him in jeans and a T-shirt, I could understand how Maya would have a hard time picturing him as just a teacher. He looked like a regular guy. "We're actually headed to a barbecue down the street."

"Darn it." She twisted a strand of hair around her finger as she spoke. "So do you live around here? I haven't seen you in the neighborhood before."

"Nah, Damian and I share an apartment closer to the school." He gestured to his friend, who was a really big guy. He wasn't quite as tall as Mr. Lund, but he looked like he spent a lot of time either at the gym or pumping up on steroids, or both. I couldn't help but wonder whether his muscles were compensation for his receding hairline. When my eyes met his, I quickly directed my attention back to Mr. Lund. He was much less intimidating.

"I don't think I've met your friends yet." Mr. Lund's eyes wandered to Kathryn and me.

"This is Emma." Maya gestured. "And this is Kathryn."

Mr. Lund held out his hand.

"It's nice to meet you officially," I said, shaking his hand. "Maya's told me how awesome psychology is this year. I wish I had room in my schedule to take your class, with how fascinating she makes it sound."

"I'm happy to hear that." He smiled. "You never really know how your first year is gonna go."

"From what I've heard around school, you've definitely made an impact." *As in, all the senior girls have a crush on you.*

I realized that the longer I stood there, the more it would look like I was a part of his fan club as well.

But before I could pull Maya away, Damian asked, "How long have you girls lived in Maplebridge? It seems like a great place."

"I've lived here since I was five," Maya replied with a smile on her full lips.

"My family's been here since before I was born," Kathryn said.

"I'm a native as well," I offered.

Damian's eyes narrowed as he looked me up and down, seeming to commit my tall, slender frame to memory. Creepy. Maya always joked that I had a somewhat exotic look, with my olive skin, dark hair, and light-blue eyes, but the way he studied me made me think we'd talked to them a little too long. This Damian guy had to think we were totally hitting on them. Maya obviously was, but I was not in the market for a man, especially not a creepy older guy with biceps bigger than my thighs.

"Anyway," I said, tugging on Maya and Kathryn's arms. "We have a party to get to. It was nice to meet you, Mr. Lund. You too, Damian."

The two men continued on to their destination, walking past a black truck that was pulling against the curb. I did a double take and gasped. *Was that Arie, the guy from the store? Could he be coming to Landon's party?*

Then I shook the thought away. Arie was probably going to the same barbecue as Mr. Lund and his friend. Wouldn't that be a coincidence if they all knew each other? Maya's crush and my new...my new *nothing*; I was on a boy-cleanse, after all. Arie was simply the guy I'd embarrassed myself in front of yesterday.

Yeah, good thing he was going to the barbecue and not the party. It would be so mortifying if everyone found out about my grocery-store incident.

———

"I'm glad you guys could make it," Landon greeted us when we finally found our way into his backyard. He and Maya had been neighbors since kindergarten, so we'd spent plenty of time playing at his house while growing up.

Landon's knucklehead friends, Derek and Kalon, soon joined us. While Landon was super chill, his buddies were cocky and thought every girl was in love with them, which—though I hated to admit it—was kind of true.

Derek sidled up to Maya and draped his arm around her shoulder. "How did you like watching me score the final touchdown in the game last night?" he asked, his wavy brown hair falling across his forehead.

"What? You were there?" Maya rolled her eyes and shoved him away. "I didn't even notice."

Derek took a drink from his cup, then said, "Ha-ha, very funny. I know you couldn't keep your eyes off me." He winked at her and gave her what I'm sure he thought was a charming smile.

"Oh yeah," she said as if remembering something. "You were the one who fumbled the ball three times. How could I forget that?"

"Burn!" Kalon slapped Derek on the back.

Maya never could resist pushing Derek's buttons. I figured he needed a little humbling, though, to keep his head small enough to fit inside his helmet.

"Okay, guys, that's enough," Landon interrupted. "Go try using your special charm on some other girls. Maya, Kathryn, and Emma are way too cool for you."

The guys began to walk away when Maya stopped them. "Hey, wait—that reminded me of something."

They stopped, probably hoping she'd suddenly become bewitched by their "special charm," as Landon had put it.

"My family is planning a date auction later this month, actually in just a couple weeks, and I'm supposed to help find volunteers to be auctioned off."

"You have our attention." Derek cocked an eyebrow.

"It's for my nephew, Braden," Maya continued. "He has to have open-heart surgery next month, so we're putting on the event to raise money to help my sister and her husband pay for the medical expenses."

"And it's going to be awesome!" I added. Maya had come up with the idea last week, and I'd been helping her and her mom with the plans since then.

"Do you guys wanna participate?" Maya tucked her hair behind her ears, looking at them as sweetly as she could...which was a feat in itself since she couldn't stand them most of the time.

"Like, be auctioned off?" Kalon asked.

We all nodded.

"I'm sure just having you guys up for bid would raise a ton of money," I added for good measure. I might as well cater to their egos while I was at it.

Derek shrugged and glanced at his buddies. "It would be fun to see the ladies fighting over me." He flexed his biceps as he spoke. "I'm in!"

"Count me in, too!" Kalon chimed, folding his arms across his broad chest. "It'll be fun to destroy Derek in this contest."

"Guys! This is *not* a contest," Maya said.

"Whatever! It's totally a contest." Derek nudged Kalon, a smug look on his face. "And I'm gonna win."

"I'm sure you will." Maya sighed. "I'll be handing out fliers at school on Monday, so you'll get all the details then."

"Sounds great!" Derek rubbed his hands. "In fact, I'll help you out right now by spreading the news that any girl can have the chance for a date with me. All it takes is a little money." And with that, he and Kalon wandered off into the crowd.

When they were out of earshot, Maya turned to Landon. "Seriously, I don't know how you can stand hanging around those two."

"Ah, they're not that bad." He waved his hand. "Once you get to know them, they're actually pretty funny."

"I think we'll just take your word on that," I said. "No need to spend any extra time with them to see if you're right." My eyes caught on someone in the crowd. I leaned closer to Kathryn and whispered, "Conner's here."

Her fair skin immediately turned pink.

"Let's go say hi," I said.

We were on our way to the table when I felt a tap on my shoulder. Brian Dastrup, my fifteen-year-old shadow, was standing behind me. *What was he doing at a senior party? And why hadn't my guy-dar warned me of his approach?* Oh yeah—this was Brian. The butterflies in my stomach were immune to him.

Brian was a few inches shorter than me, with black-rimmed glasses framing his hazel eyes. I first met him last year in concert choir, and I think he developed a crush on me while I was still dating Nick. He hadn't asked me on a date since my breakup, but I figured that was only because his parents had the rule that he needed to be sixteen before he dated.

I quickly told Kathryn and Maya I'd catch up with them in a minute, and then I turned back to Brian.

"Hi, Brian," I said warily, hoping he wasn't about to ask me out. I'd seen him driving his blue car to school last week, which meant he'd turned sixteen over the summer.

"Hey, Emma." He seemed to be piecing his next sentence together in his mind before he spoke. "Has Mrs. Jolley said anything about who she chose for the open spot in Madrigals yet?" Madrigals is the audition chamber choir at our school and one of the choir's best baritone's had just moved. I had tried out each of the past two years and had been thrilled when I made the cut last spring.

"No." I shook my head. "Did you audition for it?"

He nodded.

When he didn't offer anything more, I asked, "How'd it go?"

"I thought I did great, but apparently, some other jerk will be stealing my spot," he huffed.

"Really? That's too bad." I made a show of frowning, though inside I was singing praises to Mrs. Jolley. "Do you know who she picked instead?"

"She wouldn't tell me. She said she wanted to surprise everyone on Monday. That's why I was asking you since you're the teacher's aide."

Oh yeah, of course.

"I wonder who it could be," I said, my gaze drifting past Brian's ear to spy on Conner and Kathryn. She looked nervous, but it seemed like they were having an actual conversation this time...Maya wasn't even having to say much.

Brian continued to talk to me for a few more minutes, giving the lowdown on every guy he knew had auditioned for the choir—all of whom sounded just fine to me, though Brian had a few arguments on that front.

Eventually, I broke away and was able to hear the tail end of Conner and Kathryn's conversation.

"So tomorrow at four?" Kathryn said.

Conner nodded, his boyish face beaming about the prospect of whatever it was they were planning. "See you then."

And with that, the conversation was over, and Conner and his best friend Troy were walking off with their cookies.

"What did I miss?" I asked once they were gone. From the smile on Kathryn's face, it looked like I'd just missed some sort of miracle.

"He asked if I wanted to work on our English assignment together tomorrow."

"Ooh, so like a date!" I squealed. I might be on a boy-cleanse myself, but I could still be excited for my friend. Conner didn't seem like the cheating kind of guy.

"It's not a date," Kathryn said. "It's just homework." Though the huge smile on her face suggested otherwise.

"Whatever it is, I'm so happy for you!" I hugged Kathryn.

"You better call me after your *date*." Maya grabbed a cookie from the table. "I'll be expecting a play-by-play."

"Me too," I said.

The rest of the party wasn't nearly as eventful as the first part had been. But we had a lot of fun hanging out with all our friends and dancing to the loud, upbeat music. By the time Landon's parents shut the party down, I was tired and more than ready to leave. I almost tripped over my own feet when I spotted Arie among the departing crowd. He was standing against a tree a few feet away, by himself, looking at his phone. I didn't think he saw me, but I did notice his lips twitch a little when I stumbled, like he was fighting a smile.

What was he doing at a high school party anyway? I thought he was a few years older than me.

Maybe he was friends with Landon's older brother?

4

EMMA

AFTER LUNCH ON MONDAY, I met Kathryn by our lockers and walked with her to choir. Choir was one of my favorite classes for a couple of reasons: First, I never had homework assigned from it, which was always a plus. And second, I just really loved to sing. As an alto, I didn't sing the melody in most songs, but it was fun harmonizing and figuring out where my notes fit in with the group. Kathryn was also an alto, so we were able to sit by each other during class, which was fun.

"How did your study date with Conner go yesterday?" I asked as we walked past the auditorium on the way to the choir room.

She blushed and bit her lip. "It was good." Then in a low voice she said, "When we were sitting at the table, he sat close enough that our arms brushed a couple of times."

I laughed. Brushing arms with someone wasn't usually that big of a deal, but when the guy you liked brushed arms with you, it was the best thing in the world. It had all sorts of hidden meanings that could be analyzed for hours.

"I think he may like you," I said in a singsong voice.

"I don't know. I-it probably meant nothing."

"I doubt it," I said, smiling.

We soon arrived at the choir room and found our seats. I glanced around the classroom and noticed someone new sitting in the bass section directly behind me. I had to take a second look when I realized it was Arie. What in the world was he doing in Madrigals? Was he like a student teacher or something? I'd never bumped into a stranger so many times in just a few days.

Before I could say anything to him, Mrs. Jolley, our choir director, tapped her baton on the music stand.

Mrs. Jolley was in her midthirties and had been teaching at Maplebridge High for the past ten years. She was short and peppy, and the students all loved her. "Welcome, students," she said. "As you may have noticed, we have someone new in our class." She gestured for Arie to join her at the front. He stood and made his way next to her, making her look like a midget next to his tall frame.

"Everyone, this is Arie Blackwell, a new senior at our school. He just moved to Maplebridge and will be singing baritone in our choir. As you all know, I've been holding tryouts to fill the open spot. Lucky for us, Arie saw the sign-up sheet and came in. Once he auditioned, I knew I'd found the baritone for our choir. I'm sure you'll agree with my decision once you hear him sing. He will also be joining in the All-State Choir this year." Arie looked a little embarrassed at having Mrs. Jolley talk so much about him, but it could have been an act. "You may take your seat now, Arie."

Mrs. Jolley went on. "Speaking of All-State Choir, practices start this Saturday and will be held at Ridgecrest High. We don't have a bus going down to these rehearsals, so I want to remind those participating that they are responsible for finding their own transportation."

I'd already made plans to drive with Kathryn, so I didn't have anything to worry about.

Later, as Mrs. Jolley led us through warm-ups, I couldn't help but notice the deep melodic sound coming from behind me. Mrs. Jolley hadn't been exaggerating when she said Arie had a great voice. His voice was warm and smooth, like melted chocolate drizzled over a strawberry. After listening for a moment, goose bumps rose all over my arms and neck against my will. Kathryn glanced at me and mouthed, *"Wow."* I raised my eyebrows and nodded back. How could he get those looks *and* have that voice?

When class was over, I tried to quickly stuff my folder into my backpack and get out of the classroom before I accidentally flirted with him. I couldn't ruin my twelve-day streak. This was the longest I'd made it so far with my boy-cleanse.

I peeked behind me as I zipped up my backpack, which was a mistake because Arie was looking right at me.

"Hey," he said when our eyes met. "I don't know if you remember me. We met at the store on Friday."

I gave him a bashful smile, remembering the embarrassing experience. "Yeah. That was me in all my glory."

"It's Emma, right?" *He remembered my name? Wow!*

I mean, not wow. Of course, he remembered. Players always did things like that to make a girl feel special.

"That's me. I'm surprised you remembered." I only added that last bit so he wouldn't realize I was already on to him.

He leaned forward and whispered, "Who could forget you after that fateful muffin attack?"

I blushed. "I'd hoped you might have somehow forgotten that little incident."

He smiled. "Sorry, I'll try to forget it now." He closed his eyes briefly and then looked back at me again. "Okay, it's forgotten." He scrunched his eyebrows together and pointed a finger at me. "Have we met before? You seem really familiar."

"Har, har." I shook my head and smiled despite myself. "Anyway," I glanced at the clock, "it was good to see you again, Arie. I hope you have a great rest of your first day here." I really needed to get away before I started falling prey to his charms. I was already having a hard time keeping my eyes off the cute dimple that formed when he smiled.

"Hold on." He reached into his backpack and drew out a folder. "Could you point me in the direction of AP English with Mrs. Hendrix?" He rifled through the papers in his folder until he found his class schedule. He studied it for a moment. "This says it's in room 2B, but I've been turned around all day."

That was my next class. I groaned inwardly. How was I supposed to continue with my plan of ignoring all the hot guys this year if I had the most tempting one ever constantly in my path?

I pasted on a smile so it seemed like I wasn't fazed by the idea of having one more class with him. "Actually, that's my next class. I'll walk you there if you like." I should earn an Oscar for this performance.

He stood. "That would be awesome. It will save me from ending up in the wrong classroom like I did this morning." Arie looked down at me, and I noticed his eyes were a brilliant blue surrounded by dark lashes. "Is there anything I should know about AP English or Mrs. Hendrix before going into class?"

I led him down the crowded hall. "Yeah, she's super ornery and will give you detention if she hears you whispering to your neighbor. Oh, and don't stare at her glass eye; she *hates* it when people do that."

Arie cocked his head to the side. "Glass eye?"

I laughed. "Just kidding! She is the nicest little old lady, and

I'm sure she'll even give you special treatment. She always goes easy on the tall, dark, and handsome sort."

Arie looked quizzically at me.

I gasped, realizing I just told him how attractive *I* thought he was. "Umm, I mean, it's like any other AP English class. Mrs. Hendrix is really nice, she's been teaching forever. Right now we're reading *Jane Eyre* and talking about poetry and stuff."

"That doesn't sound too bad. Thanks for the heads-up."

"No problem. I'm sure you'll do fine." We soon reached Mrs. Hendrix's room. "This is it." Arie opened the door for me, then followed me inside the classroom. I went and sat in my usual seat near the back while Arie introduced himself to our teacher. She then motioned for him to sit in an empty seat on the front row.

As he sat down, the girls around him twisted in their seats to get a good look at him. From the expressions on some of their faces, they weren't immune to his good looks, either. This made me feel slightly better. Rachel, the long-legged cheerleader to Arie's left, introduced herself to him. Rachel had a way of getting any guy she wanted to ask her out, with her super short skirts and curves in all the right places.

I smiled to myself. If she wanted him, she could have him. It would be nice to see her get played for a change. Instead of watching Rachel work her magic, I pulled out my binder and readied for class to begin. If she had her way, I wouldn't even have to worry about keeping my defenses up around Arie because he'd never think twice about me again.

"Did you see the new guy today?" Maya asked when we got to her mom's van after school. Her car was still in the shop, so her mom had let her borrow the family van today so we could take some of the fliers to the college. It wasn't the coolest vehicle in the world, but it worked a lot better than my invisible car.

"Do you mean Arie?" I asked as I buckled my seatbelt.

"Of course! Who else would I be talking about? He was in my psychology class this morning, and thanks to him, I had a hard time concentrating on Mr. Lund's lecture," Maya said as she backed out of her parking spot.

"What's this? You found someone besides your teacher to drool over?"

Maya shoved me playfully. "Well, I still think Mr. Lund is handsome, but this Arie is totally gorgeous and our age."

"I'm glad to hear you've moved on to someone you can legally date."

"Yeah, yeah. So how do *you* know about Arie?" she asked as she pulled into the long line of cars waiting to exit the parking lot.

I shrugged. "He's in Madrigals and English with me. I walked with him to English after choir, and he seems nice." There was definitely no reason for me to tell her how I initially met Arie. I could only hope he, too, would keep that embarrassing moment between us.

"We need to find a way to snatch him up before the other girls do." Maya turned in her seat, looking at me with bright eyes. "Let's invite him to hang out with us on Friday. That will give me a reason to talk to him tomorrow in Psychology."

As if she ever needed a reason to talk to a guy. "I don't know. We don't really know much about him."

"That's kind of the point of inviting him to hang out with us." We finally made it to the edge of the parking lot and pulled into traffic, heading toward Main Street.

I leaned against the headrest and sighed. I had watched him and Rachel interact during English and was sure she was already well on her way to snagging him. But instead of turning Maya down and seeming rude, I decided to let her try and fail. "Go ahead and talk to him. We should get Kathryn to invite Conner to hang out, too, while we're at it."

"Awesome! Should I tell him we're getting together at your house or something?" Maya asked. "I'd rather not have my brothers bugging us the whole time."

"Sure, we could go out back and roast hot dogs and marshmallows in the fire pit if you want." Kathryn would probably be more comfortable with that, too, so it sounded like she was inviting Conner to something more than sitting around in my basement. We would have full reign of the house anyway, since I was the only kid living at home now.

"That sounds perfect," Maya said. "Then if it gets chilly, maybe Arie will offer to warm us up by the fire."

"He's all yours." I smiled at her ridiculousness.

It only took us a couple of hours to hang up most of the fliers Maya had printed off for the auction. Once we were done, she dropped me off at my house.

I lived in a two-story brick home that my family had built when I was young. I grew up here with my older brother, Carter, and sister, Lily, who were attending college now. It was kind of weird to be the only kid at home now, but thankfully, my parents were pretty cool most of the time, if not slightly overprotective.

"Hey, Mom," I said as I plopped my backpack down on the kitchen counter where my mother was cutting fabric for her latest project. She was big on crafts and currently working on a new quilt.

"Hey, honey, how was school?" Mom glanced at me through black-rimmed glasses hanging at the end of her nose. My mom was beautiful and looked much younger than her forty-five years. Growing up, I'd always envied Lily, who'd been blessed to look more like my mom.

My mom and sister had blonde hair, while I had brown. They had green eyes; mine were blue. They were both a little shorter than average, but I was taller. I never saw the resemblance between me and my family like I noticed in other families. When people asked where I got my darker features from, I always made a joke of saying I was switched at birth. Even though I made light of it, there was a small nagging voice in the back of my mind that wondered whether Mom might have been a little too friendly to a salesman one day while Dad was at work. I hated to think that about my mom, but it would have explained a lot.

"School was fine." I reached into the cookie jar that my mom always had filled with homemade chocolate chip cookies. I watched her work for a few minutes before going up to my room. As I studied her, I reminded myself, like I had so many times before, that a woman who sewed quilts and baked cookies every week would never have a secret affair. My genes had just gotten mixed up in different combinations than everyone else's had.

5

ARIE

I WAS SITTING in Psychology Tuesday morning when someone tapped me on the shoulder. It was the short brunette to my left. I recognized her as Maya, from the photos Jason and Sophie had shown me.

"Hey, I didn't have the chance to introduce myself yesterday." She held her hand out to me. "I'm Maya."

"Nice to meet you." I shook her hand, pretending to know nothing about her. "I'm Arie."

"Oh, I know," she giggled. It seemed like most the girls who'd talked to me since coming to school yesterday had giggled constantly. If only I'd had this much attention back when I was actually in high school. "How are you liking Maplebridge so far?"

"It seems like a nice place." I hadn't done much exploring of the town yet. I'd been busy getting briefed on the history of Emma's case, reading all the notes from her previous guards. Even though she'd been watched from a distance her whole life, there weren't a ton of close calls—mostly just notes from my superiors, Jason and Sophie, about the status of her enemy.

"It is. I'm sure you'll love it here. Have you made any friends yet?"

"Not really. I've only talked to a few people." I wasn't here to make friends. I only needed to get in with Emma's group since she was the whole reason I was here. It would be a good excuse to hang around her without looking like a stalker.

Maya brightened at my answer. "My friend Emma and I are planning a little get-together this Friday. We'd love to have you come."

That made my job easier—*they* were coming to *me*.

I smiled at her. "That could be fun. Is this Emma in Madrigals?"

"Yep, that's her," she said.

Perfect.

6

EMMA

FRIDAY, AKA day sixteen of my boy-cleanse, came fast with all the things I had going on. Only five more days until I conquered my own twenty-one-day boy fix. I was killing it!

Maya and I had handed out the rest of the fliers, and the kids at school seemed excited about the date auction. Actually, quite a few had volunteered to be auctioned off. And Maya was still getting texts from all the college kids who wanted to be part of it as well. This whole thing was going to totally rock!

At Maya's invitation, Arie joined our table during lunch the last half of the week. I wasn't so sure about it at first, worried I might get lost in those sparkly blue eyes of his as he sat across from me, but so far it hadn't been an issue.

After school on Friday, I went on a quick shopping trip for groceries with my friends, and then we hurried to my room for some last-minute primping.

"I'm so excited Arie's coming tonight," Maya said as she sat in front of my vanity, touching up her makeup.

"And I'm excited to hang out with Conner!" Kathryn looked like she was about to burst at the seams with excitement.

"Thanks for getting me to invite him. I don't know what I was so afraid of in the first place." She stood behind Maya, trying to figure out which way to wear her hair, holding it up one moment and then letting it fall around her shoulders the next.

"Lucky for Emma, he's bringing Troy." Maya glanced back to where I sat on my bed, already wearing my hooded sweatshirt with my hair in a ponytail. Thanks to my boy-cleanse, I had no reason to primp. "I bet he'll be more than happy to keep you warm by the fire."

"Thanks, but I think I'll stick with my trusty blanket." I rolled my eyes.

"Suit yourself." Maya turned back to the mirror, applied her red-wine lipstick, and then smacked her lips together. She was daring when it came to makeup. She went all out, and it looked good on her. I, on the other hand, usually focused on my eyes. I felt way too overdone if I used lipstick. To be honest, I didn't feel comfortable wearing it. I was always worried it would get smudged, or I'd press my lips together without thinking and end up looking like a clown and not even know it.

Once they finished their preening, we went to set things up outside. My house was in the older part of town, so our backyard was a lot larger than the yards of the newer houses in Maplebridge. We had a grassy area right outside the back door, and to the right, there was a cement pad with a fire pit my dad had built when I was younger.

We arranged the bags of chips, hot dogs, and buns on the patio table nearby, and then we gathered a few benches and camp chairs from the shed to set around the fire pit.

"Do you think we should start the fire before the boys get here?" I asked, looking at the progress we'd made. I had never built a fire myself, so I didn't know how long it would take to get it burning.

"We should wait and let the guys show off their man skills," Maya said.

I laughed. "Maybe we should let them carry the firewood over, too."

"Of course!" Kathryn said. "Gotta let them show off their muscles."

"Good thinking, Kathryn." Maya rested her hands on her hips. "I definitely wouldn't mind seeing Arie put his muscles to good use."

I shook my head. I really hoped Maya wouldn't be too disappointed once she discovered what kind of a guy Arie probably was. I should warn her, but I didn't want to ruin her night before it even got started. She was tougher than me anyway. While I had barely been able to think of anything to say when I caught Nick and his *good friend* making out in his car outside his house, Maya had gone right up to him, knocked on his car window, and told him off. Maya was a firecracker, even if she didn't look it in her petite body. If she did end up in some sort of relationship with Arie, she could handle it.

I set one last chair around the fire pit. "I think we're pretty much done out here. Let's go inside and wait for the boys."

We'd only been inside a few minutes when the doorbell rang.

My heart pumped with anticipation, and we rushed to the living room. "We got it," I called to my parents before they could try to answer the door. We didn't need them giving the guys a full-on interrogation like they always did. My parents were cool and all, but sometimes it would be nice to not be watched so closely all the time.

Maya opened the door to find Arie holding a plate of brownies awkwardly in front of him. "Hey, Arie, come on in."

"Thanks." He stepped through and held the plate out to

me. "My aunt said I should bring something over. I hope you like brownies."

"I love brownies, actually." I squinted at him. Was there some secret handbook guys had that told them how to weasel their way onto a girl's good side? Because if there was, Arie definitely had it. Actually, he'd probably written it. He was too nice, and guys were only nice like that when they wanted something. "How did you know brownies are my favorite?"

He frowned. "I didn't."

Maya glared at me, and I knew she was wondering why I was acting so weird. But I couldn't help it. Normal high school guys didn't do sweet things like bring brownies to a cookout.

Maya scooted up to Arie's side. "We're out back." She took him by the arm and guided him to the back door. "Do you think you could help us carry some firewood over to the pit?" Maya asked, and then she turned around to wink at Kathryn and me before stepping outside.

Conner and Troy arrived a minute later and we led them out back. As I shut the back door, I caught a glimpse of my parents spying through the kitchen window as we joined Maya and Arie. My parents were so weird.

"It looks like we have more than enough firewood," I commented as I set the brownies on the table. Next to the fire pit, there was a pile of wood big enough to start a bonfire. "Thanks for helping us out."

Arie gave Maya a crooked grin as he dusted his hands off on his dark jeans. "Maya kept telling me to get more while she sat and watched as I worked."

I bet she did.

"I thought I'd let you impress me with your mountain-man skills." Maya grinned. "Plus, you wouldn't want me to get my new shirt dirty, would you?"

"Now *that* would be a tragedy," Arie said sarcastically and plopped down in one of the camp chairs.

I bent over the fire to roast my marshmallow until it was perfectly golden brown. It was dark now, with only the light of the fire to see by. I loved campfires. There was something about them that made me feel happy and content. The sparks flying up in the air and away into the night, the crackling of the wood, and the campfire smell were soothing to me.

When I turned around to go back to my seat next to Maya, Troy had stolen it and was now flirting with her. The only seat vacant was next to Arie, so even though it was against the rules of my boy-cleanse, I had to sit there or risk looking rude.

Arie was looking around my backyard as if there was something interesting to see, so I took the opportunity to study him while he was distracted. He had been the perfect gentleman all evening, helping us carry out the salads my mom had made for us, running after napkins that blew away in the wind, and other things like that. He hadn't shown a single symptom of being the egocentric jerk I'd made him out to be in my mind. I probably shouldn't have been so hard on him from the beginning—even if I had kept most of my skepticism to myself.

He turned toward me and began cleaning his roasting stick in the ashes. "How are you getting to the All-State Choir practice tomorrow?" he asked.

"Kathryn and I are driving down together."

"Oh." He nodded. He pursed his lips as if debating whether to say something. "Do you guys have room for an extra? I still don't really know anyone in choir yet."

If I hadn't been thinking so many bad thoughts about him all week, I probably would have already thought to invite him.

I'd started my boy-cleanse as a defense against getting hurt again, but all it seemed to be doing was turn me into someone I didn't like. "Of course. I should have invited you sooner."

"Awesome." The firelight danced across his face, making it hard not to stare. Seriously, his jaw could have been chiseled from stone.

"Should we pick you up at your house, or would you rather meet here?" I asked.

"I'll meet you here. My house is only a couple of blocks away." He set his stick on the ground and then leaned back in his chair.

"Really? Where do you live?" I leaned back in my seat as well, feeling more comfortable around him now I'd let down my guard a little.

"Just over on Miller Circle." He motioned with his hand in the direction of that street. "It's the brick house at the end of the cul-de-sac."

"I think I know what house you're talking about. Anyway, practice starts at nine, so we'll need to leave here around eight. Do you want to meet a couple of minutes before that?"

"Sure." A gust of wind blew a cool breeze through the trees. Arie pulled the hood of his jacket over his head, casting even more of a shadow across his face.

"Where are you from, anyway?" I couldn't believe I hadn't thought to ask him before now.

"I grew up in central New York, just outside of Syracuse."

"Really? I hear it's beautiful there. I've always wanted to visit back east where everything is so green."

"It is beautiful, but it sure rains and snows a lot."

"I don't think I'd mind the rain, we don't get nearly enough here in Maplebridge." I sighed. Utah was one of the driest states in the United States, so I couldn't understand how some people could get sick of the rain. "What brought you here, anyway? You mentioned something about your aunt earlier..."

A guarded expression spread across Arie's face under his hood. He didn't answer right away. He was opening his mouth to speak when Maya turned to us.

"Troy and I were talking and thought it would be fun to play campfire games." Maya's eyes brimmed with mischief and delight. "How do you guys feel about going back to our elementary days and playing Telephone?"

Arie raised his eyebrows and looked at me as if asking whether Maya was serious.

"Come on, it'll be fun," I said. "Embrace your inner child."

He shook his head and smiled. "Okay, let's play Telephone. I don't think I've played it since I was ten."

"You've been missing out. We play Telephone like every day," I said.

"Seriously?"

"Right after we play with dolls in my old playhouse." I pointed a thumb over my shoulder in the direction of the wooden playhouse my dad had built for Lily and me when we were younger.

"You're hilarious, Emma." Arie smiled in a way that made my heart stop one second, then double its pace the next.

"Well, you know." I shrugged, hoping I wasn't blushing. "Life's too short to be serious *all* the time."

A second later, Maya started the game off. She placed an arm around Arie's shoulder and a hand next to her mouth as she leaned in close to whisper in his ear. Arie smiled and shook his head like he couldn't believe what he'd been roped into saying. A moment later, he leaned right next to me and whispered in my ear. A whiff of his cologne wafted to my nose, and man, did he smell good. If I'd had my guard up right then and remembered my boy-cleanse, I would have recognized it as Sign of a Player Number Fifty-Six: they always smell good. But my guard was lower than low at that point.

I didn't quite catch what he whispered because I couldn't seem to focus with the way his hot breath in my ear sent chills down my spine. It sounded a lot like, "Big crowd bears match me baboons." It didn't make any sense, but maybe that was Maya's strategy. Plus, it was the best I could do at the moment. I turned to Conner and whispered the sentence into his ear, then he turned to Kathryn who then whispered in Troy's ear.

Troy scrunched up his face and shook his head. "Was it supposed to be, 'Big crown beards match my balloons'?"

"How in the world did it end up like that?" Maya asked. "That's not even close!"

That was probably my fault. "What was the sentence supposed to be?" I asked, hoping it wasn't me who'd completely botched it up.

"Being around barns makes me croon," Maya and Arie said in unison.

I was way off. "Oops." I smiled guiltily and shrugged.

"Did you purposely sabotage my game?" Maya asked, crossing her arms.

"Of course not," I said. "I think my brain shut down temporarily." Definitely a sensory overload with Arie nearby. I resolved not to be so pathetic again.

Later, as everyone was putting the camp chairs back in the shed, I noticed Conner pull Kathryn aside.

I couldn't help but watch them as they stood under the big apple tree a few yards away. Conner rubbed the back of his neck before stuffing his fists in the front pockets of his jacket. He appeared to be speaking rapidly. Kathryn nodded to whatever he was saying, and then a huge grin spread over her face. When they finished their conversation, Conner, Troy, and Arie all said goodbye and slipped out the side gate.

Once the guys were out of sight, Kathryn walked up to Maya and me. "Guess what?" She practically trembled with excitement. "Conner asked me out on a date for tomorrow! A real live date!"

Maya and I squealed.

"I *knew* he liked you," I said.

"I can't believe this is actually happening." Kathryn shook her head in awe. "Are you sure I'm not dreaming?"

Maya pinched Kathryn.

"Ow!" Kathryn jerked away and rubbed her shoulder.

"Nope. Looks like you're awake, definitely not a dream," Maya said with a smile. "Conner really asked you out."

"Did he tell you what you'll be doing?" I asked.

"No, he said it was a surprise. He did tell me to dress warmly, so I assume we'll be outside for at least part of it."

"I'm so excited for you!" It was wonderful to see Kathryn finally get what she wanted after crushing on Conner for forever. I turned to Maya. "How do you think tonight went with Arie? Do you think he likes you?"

Maya thought for a second before shrugging. "I don't know. It was fun and all, but I had a hard time getting a read on him. He seemed distracted whenever I talked to him. Actually, I noticed his eyes wandered to you quite a few times."

"I highly doubt that." I laughed. Guys never looked at me when they could check Maya out instead.

Maya shrugged. "Maybe he has a girlfriend back home. A guy like that would have no trouble finding a girl to fall in love with him."

"That's probably it," I said, not sure how I felt about that possibility. "I mean, we don't know everything about him yet."

"You guys need to find out tomorrow. You're all going to Ridgecrest, right?" Maya asked.

"We're actually going to carpool with Arie." I turned to Kathryn. "He asked if he could ride down with us, so I told him to meet here tomorrow at eight."

"Sounds good. I guess I better get home and get some beauty rest if I'm going to look good for my hot date tomorrow night," Kathryn said, smiling.

"Make sure to hydrate your lips before going to bed. You'll want them nice and supple for Conner," Maya said.

"Ooh." Kathryn's eyes grew big and she wrung her hands in front of her. "You don't think he'll try kissing me on the first date, do you?"

"You never know." Maya winked and smiled wickedly. "It's always good to be ready though, just in case."

Kathryn looked like she was about to jump out of her skin.

"Don't worry, Kathryn," I said. "I'm sure he won't try anything you don't want. He's a good guy."

This seemed to calm her down a little. "I really better get going, though I'm sure I'll never sleep now!"

7

ARIE

I HAD FINISHED my first week on the job and felt good about it. Sure, being in high school again wasn't great, but it's not like it mattered what grades I got, since I'd already graduated early from college. Surprisingly enough, I'd enjoyed hanging out with Emma and her friends last night, even if I couldn't quite figure Emma out. She was cold and distant, almost annoyed with me one minute, but then normal and fun the next. It was like she had a split personality, and I worried I might get whiplash from it.

I figured the nice Emma was her real personality; otherwise, I might have to turn up the charm. I hoped it wouldn't come to that, though Sophie wanted me to stay close...no matter the methods it took. But the last thing I wanted was to create a fake relationship on top of all the other lies I had to tell to keep my cover.

After I returned from choir rehearsal, I typed up my report for the week and emailed it to Sophie. My mom had called a few times this morning while I was with Emma and Kathryn, so I decided to call her back now before she started to worry. She was famous for freaking out when I didn't get back to her within an hour.

My mom picked up after the first ring. "Arie!" she gasped like she'd been anxiously waiting for me to call.

"Hey, Mom." I smiled as I walked up the stairs to the second floor of my new living space and went into my room. My room was pretty basic with the regular bed, desk, and dresser you'd expect a high school student to have. The blue walls were bare, but I liked them that way. I hadn't brought much with me when I moved here, just a couple of suitcases filled with clothes and other essentials. "I'm alive." I chuckled, imagining how my mom probably looked right now, hand pressed to her chest as she slumped back into a chair, finally able to relax. She'd been through so much with my dad already, so I knew better than to give her too hard of a time.

"If you're alive and well, then why didn't you answer any of my phone calls? I thought you had Saturdays off."

"Normally, I do, but there was a special rally I had to go to this morning. I would have answered my phone, but my boss doesn't like me to use it while I'm on the clock." And so the lying continued. Since my job was top secret, I had to make up a story to tell her. As far as she knew, I was working as an intern for a senator in town.

"This working all the time can't be healthy. You're young; you should be having some fun, too. I bet there are plenty of college girls there who'd love to spend time with a handsome young man like you."

There she went again, still trying to match me up with someone, even though she lived thousands of miles away. "I'm not looking for that kind of fun right now, Mom. I need to focus on my job." I might only be working at an obscure rent-a-body-guard-type job. But it was a stepping-stone in the right direction, and I intended to take it seriously.

"And how was your first week?"

"It's been good. I'm getting the hang of things." Meaning, it wasn't quite the thrilling adventure I envisioned when I applied for the internship. Though my presence was only a precaution for now, since the threat was still locked away for the time being, I was itching for more action—something to make my time here seem worthwhile. I didn't want Emma to be in any real danger, of course, but at the same time, I was getting restless.

"That's good. I know you were hoping for some exciting protests at those rallies, but this mom will be quite happy if things stay calm over there."

"I know, Mom." She'd made that point several times in the past month.

"How are your roommates? Are they nice?" She thought I lived with a couple of college guys; I hadn't known how to explain why I was living with Jason and Sophie. I thought it might be weird, living with a married couple in their forties, but they were surprisingly cool.

"Yeah, they're great." My mom let out an audible sigh of relief.

When I first arrived in Maplebridge, I assumed things would be uptight and serious all the time, but I soon discovered Jason was a goofball when he was off duty. There wasn't a day that had gone by that Jason hadn't found an opportunity to tease me about being in high school again. He also thought he needed to constantly remind me I couldn't date any of the girls I went to school with. Did he assume every guy in their twenties was desperate for some action? Because even if I were, I would never go after someone that young.

Sophie, on the other hand, was the sweet, motherly type. She and Jason were never able to have kids of their own, so I think she enjoyed having a younger person around to mentor. I appreciated having kind people to work with and learn from on my first job fresh out of college.

I talked to my mom for another ten minutes, then hung up before she could remind me, again, that she wanted grandbabies one day and the only way that could happen was if my sister or I took time out of our busy schedules to find someone and get married. Mom was eighteen when she married my father, so she assumed my nineteen-year-old sister and I would want to follow suit and marry young. She seemed to forget all about the fact that the last thing I wanted was the type of marriage my parents had. My sister and I somehow turned out okay despite all the turmoil, but what I'd witnessed had definitely made me question whether true love actually existed. I was convinced that kind of thing only happened in the movies.

To get my thoughts off the past, I decided to go outside and do some yard work. Physical labor had a way of taking my mind off things, and since Jason and Sophie didn't work much in the backyard, there was plenty to keep me busy for a few hours.

8

EMMA

I WENT to clean the office after getting back from choir practice. I turned my music up high and sang at the top of my lungs to make the time pass as I set to work dusting the desks, cleaning windows, vacuuming and mopping all the floors, cleaning the bathrooms, and emptying the trash. I was done in two hours and called Maya on the drive home to see whether she wanted to hang out this evening.

Maya had been busy working on the date-auction preparations all day with her mom, so she jumped at the chance to get out of the house for the evening. She suggested we kidnap Arie and take him on a tour of Maplebridge. I was hesitant at first, worried about compromising my boy-cleanse, but since she had obviously made her claim to him, there was no reason for me to be worried about falling prey to his charms anyway.

I'd been so caught up in worrying about my weakness toward attractive guys like him I hadn't even stopped to realize he hadn't done anything to show he was even interested in me. So far, he'd just been the nice new guy in town who talked to me because we'd met before. I couldn't believe how messed up I had acted, all because of what had happened this summer.

I had gone over two weeks without messing up on my cleanse, so I could totally handle talking to Arie without any feelings getting involved. And there was nothing in the rules against being nice to the new guy. It had to be rough, moving away from home and switching schools during his senior year. I'd die if my parents made me move at any point during high school, let alone my final year when I'm already established.

When five o'clock rolled around, I drove my dad's truck to Maya's house. "I'm glad your parents took their car on their date," Maya said as she climbed in after dropping her picnic basket in the bed of the truck. "This way I get to cuddle up with Arie."

"Somehow I knew you'd like this arrangement." I laughed as I shifted into drive.

A few minutes later, we pulled up to what I hoped was Arie's house from what he'd said yesterday. My stomach twisted up in knots as we strolled up the walk to the large brick house. It felt presumptuous to show up out of the blue. How would Arie react when he saw us? Would he be happy? Or would he feel like he was being stalked? The last thing I wanted to do was come on too strong.

Arie's house looked sophisticated, and the yard was neatly manicured, smelling of freshly cut grass. Maya knocked on the door, and I tried to right my stomach. About thirty seconds later, we were greeted by a tall woman with an athletic build. Her blonde hair was pulled back in a short ponytail, and her warm brown eyes crinkled at the corners when she greeted us. Arie had said something about his aunt yesterday, so I assumed this was she.

Maya introduced us and then asked, "Is Arie home? We're hoping to steal him for the evening."

"Yes, he's out back." She spoke with a slight accent I didn't recognize. "Come on in." She stepped back from the doorway and gestured for us to enter.

We walked into a very lovely home. The floors were all dark wood, the furniture and decor all modern. There was an industrial chandelier with old-fashioned lanterns hanging from it with light bulbs inside. So cool. My eyes wandered from the chandelier to a huge painting of a forest at dusk. "Your home is beautiful!" I said after deciding it needed to be featured in one of those interior-design magazines my mom had.

"Thank you," Arie's aunt said. "It's taken me years to get it to look like this."

"You've done a great job." I wondered what Arie's uncle did for a living. They appeared to be *very* well off.

"I'll go find Arie. Make yourselves at home." She turned and walked out of the room.

A few minutes later, Arie came inside. He was wearing a plain white T-shirt and faded blue jeans with dirt and grass stains across the front. Even with grubby clothes and messy hair, he still looked like he could have just stepped off the set of a men's fragrance commercial. My palms got sweaty just seeing him, and my mind tried to convince me that my seventeen-day boy-cleanse had gone on long enough.

"To what do I owe the pleasure of your company, ladies?" he asked in a cadence from times gone past as he sauntered over.

"We thought it would be fun to give you a proper tour of our town," Maya said. "We didn't know if you'd seen the local sights yet and figured, who better to show you than a couple of Maplebridge veterans?"

Arie wiped the dirt off his hands and onto his pants. "That sounds like fun. Do you mind if I shower first?" He gestured at his dirty clothes and shot us a lopsided grin. "I'll be quick."

"Yes, please," Maya said. "I mean you look great and all, but we want *you* to be comfortable."

"I'll be right back." He rushed up the stairs.

Maya and I sat on a leather couch to wait for him. His aunt was sweet and brought us water and cookies while we waited. Arie was back in less than ten minutes, wearing jeans and a dark-blue T-shirt that brought out the blue in his eyes.

"That was fast," I commented, trying to be discreet as I wiped the cookie crumbs from my mouth.

"Where are you two taking me?"

"It's a surprise," Maya said as we stood.

"But don't worry," I added. "We'll have you back before midnight."

"Oh, good. That way you'll miss seeing me when I turn into a pumpkin." He smiled as he ushered us out the door.

"I hope you don't mind the tight quarters, we're driving my dad's truck tonight," I said.

"I don't mind, but I bet you're grateful I showered before we left," he joked.

We laughed and climbed inside the truck. Maya was so short-legged she had a hard time getting up into the cab. I always joked that I needed to keep a stool in the back for her to use. After struggling for a moment, she asked Arie for a boost. She didn't usually have this much trouble getting in, but I guessed maybe she did it on purpose, just to have a reason to touch Arie. I had to chuckle at the ridiculousness of what she was doing. Arie gave her a helping hand and then climbed in after her.

"So, Arie." I turned to look at him as I started the engine. "Do you know where Maplebridge got its name from?"

"Not a clue."

"Good, then that's where we'll take you first." I put the truck in gear and headed for the outskirts of town.

———

"Here we are." I pulled to the side of the road. We'd driven about ten miles out of town to where the grass grew tall and the leafy trees climbed their way up the mountain. "This is the path to the famous bridge our town was named after."

We all climbed out, and I reached in the bed of the truck for the picnic basket that Maya had packed for us.

"Here, let me carry that for you," Arie offered.

"Thank you." I handed the basket to him, our fingers brushing in the exchange.

As Maya led the way into the woods, she explained, "I know you're probably thinking there's some awesome story with the bridge up ahead since our town was named after it and all"—she glanced back at Arie, who was a few steps behind her —"but I'm sorry to say that we don't even know if there's a story behind this place. We just think it's a great site to see."

"Yeah," I said, coming up beside Arie. "I guess we probably should have looked it up online or something before giving you this tour." I frowned as I set my hands on my hips. "The trees around here must be maple trees. I'm not really sure." Now that I thought about it, it was kind of embarrassing how unprepared we were for this excursion. Hopefully, Arie didn't mind being taken on a tour by the least knowledgeable tour guides ever.

Arie chuckled. "I can't wait to see this famous landmark of yours that needs no special story to make it awesome."

We continued walking the dirt path a few more minutes until we came to the bridge. It wasn't very big, just wide enough for two people to walk across together. The wood had grayed over the years, but it was still beautiful. Today, everything was covered in yellow and brown leaves. The river below shimmered in the afternoon sunlight peeking through the trees.

Arie set the picnic basket on a rock nearby. "This *is* a beautiful area." He stood with his hands in his pockets, pivoting around to fully take in the view.

"It is," I mused as I soaked in the sun. "I love coming out here when I need to get away from the noise in town."

"It is peaceful. I can see why you guys like it so much." He looked sideways at me.

"Come on, guys, let's eat." Maya was already across the bridge, motioning for us to join her in a spot shaded by trees. We all sat down in a circle on the tablecloth Maya had packed, and Arie placed the picnic basket in the center.

"I hope you guys like peanut butter and jelly," Maya said as she handed us our sandwiches. "We also have string cheese, chips, cookies, and apples—delicacies at my house." She took the food out and spread it on the tablecloth. "Oh, and don't forget the juice boxes."

I leaned over and mock-whispered to Arie, "Would you guess that Maya's mom is a preschool teacher?"

"That makes sense," Arie said. "I do love juice boxes and string cheese." He winked at us as he took two of each from the pile.

"So Arie, what brings you to Maplebridge anyway? Have you always lived with your aunt and uncle?" Maya asked.

Arie swallowed and took a sip from his juice box. "Actually, my mom sorta sent me here as a last resort."

My eyebrows arched. "A last resort?"

"Yeah, after my dad died, I started hanging out with a rough crowd." He shrugged. "After a couple of years of trying everything she could, my mom decided the best thing for me was to live with my aunt and uncle."

What? Arie was a troubled teen? "I never would have guessed that was your story in a million years," I said, not knowing what else to say.

"Well, I did take out my piercings and had my tattoos covered when I first got here." He winked at me as he unwrapped a string cheese. "I try to make a good first impression."

Did he just wink at me? I quickly busied myself with putting the straw in my juice box, hoping he wouldn't notice the blush rising to my cheeks.

"Did you really have earrings?" Maya asked, leaning closer to get a better look at him. "It doesn't look like you have holes in your ears."

"No, of course not." He smiled, obviously enjoying teasing us. "You two are so gullible."

That was definitely true in my case. I was too trusting of people and had been burned by that fault too many times in the past.

I wanted to ask him more about how his dad had died but decided against it since the conversation had already veered away from the subject. Plus, I probably didn't know him well enough for him to divulge those kinds of details. I tried to imagine how I would feel if my dad died right now but shook the thought away. I didn't even want to think about something so horrible.

Once we finished our picnic, we walked back to the truck so we could get to our next destination before the sun went down. In the parking lot, we found a dark-blue sedan parked right next to my truck. It was so close I couldn't open the driver's-side door wide enough to climb in.

"Nice parking job," Maya said sarcastically.

"For real." I looked around to see who would be rude enough to park that close when there were about ten other parking spots free.

"I guess we'll all be climbing in through the passenger door this time," I said as I tramped over to the other side of my truck.

Once we were all in, I carefully backed out, half tempted to *accidentally* scratch along the side of the blue car. My conscience won out, though, and I made it out without damaging the vehicle. We pulled out of the parking lot and drove a little farther down the highway, taking a turn off the main road to go up the mountain.

"Where are you taking me now?" Arie asked. "We're not going to a secret hideout in the woods where you tie me up and leave, are we?"

"Wow, it's like you have ESP or something," I said. "That's *exactly* what we planned."

"Don't worry, you won't be tied up there for long. There are all kinds of bears and mountain lions in the area that come out at night to hunt their prey," Maya added.

"At least I got to see the famous bridge before I die," Arie shrugged, resigning his fate to us.

Maya scooted a little closer to Arie and placed her hand on his knee in a flirtatious manner. "Actually, we're going to Duncan Hill—AKA Make-Out Point."

Arie's eyes widened. "Are you serious?"

"Dead serious," I said. It was the truth.

"Don't you think it's a little soon for that?" He leaned away from Maya. "I mean, you two are gorgeous, but we just met."

"You don't have a girlfriend back home, do you?" Maya looked up at him with her big brown eyes.

"Um, no." He was backed up against the door now.

"Then what's holding you back?" Maya scooted even closer to him.

From the look on Arie's face, he was about to jump out of the truck.

"Okay, Maya, I think that's enough." I laughed. "We've had our fun, and he passed the test."

Maya nudged Arie in the side and slid back to the center of

the bench seat. "Sorry if I made you nervous. We like to make sure guys aren't just with us because of our unearthly beauty." She flipped her hair.

I nodded. "We just wanted to take you up here to see the awesome view of the city before the sun sets."

Arie breathed a deep sigh of relief, and his shoulders relaxed. "You had me going there for a second."

We reached the scenic overlook a few minutes later and walked toward the cliff edge. I was afraid of heights, so I gripped the guardrail tightly.

"This is it," Maya said, gesturing to the view of our town below.

"I can see why it's called Make-Out Point." He raised his eyebrows at us and smiled.

I shrugged. "I imagine most people who come to make out don't appreciate the view like we're doing tonight."

"You're right, Emma. The view isn't nearly as fascinating in the dark." Maya winked at me.

Arie chuckled. "You sound as though you've been here before, Maya."

Maya smiled broadly up at Arie and batted her eyelashes. "Maybe, but then again, maybe not. I'm not the type of girl who kisses and tells."

Arie turned to me. "What about you, Emma? Do you come here often?"

"I, uh..." I hesitated, trying to find a way to be honest without sounding pathetic.

"No, her standards are too high to come up here," Maya answered for me. "She prefers more refined places like Ferris wheels and porch swings." Maya pointed a finger at Arie. "So don't press your luck. Many guys have tried, but not even Nick was able to get Emma to break her rule."

"Oh, um, uh..." Arie dug his hands into his pockets.

I felt the color drain from my face and glared at Maya. Had she really said all that? She'd just made me sound like a total goody-goody. It wasn't that I was averse to kissing. I enjoyed it as much as any other girl. I just knew making out in the backseat of a car often led to other things, and I didn't want to give a guy the wrong idea.

Maya's cell phone rang.

She pulled her phone from her back pocket and glanced at the screen. "It's my mom. She's probably freaking out over the date auction again." She strode away with her phone to her ear, her feet crunching on the gravel as she went.

"Sorry about that." I fiddled with my bracelet while looking at Arie's shoulder. "Maya says whatever comes to her mind."

"That's okay." Arie tilted his head to the side. "I can see it's the way Maya is. She reminds me a lot of my sister."

"Really?" I said. "How old is your sister?"

"She just turned nineteen."

"Oh, so you're the baby of the family?" I asked. "So am I."

A confused look crossed his face. "No..." Then his expression changed. "I mean, yeah, I guess that would make me the baby of the family."

It was weird how he said that. Maybe being as close in age as they were, he'd seen himself as being the same age?

Arie coughed, then pointed ahead of us. "That's quite some sunset, isn't it?" He scooted closer and leaned into the railing. The sun was falling behind the horizon now, turning the sky shades of orange, pink, and purple. Arie and I stood in silence for a moment, looking at the scene unraveling before us.

It felt oddly intimate to be alone with him, watching the sun sink behind the mountains across the valley from us. I still didn't know him well, so I wondered what he was thinking about—what he thought about Maya and whether he was starting to like her like she hoped. But then he'd said the whole thing about Maya reminding him of his sister, so that probably wasn't a good sign for her.

"Who's Nick?" Arie turned toward me, his eyes squinting in the sunlight.

I blew out a breath. "My ex. You know, the guy I was hiding from in the store."

"Ah. *That* guy." He strummed his fingers on the guardrail for a moment. "Did you guys break up recently, then?"

"I caught him and his now-girlfriend kissing a few months ago."

"Dang. That's rough."

I turned away from the sunset and leaned back with my elbows on the railing. "I was headed to his house to surprise him after getting back from vacation. When I found him in the backseat of his car, all he could say was, 'I thought you were supposed to get back tomorrow.'" I shook my head, remembering the moment and how betrayed I'd felt, how angry and hurt I'd been. "Even though Maya can sometimes get carried away with whatever comes out of her mouth, I've never been more thankful to have her with me than I was that night. She'd come to help me decorate his room as part of the surprise. Instead of leaving his carpet scattered with heart-shaped confetti, Maya left him with a good scolding, which I'm surprised didn't make his ears bleed. Then I poured what was left of my soda all over him and his car...not my finest moment, really."

Arie smiled. "I hope his car upholstery was stained after that."

"It was." I returned his smile, happy he saw my side of things. "I saw his car parked downtown a few weeks later, and there was still a red stain on the backseat. I figure it's something he can remember me by."

It was then I noticed a dark-blue car driving slowly past the parking lot and down the road. It was going at the slow pace you'd expect a car to drive when the driver is lost or uncertain of where they're going.

Arie stiffened beside me.

"Does that look like the same car we saw at the bridge?" I asked Arie. It was hard to tell in the dimming light, but it looked very similar.

"I was wondering the same thing." Arie scooted closer to me. I could have been imagining it, but there was almost something protective about the way he stood so close.

We stayed silent for a moment as we watched the car make a U-turn on the road. When it turned into the parking lot, I couldn't shake the feeling someone had followed us.

9

EMMA

AS SOON AS the car pulled into the parking lot, Arie grabbed my arm with a firm hand. "Hurry, hide." He pulled me away from the railing. We ran in a crouched position to hide in front of my truck, my heart racing.

"What's wrong? Why do we need to hide?"

He didn't seem to hear my question. My eyes searched his face, but all I saw was intense concentration as he peeked over the hood to watch the approaching vehicle.

When the car pulled up next to the passenger side, Arie grabbed my arm again and pulled me onto the other side of the truck. We stood there, listening. I heard a car door open and then the crunching of feet on gravel as the footsteps approached. Then they stopped. I didn't know what to do. Was something going on? Arie certainly seemed to think we could be in some sort of danger.

I crept up to check whether I could see whoever it was through the window.

I sighed and rolled my eyes.

"It's just Brian." He was looking through the window, probably checking to see whether anyone was making out in there. He'd probably recognized my truck since it had my dad's company's name on it. Which meant he was checking to see whether *I* was making out in there. *Gross.* "He's a kid from school."

Arie's eyebrows squished together. "Brian? Have you known him long?"

"He moved here about a year ago, I think. He's a junior."

For some reason, that helped Arie relax a little. But why had he gotten so anxious in the first place? He'd said earlier that he'd hung out with a rough crowd back in New York. Maybe he had a lot of experience running from cops or other people, so hiding was a reflex?

"Hey, Brian, what are you doing here?" I heard Maya's footsteps on the gravel as she approached from the opposite side of the parking lot. "Have you seen Emma and Arie?"

That was my cue to come out of hiding. I stood up the rest of the way and walked around the vehicle. Arie followed.

"We're here," I called. "I dropped my bracelet earlier, and Arie was helping me find it." I might as well help Arie save face for acting so weird a minute ago.

"Sure you were." Maya winked at me. Obviously implying we'd been more romantically occupied.

I cringed inwardly, wanting to tell her she was totally wrong, but decided to shake it off. Maybe it would be good for Brian to think I was doing that. I turned to Brian. "So what are you doing up here? And why were you peeking in my truck?"

Brian stuffed his hands in his pockets and looked down. "I was out for a drive, looking for something to do. I noticed the sunset and thought to stop here to get a better view of it."

Sure you were. But whatever, I wouldn't call him out on it.

Maya looked at the sky behind us and frowned. "It looks like we both missed the sunset, Brian." She turned back to us and shrugged. "Would you like to join us at Kiki's for ice cream?"

"That would be great," Brian said. He looked at me and smiled. "Their cookie-dough shakes are the best!" He cleared his throat. "Would one of you like to join me?" He glanced toward my truck, then back. "It looks like you've been pretty crowded in there."

I held up the keys. "I'm the one driving." Thankfully.

"I'll stick with Emma, if you don't mind," Arie interjected. "I've already been informed about the mountain lions that come out to hunt their prey. It's probably best they have one of us tough guys around to protect them." His lips quirked up into a lopsided grin, showing off that dimple again.

Brian seemed disappointed I wouldn't be driving with him, but at Arie's mention of him being tough he stood a little taller and puffed up his chest. "I think I heard about an attack last month. You better come with me, Maya."

Maya mouthed "help" to me. But I simply shrugged and smiled back. She was the one who invited Brian in the first place. She might as well be the one to keep him company while she was feeling generous.

Maybe I was a mean friend, but since Arie didn't want to drive down with Brian, there really was nothing I could do.

During lunch on Monday, I couldn't help but notice that Kathryn was glowing. She'd had her date with Conner Saturday night, and I really hoped she'd had a better time than I'd had that same evening. Getting ice cream with Brian had almost turned into a weird double date. Once we went into Kiki's, Maya all but clung to Arie's side, which left me to entertain Brian. It hadn't been horrible, except Brian might have gotten the wrong impression. Because I sat and talked to him, he might think it's okay to ask me out on a real date next time. And that was scary because he was sixteen now.

"How was your date with Conner?" I asked Kathryn.

"Ooh, yes! We need details!" Maya chimed in.

A big smile swept across Kathryn's face. "It was amazing!" she said. "We doubled with Troy, of course, and went up the mountain to watch a movie. They had a couch set up out there and everything."

I raised my eyebrows, impressed. "Wow! How did he work that?"

"He hooked his laptop to a projector. I never would have even thought to do something like that. It was *so* fun!"

Maya leaned forward over her lunch tray. "Did he kiss you?"

Kathryn glanced at Arie. She looked like she didn't know whether she wanted to be talking about this in front of him. He seemed to notice her hesitation and concentrated on his mashed potatoes—giving her a little privacy. "No," she whispered. "But he did hold my hand." She sighed blissfully.

"That's a good start. Do you have plans to do anything this week?" Maya asked.

"Not yet, but I think I'll invite him to go to the date auction with me on Saturday to watch the bidding."

"Speaking of the date auction..." Maya turned to Arie, a sly look on her face. "What are *you* doing Saturday night?"

Arie sat up straighter, his expression wary. "Umm, I'm not sure. Why?"

"I had the most fantastic idea," Maya said, her voice energized with her excitement. "How would you like to be a part of our date auction? I bet all the girls at school would go crazy over the chance to go on a date with you."

Yep, it was a loaded question.

"Didn't you say you had enough guys for the auction already?" he asked.

"Maybe." She scooted her chair closer to him, grabbed his bicep, and looked up at him sweetly. "But there's always room for a big-ticket item like you."

"Oh come on, I'm not gonna go for any more than the other guys," he said.

"Now don't be humble, Arie. You know half the girls in school are infatuated with you."

He shook his head. The skeptic in me thought he was a little too good at pretending like he didn't know he was hot.

Maya unleashed the big guns, with her pouty face and puppy-dog eyes. "Pleeeease, we need your help. For my nephew."

I could tell from the look on his face he was having an internal battle. He thought for a while and then held up his hands. "Okay, I'll do it." He pointed a finger at Maya. "But only because it's for a good cause."

10

ARIE

I'M SUCH A CREEPER, I thought as I did another walk around the building Emma was cleaning. Now that we were becoming more like friends, my job suddenly felt more like stalking than actual work. Thankfully, Jason, Sophie, and Bruce were usually the ones doing the creeping around, since my shifts were typically in Emma's presence while we were at school or hanging out. But since Jason and Sophie were celebrating their anniversary this evening, and Bruce had the late-night shift, I had offered to put in extra hours.

Once I was sure no one else was poking around, I settled back into my spot behind the dumpster to watch Emma. The blinds weren't closed all the way in the office she was working in, and the light from inside made it easy for me to see her. A smile spread across my face. She did a lot of funny things when she thought no one was watching. Right now she had her earbuds in, and I could tell from the way her mouth moved that she was singing at the top of her lungs. I had heard her sing in choir, so I knew she was good, but I hadn't seen her jam to the music like this before. It was actually kind of cute.

Out of the corner of my eye, I saw a dark figure move from beneath the trees along the parking lot. My body went on high alert, eyes wide, ears perked, muscles tense. I watched the person in a dark hoodie creep along the sidewalk toward the building. I wasn't sure whether it was a guy or a girl since the baggy clothing didn't reveal much, but I assumed it was a guy based on the way he moved.

I felt the back of my pants to make sure my gun was still there, and then I moved from my spot behind the dumpster to hide behind a tree for a better view. The mysterious person seemed to look inside the windows and watch Emma for a moment before he slunk next to Emma's car. He pulled something out from the front pocket of his hoodie. My stomach tied in a knot. What was he holding?

My mind buzzed through a dozen different possibilities. It could be anything, but there was one possibility that sent my adrenaline over the edge. What if he knew who Emma was and was placing a bomb on her car?

I yanked my gun from its clip and snuck up on the guy. I was four feet away when I saw the hooded man was holding a piece of paper, folded in half.

Not a bomb.

Whew.

A second later, he turned his head and looked right at me.

"Brian?" I asked, quickly jamming my gun back into its holster—hoping he hadn't seen it. "What are you doing here?"

"Just out for a run." He noticed me eyeing the paper, and before I could grab it, he stuffed it down the front of his pants.

Yeah, I'm not going after that.

But what could be on that paper? He certainly didn't want me to know. It seemed far-fetched, but could he be working for the enemy? He certainly had a great track record for stalking Emma. But then again, it could have been a love letter. He was the type of guy who would write creepy notes to a girl, moon-lighting as her secret admirer.

"What are *you* doing here, Arie?" he asked, squinting at me.

"My, ah, *neighbor* owns this building," I fumbled for something believable to say. "While he's out of town, he asked if I could make sure it's locked up each night."

"Really?" He said the word slowly as if he didn't believe me. Which, for all I knew, meant he knew who the real owner was.

Lights went out of the office Emma had been cleaning. My chest tightened. If she was following the regular routine that Jason and Sophie had told me about, she'd be coming outside any minute to empty the trash. If I didn't get Brian to leave so I could get back to my hiding spot, I would be caught.

11

EMMA

WEDNESDAY AT WORK, I was finishing up when I had the feeling someone was watching me. My neck prickled the whole time I vacuumed the floor.

I worked in a large two-story building, with a few small businesses inside. There was a lobby on the main floor with four different offices, along with restrooms. The second floor was designed the same way. I was in charge of cleaning the main floor while another guy did the second floor. He usually cleaned early in the morning, so I had assumed I was all alone in the building.

I turned out the lights and peeked out the window of the adoption agency I had just finished tidying. Since it was easier to see with the lights off, I expected to spot someone coming in from outside. But no one was out in the lobby, and the other offices were dark. I waited a little while longer, but when no one appeared, I opened the heavy door, grabbed the trash bags, and crept down the hall with them.

This was the part of the job that freaked me out most. I had to walk down a long corridor, passing a few doors on my way out. If I worked here during the day when it was busy with people, I'm sure the hall wouldn't be so scary, but at night it creeped me out. I never knew whether a door was going to be jerked open by someone working late, which had happened to me a few times. At the end of the hall was a dark staircase right before the back exit. I always imagined someone might be lurking there behind the corner, and I would never even know until they grabbed me. I knew my imagination was running wild, but it still scared me.

When I reached the door, I stuck a rock in it to keep it from shutting all the way, then rushed to the dumpster twenty yards away to throw the trash in. I almost jumped out of my skin when something shuffled behind the dumpster. My feet were unsteady as I scrambled back to the building, locking myself inside. My pulse continued to pound through my head the whole time I packed everything up.

Once I was in my car with the doors locked, I drew in a deep breath. From the corner of my eye, a light flicked on in the second floor. I waited, trembling with fear, until I saw the other cleaning guy start washing the window. *It was him all along.* I leaned back in my seat, threw my head back, and laughed—somewhat hysterically.

My mom and I went to the school Saturday afternoon to help Maya's family get everything ready for the date auction that evening. After a few hours, the stage was transformed to look like the backdrop of a fashion show. The podium was set in the center of the stage where Mr. Naylor, the biology teacher who was famous for his commanding voice, would be the emcee for the event.

The stage was set up so the "date" would walk out from backstage through the doors on the side. They could strut their stuff across the stage if they liked and then stand next to Mr. Naylor for the bidding. I could only hope that when it was my turn, I wouldn't trip in the high heels I planned to wear for the event.

As showtime neared, I rushed to the dressing room to change into my lacy blue, knee-length dress. Running my fingers through my hair, I gave it one final fluff, touched up my mascara and lip gloss, and waited backstage with the other contestants.

When Arie walked backstage, he glanced around at the groups of people for a moment before noticing me. My body flooded with warmth when he smiled and strode toward me. He looked so handsome in his light-green, button-up shirt and dark denim jeans. I wouldn't be surprised if he had college-aged girls bidding on him as well as all the high school girls.

"You look great," Arie said after studying me for a moment.

"Thanks, so do you." My face flushed at the compliment. I hoped it wasn't noticeable.

"Thanks." He tugged on his collar. "I can't wait for this to be over with. I'm not really into prancing around on stage for everyone to see."

"Me neither," I said, pushing some hair behind my ear. "I'm only doing this because Maya begged me."

"We need to find a way to get her back." Arie peeked over his shoulder as if looking for someone, and then he spoke close to my ear, making me shiver against my will. "Maybe we should tell Mr. Naylor to introduce *her* as the last date to be auctioned off."

I drew in a deep breath. What was happening to me? I was on day twenty-four of my boy-cleanse. I should be immune to cute guys by now—not wondering what it would be like to go on a date with one. "She'd kill us if we did that. And knowing her, she'd find a way to get us back anyway."

"Come on, we have to do it. She conned us both into being auctioned off. I say we pay her back." His smile was so cute and convincing I couldn't say no. Plus, Maya had embarrassed me enough over the years it'd be okay to put her on the spot for once.

"Okay, let's go tell Mr. Naylor about a last-minute entry," I said before we snuck off to write up Maya's introduction to give to Mr. Naylor.

"I can't believe you talked me into doing this!" I said to Maya while pacing backstage. "I'm going to look ridiculous in front of all those people. Not to mention that they're going to think I'm some narcissistic girl who feels like every boy is dying to go out with her." Which we all knew was definitely not true.

"Don't worry about it, Emma." Maya grabbed hold of my hands and turned me to face her. "You'll do fine, and I bet all the boys will go crazy when you walk on stage."

"In my dreams," I said. "I'll be lucky if anyone normal bids on me at all."

"*Our next date up for bid is...Emma Howard,*" Mr. Naylor's voice boomed through the speakers.

My mouth went dry. I wanted to bolt, but Maya stepped right in front of me, blocking my escape.

Maya took my shoulders in her hands and looked calmly at me. "You have nothing to worry about, Emma. You're a great catch. I know there are quite a few guys out there dying to go out with you. Remember who you're doing this for, and you'll do great," she finished her pep talk, gave me a hug, and gently pushed me through the door.

The spotlights shone down on me as I stepped on the stage, feeling the weight of the audience's stare. I fingered my dress as I came to stand next to Mr. Naylor, barely able to hear my introduction over the pounding in my ears. All I caught was something about me being an honor student who enjoyed reading, singing, and hanging out with friends. *Why had I written such a boring introduction for myself?* I felt silly but smiled at everyone, trying to appear more comfortable than I was. *I'm doing this for Braden,* I reminded myself. Remembering *that* gave me the confidence to look out into the crowd for the first time.

The auditorium was filled with people of all ages. My parents and my sister, Lily, smiled and waved from the third row. I smiled back, lifting a hand at my side to wave. Maya's family was seated in the front row. Maya's cute nephew, Braden, sat on his dad's lap. He was such a sweet baby, and I hoped the auction would raise enough money to help with the surgery next month. Open-heart surgery at ten months old had to be such a scary thing for his parents to think about. They didn't need the added pressure of wondering how they would pay for it.

As Mr. Naylor came to the end of my introduction, I took a deep breath and prepared myself for the worst.

"Let's start the bid at five dollars," Mr. Naylor said. "Anyone want a date with this pretty young lady for five dollars?"

About a dozen hands went up. I squinted to see whether I recognized any of the guys raising their hands. I gasped when I saw that one of the raised hands belonged to Brian.

My stomach dropped to the floor. Brian's family was loaded. There was practically no chance of him not winning the bid if he wanted to badly enough.

"What about ten dollars?" Mr. Naylor said into the microphone.

The same hands went up again.

Mr. Naylor continued raising the bid, and Brian kept raising his hand. I tried to hold back a grimace as the bidding went higher and higher, with Brian remaining one of the main competitors.

"I'll bid two hundred dollars," Brian's voice shouted from the crowd. The current bid was only at fifty dollars, so of course a collective gasp sounded throughout the audience.

I glanced at Mr. Naylor, who looked somewhat taken aback at the sudden increase in bid. "All righty, then. The bid is at two hundred dollars. Going once." He paused for a moment. "Going twice." He paused once more, allowing for someone else to make a counter bid. He banged the gavel on the podium. "Sold to the dark-haired young man in the fourth row."

Brian smiled hugely at me from his seat in the fourth row. I managed to paste on a smile as he winked at me. One of the attendants escorted me down the stairs and out into the audience to sit with him for the rest of the auction.

I pushed some hair behind my ear when I reached my date. He smiled at me with his hazel eyes, magnified by thick glasses. I didn't know what to say. "Uh, thanks for bidding on me," would have sounded weird, so instead I simply said, "Hi."

Brian rubbed his hands together. "Do you want to finish the auction, or should we get started on our date?"

"Oh, um," I hedged. "Could we finish the auction first? I hear there's a surprise entry at the end, and I really don't want to miss it." Plus the less time I spent alone with Brian, the better.

He nodded, and we sat quietly for the next ten minutes as the auction continued. Most of the bids went as expected, until a college-aged guy got onstage. I'd noticed him backstage earlier, and remembered the way Derek and Kalon had glared at him. Apparently, they saw him as a threat to their goal of getting the highest bid of the night. And with the reaction he received from the college girls in the front row, it was obvious Derek and Kalon's jealousy hadn't been misplaced. The bidding was intense, and at the end of the bidding war, he went for a whopping $334.57.

"Next up on this evening's agenda," Mr. Naylor said a few bids later, "Arie Blackwell!" The crowd applauded, and a group of high school girls to my right erupted into cheers when Arie walked onto the stage. He blinked into the spotlight but smiled at the crowd, and for a fleeting moment I found myself wishing I were one of the girls bidding. I quickly banished that urge, though.

Arie might have said he wasn't looking forward to being auctioned off, but he still stood with an air of confidence. There was only a slight crack in his facade that let me know he was uncomfortable.

"Okay, ladies. Settle down, please," Mr. Naylor said after the cheering had gone on long enough. "Settle down." He struck his gavel on the podium several times before the crowd quieted again. Arie's eyes rested on me for a moment, and I gave him a thumbs-up sign when I saw the color drain from his face. Maybe Maya shouldn't have done this. He really didn't look like he wanted to be up there at all. It was a surprising thought, since I always assumed a guy with looks like him would love being the center of attention and have girls treating him like a rock star. But Arie was different. Yes, he did have a sort of charisma that made him instantly likable, but he didn't seem to know it about himself.

"What is it about Arie that all you girls find so interesting?"

Brian said when the bidding began. I took my eyes off Arie and saw a disapproving look on Brian's face. He obviously wasn't a member of Arie's fan club.

I shrugged. "He's nice."

Brian shook his head. "There's something weird about him. He seems like he's hiding something."

My brow wrinkled. "What makes you say that?" Had Brian even spent any time with Arie besides the night we got ice cream at Kiki's?

Brian pursed his lips like he was debating whether to answer my question. In the end, he shrugged. "It's probably nothing. I just ran into him somewhere this week, and he seemed really agitated."

"What do you mean?" I leaned closer.

He shifted in his seat. "It doesn't matter. I just wouldn't trust him. When I talked to Mr. Lund about it on Thursday—"

"Wait, you talked to Mr. Lund about Arie? Why would you do that?"

"He's my Psychology teacher. I talk to him about lots of things." He seemed to sense my irritation. "It doesn't matter, though. You guys are friends. Forget I said anything."

But I couldn't just forget what he'd been saying about not trusting Arie.

"Why don't you trust Arie?"

Brian set his jaw. "Just forget I said anything. Let's finish the show." He pointed to the stage, and I knew I wouldn't be getting anything out of him right now.

So I turned my attention back to what was happening up front with Arie's bidding. I thought I had come to terms with trusting Arie to be a good guy. Why did Brian have to go and try to tarnish Arie's reputation?

My ears pricked up when I heard a girl in the front call out, "I bid one hundred dollars."

I squinted to see whether I could tell who had yelled out the bid. I recognized the tall, blonde-haired girl in the front: Rachel, from English. My stomach hardened. Of course. I should have known she'd try to get a date with the hot new guy at school.

"We have one hundred dollars. Can I get one hundred and ten?" Mr. Naylor asked.

A few girls raised their hands. Mr. Naylor continued raising the bid, and a group of ten or more girls from school continued to raise their hands, Rachel being one of them.

I couldn't help but notice that Arie seemed to be holding back a grimace just as badly as I was. Maybe I was wrong about him. Maybe none of the high school girls in Maplebridge were good enough for him after all. But another, more pleasant thought followed just as quickly. Maybe he wasn't interested in the cheerleader and drill-team type that was currently trying to win a date with him.

In the end, Rachel won the bid for Arie for a whopping $287. Rachel jumped up and down when Mr. Naylor announced her as the winner. Arie smiled as he walked down to meet her, though it wasn't the type of smile that reached his eyes.

"We have a last-minute entry," Mr. Naylor said at the end of the night. "I'd like to call Maya Brown to the stage."

A huge smile spread across my face when I saw a shocked-and-bewildered Maya shuffle out from backstage. She looked so confused.

Mr. Naylor held his arm out and gestured for Maya to stand by him. "Now this young lady is quite the catch." He smiled at the audience. "I have it on good authority that any guy would be lucky to get a date with Maya. But I don't need to tell you myself; she has quite the introduction."

Mr. Naylor gave the audience a lopsided grin before looking down at the stack of papers in front of him.

He cleared his throat. "Maya Elise Brown is a girl unlike any other," he read. "She may only be a senior in high school, but with the list of talents she beholds, you would think her much older."

Maya pasted a nervous smile on her face as she smoothed her black pencil skirt.

Mr. Naylor continued, "Maya is an accomplished bassoon player and enjoys serenading her dates with the romantic music she's written over the years. Her most requested tunes are, *I'm Secretly in Love with You* and *Do You Wanna Taste My Lipstick?* When she isn't practicing her bassoon, she can be found rescuing ant colonies from the stomping feet of preschool children and reading bedtime stories to the animals at the zoo."

A low rumble of laughter passed through the audience. The smile that had been on Maya's face was now replaced by one of horror.

"Maya's favorite mythical creature is the unicorn," Mr. Naylor continued while trying to suppress a smile. "She loves to draw unicorns in-between homework assignments and proudly displays them all over her bedroom walls. When she isn't busy with her other hobbies, she sews various lizard costumes, which she dresses up in when she has special errands to run, like grocery shopping for her mother or taking mail to the post office. Her dream date would be to dress up in her purple dragon costume and go out with a handsome man to scour the local creek for pollywogs."

The crowd burst into laughter and applause when Mr. Naylor came to the end of Maya's introduction, and I was relieved to see that Maya was laughing as well. I'd been worried that Arie and I might have gone a little overboard.

"I had no idea Maya was so cool," Brian whispered to me.

I looked at Brian with wide eyes, unable to believe someone would actually be impressed by that ridiculous intro. Instead of telling him it was fake, I simply smiled and said, "Yeah, she's pretty awesome." I just hoped she wouldn't kill me the next time we were alone.

12

EMMA

ON MONDAY AT LUNCH, I was hoping no one would ask about my date with Brian. I didn't even want to ask Maya how much money they raised, for fear it would come up. But as soon as I sat at the table, Kathryn asked about my date.

Kathryn and Conner were officially dating now, so he and Troy ate lunch with us today.

"Um, it was all right. We ate dinner and then hung out afterward." I didn't want them to know what "hanging out" with Brian Dastrup was like. To redirect everyone's attention away from me, I turned to Maya. "Sooo...how do you think the night turned out?"

"It was great...until the big surprise at the end when I was auctioned off." She eyed me suspiciously. "I wonder how that happened."

I worked hard to keep a straight face. "Who would possibly want to enter you in the auction?" I peeked at Arie, who was fighting a smile as well. "How was your date anyway?"

"It was good," she said. "I still can't believe John Stakner bid on me." John Stakner was Mr. All-Star Quarterback at

Maplebridge before he graduated last year. Maya shook her head. "I mean, why would someone in their right mind bid on a girl whose dream date includes dressing up like a dragon and looking for pollywogs? Eww!"

Troy burst out laughing and slapped his knee. "That was, like, the best part of the whole night."

I had to laugh, too. "Sorry, Maya. Arie and I couldn't help ourselves. We had one chance to get you back, and we had to make it count."

Maya pouted for a second. Arie leaned over his lunch tray. "You know it was funny."

A slow smile spread across Maya's lips. "Okay, fine, it was funny. But in front of Mr. Lund? You guys, you're seriously cramping my style. Now Mr. Lund's gonna think I'm an immature kid who still plays with frogs at the pond. Geez!" She pointed a finger at Arie, then me. "Next time, pick on someone else, will ya?"

"Okay, I'll try not to do it again." That seemed to appease her, so I turned my attention to Arie next. "And how was your date with Rachel?"

He took a sip from his water bottle before answering. "It was fine."

"What did you guys do?" I prodded.

He shrugged. "We ate dinner at the Mexican place on Main Street, and then Rachel offered to take me to Duncan Hill."

My eyes widened, and an audible gasp escaped my throat. "Duncan Hill?" *He wouldn't go there with her, would he?* My insides bubbled at the thought.

"That little skank," Maya muttered under her breath. I guessed she was remembering the time Rachel took Maya's last crush to Duncan Hill.

Arie laughed. "Luckily, I already knew what Duncan Hill was popular for, so I got her to go to the movies instead."

Whew, I thought. Though I didn't know why I should even care.

———

After lunch, I walked to choir with Arie. He asked, "So how did your date with Brian really go? I'm sure there was more to it than going to dinner and hanging out like you said at lunch."

Why did he have to be so observant sometimes?

I drew in a deep breath. "He took me to dinner and talked for thirty minutes about some video game he'd beaten. So that was *interesting.*" I didn't want to go on with the details, but Arie seemed to be waiting for me to continue, so I did. "Then he took me to his house to carve wands out of the tree branches he'd collected." I clamped my mouth shut. Why in the world was I telling him about this?

"Wands? Are you serious?"

"Well," I said, scratching my forearm, "I didn't really mind the carving part. I used to whittle wood when I went camping with my dad. But then Brian wanted us to pretend we were wizards with our new wands."

"Wow." Arie shook his head and grinned.

"I didn't know what to do, so I went along with it. I hope the neighbors didn't see us. It was *so* embarrassing."

Arie tried to control his laughter but failed. "Where's a video camera when you need one?"

I had to laugh, too. "I know. It was ridiculous."

"I didn't say that."

I bumped shoulders with him. "You didn't have to."

"I'm guessing there won't be a second date?"

"You guessed right. I hope he got the hint when I jumped out of the car as soon as he pulled up in front of my house."

"Poor guy," Arie said, feigning sympathy.

I rolled my eyes.

We walked into choir. Arie continued to tease me about it in class and the whole way to English. He even tried to trick me into thinking Brian was coming our direction a couple of times, and even *accidentally* called me Hermione.

13

ARIE

"WHY DIDN'T you and Jason tell me about Emma's wand carving?" I asked Sophie that evening. I was sitting at the table, typing up my report from last week as she made dinner. She and Jason had told me about the stick carving, but they hadn't mentioned the sticks were supposed to be wands—or that Emma had pretended to be a wizard on a date. It was hilarious! I really wished I could have witnessed that spectacle—too bad I'd been stuck on a date with Rachel.

"I guess we didn't think you'd be interested." Sophie shrugged as she stirred the soup she was cooking. "Plus, she'd probably think something was up if you didn't act surprised when she told you."

"That makes sense. Have you guys been able to find out more about Brian?"

"Yes, a little." She set the wooden spoon on a plate and leaned against the counter. "He's been in Maplebridge for one year. He's an only child." She shrugged. "Everything seems to check out fine. We have noticed his blue car driving down her street slowly a couple of times."

"That's weird. Do you think he's a threat?"

"I'm not sure yet. He could be a lovesick teenager, stalking his crush. But then again, he might not be. Jason plans to keep a closer eye on Brian for a few days. Hopefully, we'll soon know more. For now, though, we'd like you to stay close to Emma, just in case."

"I'll do my best." Yes, I'd definitely do that. I wouldn't let anyone slip through the cracks.

Sophie opened the freezer and pulled out a bag of frozen broccoli. As she dumped it into a pot on the stove, she asked, "How'd it go with Rachel today? Were you able to keep her from pursuing you further?"

"I tried." I sighed. "But I have a feeling she's the persistent type. Won't give up until she gets what she wants."

Sophie *tsked* as she tapped the spoon on the edge of the pot. "We can't have you dating another girl at Emma's school."

"I know. And I'm not interested at all." *Definitely not.*

14

EMMA

IN ENGLISH THE NEXT DAY, Mrs. Hendrix announced that our class would be partnering up for our book reports on *Jane Eyre*. For the assignment, we were supposed to write a paper together, discussing some of the main points in the book. I had enjoyed the book, so I was eager to discuss my opinions with someone else.

Arie turned in his seat and looked back at me as if to ask whether I wanted to be his partner. I nodded, feeling breathless for some reason.

I tried not to smile when Rachel asked him to be her partner, only to be turned down. She pouted in her seat for the rest of the class period.

After class, Arie and I arranged to work on our book report at his house right after school since we had to get it done before we left for the All-State choir trip Thursday morning, even though it wasn't due until Friday.

Arie was waiting for me by my locker after the final bell, and we walked to his black Chevy together. When we reached it, he was sweet and opened the passenger door for me to climb in.

The vehicle was a few years old, but it was nice and clean inside.

He glanced at me as he drove. "Been playing wizards with Brian lately?"

"Ha-ha, very funny." I glared at him. "It may surprise you, but I made it through the day without casting a single spell. I seem to have forgotten to bring my wand to school today."

"Maybe tomorrow, then. I'm sure Brian has an extra if you lost yours already."

"What a brilliant idea! Then I'll be able to turn you into that pet chimpanzee I've always wanted."

He turned his attention back to the road and chuckled.

Arie was an excellent driver, not crazy like my brother. I had dealt with motion sickness my whole life and always got carsick while driving with Carter. He liked to wait until the last minute to stop at a stop sign, and when it was his turn to go, he accelerated as quickly as possible. I could relax while Arie drove, and that earned him brownie points in my book.

Arie's aunt was out running errands when we arrived, and I assumed his uncle was at work. So we had the house to ourselves for the time being. Arie grabbed his laptop from his room, then we settled in at the kitchen table.

He picked up his copy of *Jane Eyre* and fanned the pages absentmindedly. "What did you think of the book?"

"I really liked it." I set my copy on the table. "It's an old book, so I had to get used to the language, but after that I couldn't put it down."

"Really?" He sounded skeptical.

"Absolutely." I probably sounded like a nerd to him. "What about you?"

He folded his arms across his chest and leaned back in his

chair. I tried not to think about how the way he was sitting emphasized the size of his biceps. "It was all right. No big action or suspense scenes, so it wasn't my typical read, but it was fine. I thought Mr. Rochester was entertaining."

"What was so entertaining about him?"

"Oh, you know, just the way he liked to tease Jane all the time. He didn't seem as stuffy as other characters from classic literature."

"That's true." I had thought the same thing. "What did you think about him keeping his first wife a secret from Jane? Do you think it was okay for him to try to marry her before telling her about his past?"

For some reason, I really wanted to know his answer to this question. How Arie answered would tell me a lot about what kind of guy he really was. If he thought it was completely fine, then I would know for sure he was the type to play with a girl's heart before grinding it into the ground beneath his shoe. And the thought of that being true disappointed me.

He looked thoughtful for a moment, rubbing his chin. "I don't think it was necessarily okay, but I understand why he did it. I'm not so sure I wouldn't have done the same thing. He made a mistake early on in life, but I think he deserved a second chance at happiness."

That was an okay answer, but it still made me wonder whether honesty was as important to Arie as it was to me. "Mr. Rochester should have at least told Jane. She might have understood. I mean, I think if I were Jane, I would have tried to work through it with him. It'd be much better than being lied to the whole time."

"Do you really think so? Look what happened when Jane found out. She ran away."

I held up a finger, feeling somewhat emotional about the subject. "That's because he hadn't told her before. He waited for someone else to spill the beans on their wedding day. If he had told her from the beginning, or at least when he knew he wanted to marry her, I think they could've worked it out together. Instead, he lied and made her look like a fool when she found out on her wedding day. No one should have to find something out like that." I settled back in my chair, not realizing how I'd leaned way forward as I'd spoken. I seemed to be a lot more passionate about this topic than I'd thought.

"Maybe," Arie said. "But sometimes things are kept secret for good reasons." The way he said it made me wonder what kind of secrets he had. Everybody had a few.

"Do you have some deep dark secret, Arie?" I asked, somewhat serious, somewhat in jest. He still seemed to be a little too perfect to me; there had to be *something* wrong with him.

He looked startled and uncomfortable at my question, but then he recovered quickly. "Oh no, uh...nothing like that."

"Are you sure?" I cocked my eyebrows.

"Of course." He laughed awkwardly. "I can take you up to my tower if you really want me to prove I'm not hiding my crazy first wife up there."

"That's okay," I said, giving it a rest and bringing my heart rate back to normal. "I believe you."

"Good." He scooted his seat a little closer to me and spoke in a low voice that caused my heart to pick up the pace again. "What do you think about the age difference between Mr. Rochester and Jane?" A flirty smile played on his lips, but I couldn't understand why he'd find that question amusing.

"I think it was fairly common back then to marry someone older. I don't think I'd go for anyone *that* much older than me, but a few years older would be fine."

"What about someone who just graduated from college? Or is that pushing it?"

"I don't know." Why was he asking me this? "I mean, I'm in

high school—it's not like I spend much time around guys like that." *Wait.* My eyebrows drew together when something occurred to me. "You're not trying to find out if I'm part of Mr. Lund's fan club, are you?"

He looked confused for a moment. "No. Wait, are you?"

"Of course not!"

"Okay." He grew quiet for a moment. "What about when you graduate? You'll be going to college with guys of all ages, do you think you'd consider it then?"

I thought about it. "If I met an amazing guy, age wouldn't be that big of a deal. I don't think I'd go for anyone ten years older or anything. For a guy to say, 'Hey, I was in fourth grade when you were born,' would be kinda awkward."

Arie laughed. "Yes, that would definitely be robbing the cradle."

"What about you?" I asked.

"I think I could date a girl four years younger than me." He smiled a crooked smile. "Any younger might be weird."

"So you're saying you'd feel fine dating a fourteen-year-old right now, but dating a thirteen-year-old would be pushing it?" I knew he was probably talking about dating someone so young in the future, but I couldn't help but tease him.

"What?" He wrinkled his forehead. "No, I meant I could date someone that much younger than me when I'm older. Of course I wasn't thinking about dating a fourteen-year-old. I'm not a pedophile!" He shook his head. "I meant to say that if I were twenty-one or twenty-two, I might consider dating an eighteen-year-old."

I laughed. It was fun finally being able to tease *him* about something for a change.

We ended up getting lost in the conversation, discussing everything from the weirdest couples we knew, to our favorite movies, to where we planned to apply for college. Me: Maplebridge University because let's face it, I'm a homebody. Him: Cortland State or Ithaca College—it looked like he wanted to get back to New York.

Talking with Arie was fascinating. He was smart and witty and so easy to talk to. I'd never experienced that before with a guy.

We lost track of time until Arie glanced at the large clock on the wall. "Oh, man, it's almost dinnertime. Sophie wanted me to cook dinner tonight, since she and Jason were going to be out later than usual."

"Sorry, I didn't realize we'd been here so long," I apologized. "We still haven't even made a real dent on the assignment." Not good when I only had tonight and tomorrow to finish it.

"Don't be sorry, I've enjoyed myself." He thought for a second. "Why don't you stay here for dinner, and we can finish this up after we eat?"

"That sounds good. Let me call my mom to see if it's okay with her."

After I got off the phone, I walked into the kitchen and saw Arie had pulled out what looked like the makings of spaghetti. He was putting on a black apron as I came in. I smiled, thinking he was adorable. I mean, you just don't see manly men wearing aprons every day.

He turned around and smiled sheepishly.

"What's the verdict?" He finished tying the strings behind his back, the muscles in his arms bulging as he did so.

"My mom said I could stay." I walked to his side. "What can I do to help?" I looked around the kitchen, admiring the dark wood cabinets and granite countertop. My mom would love to have a kitchen like this.

"I'm no chef, so it's spaghetti and green salad tonight." He gestured at the ingredients on the counter.

"That sounds easy enough."

"It should be. Sophie keeps spaghetti sauce ready in the pantry for nights like these. All we have to do is brown the hamburger, dump the jar into a saucepan, and let it all simmer." He peeked at me through slanted eyes. "Would you mind doing that?"

"Sure." I turned the burners on. Once lit, I filled a big pot with water and placed it and a saucepan on the stove. I looked at Arie again, who was studying me with a thoughtful expression.

"I can tell by the way you were eyeing my apron earlier that you're wishing you had one, too," he said. "And it just so happens that I have an extra, if you'd like to wear it."

I glanced down at my lacy pink blouse. "Yes, please." I held out my hand.

He reached into a drawer next to the double ovens, pulled out a red apron, and walked over to me. Instead of handing it to me, he unfolded the apron and gently dropped it over my head. He took a step closer as he wrapped the strings around my waist. I had not been expecting this, and my face immediately flushed with heat. As I stood with my face to his chest, I breathed in his scent. He smelled so good! A clean, fresh scent that shouldn't have been overpowering at all, but I felt myself getting weaker by the minute. I dared to look up at his face as he tied the strings behind my waist. He grinned and must have known he was causing my stomach to do backflips.

So much for that boy-cleanse of mine. I didn't make it to twenty-six days. *Curse you, Arie, for being so cute.*

Arie finished tying the bow around my waist and took a step back. "I hope that fits all right." He smiled again, showing the creases in his cheeks that were his dimples.

"Yeah, it's perfect." I attempted to sound nonchalant about

the whole thing, as if having an attractive guy tie an apron around me was an everyday occurrence.

"I forgot one thing." Arie sauntered close to me again. I backed up against the counter, not sure what he was going to do this time. He leaned in closer. My heart began to hammer inside my chest. *What is he doing?* I held my breath and stood there, not sure what to do. He reached his arm behind me, brushing my shoulder in the process, and grabbed something from off the countertop.

He held up a spice jar. "Can't forget the red pepper flakes." He flashed me his signature dazzling smile. "I like to heat things up a little."

That's for sure.

I enjoyed dinner with Arie and his aunt and uncle. Jason and Sophie were nice and easy to talk to. I learned they'd lived in Maplebridge for the past eighteen years. Jason looked somewhat familiar, so I was sure we'd passed each other around town before.

They told me about how they'd always wanted to have kids but had never been able to have any of their own. They were happy to have Arie live with them, feeling it gave them the chance to be like parents for the first time.

Arie and I helped clear the table after dinner, and then we went back to working on the assignment. We kept on task this time, knowing we had a time constraint, and had the assignment completed by ten thirty.

"How about that?" I said. "Done in one night."

"We make a pretty good team." He leaned back in his chair, placing his hands behind his head.

"I agree." I saved our work and shut his laptop. "I guess it's time for me to get home." I wished I had an excuse to hang out longer. Doing this report with Arie had been fun and hadn't seemed like the chore homework usually was.

"I'll grab my keys." He disappeared up the stairs and soon returned, jingling his keys in his hand. "Ready?"

"Sure." I slung my backpack over my shoulder and followed him out the door.

As he drove toward my house, he asked, "So what is it about Maplebridge University that makes it so awesome it's the only school you're applying to?"

There were a lot of reasons. Some just sounded better than others. There were the normal ones: I could save money and live at home if I wanted, they had a great teaching program, and it was a great school for the price. But there was also the other reason that kept me from applying anywhere else. I was scared. The thought of moving away from home and my parents and living on my own caused me enough anxiety that I would probably never sleep again. It was embarrassing. I would be eighteen next Friday...in just ten days...and I still got nervous when I was away from my family overnight. It had taken me years to stay the whole night at sleepovers. And it wasn't until just last year that I'd actually made it through an overnight trip for school without having a panic attack. How in the world would I handle moving away for four years?

"Um..." Arie was still waiting patiently for me to answer. I cleared my throat and shrugged. "It's a really good school, plus Maya's planning to go there. So it should be fun." *Yeah, only my parents and siblings are allowed to know about my secret anxiety problem.*

"That makes sense." We were silent for a moment before he asked, "What else do you have going on this week, besides All-State Choir?"

"Just work. I have to clean the office tomorrow night."

"Where do you work?" He glanced at me briefly as he drove, the lights from the truck's dash illuminating his face.

"I clean an office building on Main Street on Wednesdays and Saturdays. It's a great job...while I'm in high school anyway."

"That's cool."

"Yeah, it's pretty good, except for when I freak myself out. Last week, I thought I heard a noise and was scared to death the rest of the time. But it was just the guy who cleans the second floor. I hope he didn't see me scrambling around the office after he'd scared me."

"I'm sure he would have assumed you were in a hurry." His eyes crinkled as he smiled.

"No, he probably thinks I'm some nutcase high school girl."

"You're right." He winked. "Chances are, he thinks you're crazy."

"Probably." We had reached my house. "Thanks for the ride." I unbuckled my seatbelt, opened the door, and reluctantly climbed out of his truck.

"No problem," he said. "See you tomorrow at school."

———

That night, as I got ready for bed, my phone beeped with a new text message. I picked up my phone from the soft lavender comforter and saw I had a message from a blocked number.

That's weird. I had never received a text from a blocked number before. I opened it, curious.

Your boyfriend is not who he seems to be.

I dropped my phone back onto my bed as if it had burned my hands. *What the heck is that supposed to mean?* I darted my gaze around my room, feeling as if I were being watched. I breathed through my nose to try and calm myself down, and then I texted the person back.

Me: **Who is this?**

There was no response.

I read the text again. *Your boyfriend is not who he seems to be?* I didn't have a boyfriend. Who was this person talking about?

Nick? Could it be about Nick? If so, this blocked-number person must not have gotten the memo that we broke up. It certainly would have been nice to get this text when we started dating. He definitely hadn't been who he appeared to be.

Or were they talking about Brian? But we only went on one date—if you could call wand carving a date. Had he been telling people he was my boyfriend? He was a little odd, but I didn't think he was delusional. And I was pretty sure I'd figured out what he really was like on that date. And he was definitely not my type.

Or could the text be about Arie? We'd been hanging out a lot, but we were just friends. The only time we'd even hung out alone had been tonight. Could it be Rachel who'd sent the text out of jealousy? She hadn't been happy when Arie chose to be partners with me instead of her. Maybe after their date she'd thought they'd had a connection.

Maybe they had. Perhaps they'd even had a great date, and Arie was just being a player. I mean, he had been rather flirtatious this evening. My heart sank. My first impression must have been right, and I'd been stupid enough to let my guard down these past few weeks that we'd been hanging out.

Then another thought occurred to me. Maybe it wasn't even Rachel's text at all. Maybe someone was messing with my head for fun.

Scenario after scenario ran through my mind. There was no way to know for sure until I had more information.

For now, all I could do was keep my ears open. It was always possible the text had been meant for someone else and not even me at all; maybe that's why they didn't respond. After all, it referenced me as having a boyfriend. And *I* didn't have one. Not now and not anytime in the near future.

15

ARIE

"KNOCK, KNOCK," Jason said at my door. It was Thursday morning, and I was packing for the choir trip.

"Come in." I pushed my phone charger into the front zipper pocket of my duffel bag before looking up at him.

Jason entered my room, looking more anxious than he usually did. "We just got the news. Fenris has been released from jail."

"What? Already?" I knew this was the reason I'd been brought on the job, but I hadn't realized how quickly the preparation time would end.

Jason dipped his head. "Yes. We're on high alert now. If his men have figured out who Emma is, they won't hesitate to make their move."

My stomach churned. I had known all along that this was coming. But were we ready? Was I ready? Could I do what it would take to keep Emma safe?

"I'm confident Emma will still be safe on this trip of yours, but I want you to stay extra close. Stalk the girl if you have to.

Ask her on a date if that's what it takes to keep her close. I need you by her side as much as possible. Do what it takes."

I swallowed and tried to push down the anxious feeling inside. "I can do that."

"Are you sure?" Jason raised his brow, his eyes serious and questioning.

"Yes. I can do that."

"Good. We're counting on you." He turned to leave but stopped and looked back at me. "And try not to enjoy yourself so much doing it." A half smile lifted the corner of his mouth.

I sucked in a breath through my nose. Had he noticed something between Emma and me when she was over Tuesday night? It almost seemed like he knew that last request was turning out to be the most difficult one.

16

EMMA

THURSDAY MORNING, I woke to the sound of my alarm. I hadn't slept well, so six thirty came way too early. I'd been thinking about the text all day yesterday but still hadn't been able to come to any conclusions. With the slight chance it could have been talking about Arie, it would be stupid of me to completely ignore it. So I planned to keep a close watch on him this weekend, since we'd probably have some time together. Surely after a few days I would have him figured out.

When my mom dropped me off at the school, a few kids were already on the bus. Those from the choir, band, and orchestra were all going on the same bus, since the big All-State concert included all three groups. Conner played the trumpet in the band, so I figured Kathryn would be hanging out with him on the bus.

I grabbed my bags out of the car and said bye to my mom, then hefted my duffel bag into the storage area under the bus and climbed on board. Most of the seats were already taken, which caused a thrill of anxiety to pass through me. I didn't feel comfortable asking to sit next to someone, since it was going to be a long trip and people would rather have their own seat to stretch out on.

Kathryn was already on the bus with Conner as expected, so sitting with her wasn't an option. I looked around for an empty seat nearby when a voice called my name. Arie motioned for me to come sit with him.

Relief washed over me as I hurried down the aisle and stashed my backpack—full of snacks, reading material, and other necessary items for long bus rides—in the overhead bin.

"Thanks for the seat," I said, slightly out of breath. Then after taking in his appearance, I asked, "Did you just wake up?" Maybe the text had referred to him being a night owl instead of a morning person? But who would care about that? Really?

"Of course not," he said as if insulted. "I've been up since five. It took me hours to get my hair just right this morning." Obviously he was kidding, because he had a bad case of bedhead, which was super adorable in a way. His dark hair was smashed on the left side of his head where his pillow must have been a short time before. He was slouched in the seat, wearing a hooded sweatshirt that complimented his mussed-up hair nicely.

"Oh, it looks great," I said. "I didn't know bedhead was coming in style. If I'd known that, I could've saved myself some time this morning and slept in."

"You should try it sometime. I bet with your long hair you'd look awesome with bedhead." He gently flipped my hair with his fingers. "But really, I woke up about twenty minutes ago. Don't worry, I did brush my teeth before I ran out the door."

"That's a relief. Bedhead may be the latest fashion, but morning breath isn't." I smiled and slouched down in the seat so I was no longer looking down at him. "Thanks again for letting me sit with you."

"My pleasure."

Mrs. Jolley's bright voice sounded on the bus intercom. She announced we'd be leaving in a few minutes and invited us to use the school restrooms if needed. At her suggestion, a few kids hurried off and into the school.

As we waited for the bus to depart, I considered my misgivings about Arie once more. From what I observed so far this morning, nothing seemed to confirm that the text had been about him. He didn't act like he was hiding anything. He simply looked tired.

17

ARIE

"WHAT ARE your plans for all the downtime we'll have today?" I asked Emma as we neared Salt Lake City, Jason's warning still fresh on my mind.

"Nothing much. Kathryn and I were going to do a little shopping at the mall this afternoon. What about you?"

I'm planning on stalking you. Though I would much rather be with her and have her know about it, instead of going about it the secret-agent sort of way. "I was thinking of walking around town. I've never been to Salt Lake City before and wouldn't mind seeing what it has to offer." I knew Jason had told me to ask her on a date if needed, but I didn't want to pursue something fake if I didn't have to. If I was going to date someone, I was going to do it because I wanted to. So for now, I'd just ask her to "hang-out." That would be much more appropriate than a date anyway, considering she was still only seventeen and I was almost twenty-two.

"Do you want to hang out tonight after practice?" I asked as the bus drove onto the exit ramp.

A grin took shape on her face. "That would be great."

"Cool." Mission accomplished. Jason would be happy.

We stopped at our hotel, which was next to a few shopping malls and restaurants we were allowed to visit between rehearsals.

I stashed my things in my hotel room and then waited around the lobby to follow Emma and Kathryn, hoping they wouldn't notice me lurking around. I felt so weird doing this. I tried to act casual and followed the girls from a distance as they ate lunch in the food court, then explored the mall. I watched from afar as they went into different boutiques, peeking through the doors of each of the shops they went into.

I was standing by one of those mall kiosks, trying to get a better look into the clothing store Emma was in, when the kiosk owner started talking to me. She was a short, Hispanic woman.

"You looking for something nice for your girlfriend?" She swept her hand over the items she had on display, a collection of beauty supplies.

"No, I don't have a girlfriend," I answered, still focusing on the shop Emma was in.

"Oh." The lady smiled and nodded as if she understood. "You maybe like to have your hands looking nice?"

"Sure," I said, still not fully paying attention to her.

The lady gestured to a chair for me to sit in. It had the perfect view of the shop I was watching, so I thanked her and sat down. She then asked me to place my hand on the kiosk, so I did, not thinking anything of it.

Before I knew it, the lady was holding my fingers and running some sort of sandpapery stick along my fingernails. I yanked my hand away. "What are you doing?"

"Buffing your nails." She peered more closely at my fingers. "You bite your nails, no?"

"Sometimes..."

She shook her head and made a *tsking* sound. "Here, I show you what to do."

"O-okay," I said, not wanting to insult her. I was the one who'd been dumb enough to look like I was interested in beauty supplies in the first place.

The lady resumed buffing my fingernails. My knee bounced as I glanced toward Emma. She and Kathryn were at the checkout counter. If I didn't get away from this lady soon, they'd catch me getting my nails done and wonder what kind of guy I was. I mean, I hadn't made many friends since moving to Maplebridge, and I hadn't gone out on a date with any of the high school girls besides the date with Rachel. If they caught me they'd never let me live it down.

The kiosk lady was sweeping clear nail polish on my fingernails.

I nearly fell off my chair.

I looked around again, and to my horror, Kathryn and Emma were now out of the shop and a few feet away from me. It was too late to make a run for it, so I pulled my hood over my head and ducked down.

"Is that Arie?" Emma asked Kathryn as they walked past me.

I turned my head slightly in her direction to see whether she was looking at me.

She was.

I smiled weakly at them as they walked off giggling. *Crap!* I needed to get away from this lady before anyone else saw me.

18

EMMA

AFTER OUR AFTERNOON REHEARSAL, Kathryn and I hurried back to our hotel room to freshen up before the evening's activities. Even if tonight was more about researching Arie and who he really might be, I still wanted to look my best. I wore a dark-purple blouse and white jeans with my favorite glittery heels. They weren't the most sensible shoes for walking around downtown Salt Lake, but they looked awesome. Also, since Arie was so tall I felt I could get away with wearing them. Those seemed like good enough reasons to wear the shoes in my book. Fashion over function.

There was a knock on our door. Kathryn went to answer it. It was Conner.

"Hey, Conner," I called from around the corner as I inspected myself once more in the large mirror.

"Hey," he said as Kathryn grabbed her jacket.

"What are your big plans for tonight?" I asked him. A section of my hair refused to curl the right way, so I worked with it until it finally obeyed.

"We're going to dinner and hoping to find a movie that ends before that dumb nine-o'clock curfew Mrs. Jolley set."

I laughed. "Good luck with that."

"How about you? Looks like you're all dressed up for something special."

I gazed at my reflection again and straightened my shirt where it rested over my hips, hoping it wasn't too much. I wanted to look good, but not like I was trying too hard. I didn't want Arie thinking I'd assumed this was a date, though I kinda hoped it might be. "Um, nothing special. Just hanging out with Arie."

"Oh, so *you're* the girl he's going out with tonight." He smiled like he knew something I didn't.

"What do you mean by that?" I turned away from the mirror to face him.

"It's just that we're staying in the same room, and I've never seen a guy take so long on his hair."

What? Warmth radiated through me. Had he done that for me?

Kathryn stood next to Conner. "Ready to go?" She looked excited to get on with their evening.

"Yep." He gave her a once-over and smiled. "You look great, by the way."

"Thanks." She blushed. Turning to me, she said, "Bye, Emma. Have fun tonight."

"Thanks, you too."

I walked down to the hotel lobby at six thirty to meet Arie. He was already waiting, looking out the window at the busy street with his hands in his pockets. His hair was no longer smashed to the side of his head as it had been this morning. I couldn't tell whether he'd taken forever on it, like Conner suggested, but it looked good. He wore a gray jacket that accentuated his broad shoulders and muscular physique.

He turned toward me when he heard my heels clicking on the tile floor. A smile crept up on his face. "Look at you!"

Maybe I had overdone it with the heels. I tried not to blush. Then I remembered what Conner had said. "Nice hair."

He shrugged. "Thanks. Thought I'd try and look more presentable than I did this morning."

"But isn't bedhead the latest fashion?"

"Oh, it is. I just don't think the people of Salt Lake know it yet. I didn't want someone to see me and try to steal my look."

"I bet." I reached out and lifted his hand to study his finger-nails. "I love what you've done with your nails, by the way."

He pulled his hand away, and hid his nails in a fist. "It's not what you think."

"I'm sure."

Maybe the text I received Tuesday night was referencing the fact that he secretly liked to keep in touch with his feminine side. I didn't have a problem with a guy who had good hygiene, but if he got manicures more often than me, it might be a little overboard.

"No really," he said, still trying to convince me. "Let's just say I was in the wrong place at the wrong time."

After grabbing a quick bite to eat at a sandwich shop, we walked around the town, trying to find something to do that we couldn't do back home. The street was busy tonight with cars and trains hurrying on to their destinations as darkness crept over the city. I wasn't used to so much noise and felt more jumpy than usual. When we passed a group of shady-looking guys, I was thankful Arie was as well built as he was. Walking next to him made me feel much safer.

"How do you feel about ice-skating?" I asked when I spotted an ice-skating rink across the street.

"It sounds fun. Back in the day I was dang good at ice hockey."

"Really?" I tilted my head to the side. "I've never been skating before, and I'll probably be horrible. But I'd love to try."

"You deprived girl! We have to go." He tugged on my arm and pulled me in the direction of the rink.

Arie paid for me when we got in, which I tried not to read too much into. We rented our skates and put them on. I made my way onto the ice, holding onto the wall for balance. Arie, on the other hand, glided on the ice like a pro.

The rink wasn't too crowded—just a few families and a handful of people our age. I watched in awe as a girl who looked about nine or ten years old zoomed past me before jumping and spinning in the air. I definitely felt out of my element as my legs wobbled on the slippery ice.

Not wanting to be shown up completely, I tried to move forward a little and lifted my hand off the padded wall for a second, only to immediately grab it again for support. *Maybe this wasn't such a brilliant idea after all.* I didn't want to look like a fool in front of Arie and fall flat on my face. How did the ice-skaters on TV make it look so easy?

Arie skated over to me, skidding to a stop at my side. "You know, most people like to skate when they come here, not stand against the wall."

"I know. I'm getting used to the feel of these things." I gestured at my feet.

He looked thoughtful, and then he offered me his hands. "Come on. Let me help you."

"Okay." I tentatively placed my hands in his and let him

guide me away from the safety of the wall. His palms were warm and calloused, and just this little touch caused an electric current to rush through me.

Arie continued to drift backward for a while, pulling me along the edge of the rink. I didn't dare move my feet, for fear I'd crash, so I stood there with my hands outstretched and my butt sticking out for balance. Yeah, super attractive.

"See, it's not so bad, is it?"

"Sure. Just don't let go," I said.

"Don't worry, I won't." He squeezed my hands. "You're doing well, it just takes a while to get used to the ice. We'll move like this for a bit, but then we're going to try something more difficult."

"I think this is pretty good. No need to change what we're doing," I hurried to say. Being towed around the rink seemed much safer.

"You can't improve if you don't push yourself." He looked at me gently. We finished the first loop around the rink. The ten-year-old girl went whipping by again. "I'm going to let go of one hand and move to your side." Arie released my right hand and did as he'd said. I wobbled and squeezed his hand tighter for support. He chuckled. "Don't worry, I have you."

"I can't believe I always thought skating would be so much easier," I said, daring to push off with my feet to move faster. "They always make it look so effortless on TV. I can't imagine doing what the pairs skaters do. How in the world does a guy keep his balance on the ice as he lifts a girl over his head?"

"Lots and lots of practice." Arie started to move faster, bringing me along with him.

"Did you play hockey a lot when you were younger?"

"I was on a hockey team for a couple of years when I was ten and eleven. It was fun, but when I discovered how much I liked basketball, I focused on that during the winter instead."

"You didn't get all violent like the pro hockey players do, did you?"

"No, not too violent anyway." He looked sideways at me and smiled. "I only got thrown in the penalty box a few times."

I was so caught up in the conversation—and a little distracted by Arie's smile—that I didn't realized how fast we were moving. I tried to slow down by using my toe pick—and immediately lost my balance. I yanked my hand away from Arie's to brace myself on the ice as I fell. Right before I hit the ground, Arie wrapped his arms around my waist, lifting me on my feet again.

"Uh, thanks," I breathed, caught off guard and somewhat overwhelmed by his sudden closeness.

"No problem." He let go of me, looking as surprised as I was to be standing so close. "That ice isn't the softest place to land."

After my almost crash, I eventually let go of Arie's hand and was able to skate around on my own. I even tried to do a few slow turns. Ice-skating wasn't all that different from in-line skating, after all. I wasn't about to try a triple Lutz or anything like that, but I felt competent for it being my first time.

"Do you think Kathryn and Conner are back from their date yet?" Arie asked as we came to stand in front of the door to my room after we'd made it back to the hotel. "Conner seemed pretty excited about it earlier."

I leaned against the wall and tilted my head back to see his face better. "Kathryn was looking forward to it, too. I imagine they're already back, unless..." I stopped myself before saying my thoughts out loud.

"Unless what?" Arie asked, leaning his shoulder against the

wall.

"Umm..." I blinked, having a hard time keeping my thoughts from scrambling. Standing so close to Arie, with his attention focused solely on me, was overwhelming.

"You weren't about to say, 'Unless they found a couple of sticks on their way back and decided to pretend to be wizards,' were you?"

I giggled, though I knew he was teasing *me*. "Umm, no that's not what I was thinking, but I can see how that might be a possibility." I fiddled with the charm on my necklace.

"Then how about this? 'Unless they fell into the sewers and got caught in a fight with a few giant rats.'"

I laughed again. "Nope, not that, either."

"Then tell me, because I'm stumped."

He wasn't going to give it up. I blushed as I told him what I almost said before. "I was going to say, 'Unless they found some secluded place to make out or something.'" I looked down, unable to meet his eyes.

"Oh," he said in a knowing voice. "Now why would you think that?"

"Because that's what people like to do when they're dating."

"If only we had a reason to find a secluded place, too." He winked.

My mouth went dry, and my stomach jumped to my throat. "W-what do you mean by that?"

He leaned closer. "I think you know."

Did he just glance at my lips? A thrill went through me, but I tried to push it away, knowing he had to be messing around.

"Well, I have this rule." I pushed his chest gently, and slid out from where he was leaning toward me. "You see, I don't kiss boys outside hotel rooms."

"We can go inside if you'd prefer." He smiled

mischievously, eyeing the door.

Yeah, he was totally playing with me, probably loving the way he was making me squirm.

"You know that's not what I meant." I arched my eyebrow, because that's what someone who was completely calm and collected would do at that moment. Fake it till you make it.

Arie laughed. "Too bad."

I was about to call his bluff when something flashed across his face, as though he remembered something suddenly.

"I better let you get some sleep." He straightened and stuffed his hands in his pockets. "Thanks for hanging out with me tonight. It was fun."

"I had a great time as well." I pulled my room key out of my back pocket and unlocked the door. "See you tomorrow."

He left for his room down the hall. I watched him for a moment, only then realizing I was trembling. What had just happened? And why did I feel sad I hadn't taken him up on his offer?

Friday was so jam-packed with choir practices and other group activities I didn't get another chance to be alone with Arie to find out whether he'd been simply flirting with me outside my hotel room or had been serious.

That night, I received a late-night text from Maya about Emmy, a girl from our school, who was almost kidnapped at the football game that evening. Maya had no details to give me since she'd heard about it secondhand, but that hadn't kept Kathryn and me from staying up all night talking about how crazy it was for something like that to happen in Maplebridge.

The next day when we talked to Arie about it, he seemed really concerned. He asked me whether I knew Emmy well, what she looked like, and other random things—which apparently helped him make sense of why someone would want to kidnap her. Who knows, maybe kidnappers were looking for tall brunettes. When I tried to make a joke about me being next on the kidnapping gang's hit list based on those characteristics, he didn't find it very funny.

The performance went well on Saturday. It was a long concert—what with the band, orchestra, and choir all performing—but it was wonderful. The most talented young musicians from all over Utah were together, and the outcome was remarkable. It was also a great honor to perform in the Conference Center. Many famous operas, choirs, and orchestras from around the world had performed there.

By the time the concert was over Saturday night, I could barely keep my eyes open in the bus. I tried to find a comfortable position, but I was sitting with Arie again and I didn't want to invade his space—especially because I wasn't sure what was going on between us, not after the flirting outside my hotel room. I hoped there were some real feelings developing between us, but I didn't want to scare him off if he was on the fence. So to be safe, I ended up hunching forward, resting my elbows on my knees, my chin on my hands, my head against the seat in front of me. Not the most comfortable position, but it'd have to do.

Arie was next to the window, so he was able to lean against the side of the bus to rest.

"You look comfortable," he said after a minute, his tone playful. He was looking at me with half-shut eyes, but there was a smirk on his lips.

"I'm tired enough that I'm sure I'll be asleep in a little while, no matter what position I'm in."

"Maybe," he said.

After a minute, I shifted around again. I moved my hands

to my neck, so my jaw rested on the side of my hands. I tried slouching down in my seat, but since I was still in my choir dress, it was hard to breathe that way. I sat up again, and eyed the floor, but it was filthy and I didn't want to ruin my dress.

I peeked at Arie to see whether he was sleeping yet.

He wasn't. He was looking at me with a crooked grin. Had he been watching me that whole time?

"Come on, Emma, just lean against me." He reached over and tugged on my arm. "I may not be soft, but I'm sure we'll both sleep better than with you fidgeting around like that."

"Okay..." My heart raced as I scooted closer to him. *Was he serious about this?*

He tugged on my arm again, so I moved to lean against him. Right before my head touched his chest, I stopped. "What if my makeup gets on your shirt?" I didn't usually wear a ton of makeup, but when I performed with the choir, I always added extra so I wouldn't look washed out on stage. Once after a concert last year, I'd forgotten about it and accidentally gotten some on Nick's favorite shirt as we cuddled. He'd been furious, even though I'd apologized and offered to wash it myself. I would hate to do the same thing to Arie's nice white tuxedo shirt.

"It will wash off," he said. "I'm really not worried about it."

My anxiety lessened somewhat. "Are you sure?"

"Yes."

I leaned my head the rest of the way down.

He was right about not being soft. His torso was all hard, lean muscle, but it was much more comfortable than the positions I had tried earlier...and much more enjoyable.

He rested his arms around me, pulling me in closer. "Is that better?" he asked, speaking into my hair.

I smiled and nodded, breathing in his cologne. He smelled amazing. "Much better."

19

ARIE

"HEY, ARIE." Jason looked up from his newspaper as I dragged myself into the kitchen Sunday morning. He was sitting at the table, eating breakfast before he and Sophie would relieve Bruce from the late-night shift of watching Emma's house.

"Good morning." I yawned and rubbed the sleep from my eyes. We'd gotten back from the choir trip late last night, so I hadn't slept as long as I'd liked. Sure, I'd dozed off on the bus with Emma, but I had woken after a little while. I hadn't been able to fall asleep again because I was too distracted by the beautiful girl I held in my arms. I'd spent the rest of the ride trying to figure out what I should do about the complicated situation I'd gotten myself into.

I couldn't ignore the attraction I felt. But what was I supposed to do? She was way too young for me, even if she didn't know it. Her parents would undoubtedly object to her dating someone so much older, and Sophie would probably fire me if she discovered I was interested in being more than friends with Emma.

I pondered on those thoughts as I made my usual green

smoothie. Once it was blended, I toasted some bread, then sat down at the table where Jason was reading the newspaper with a serious look on his face.

He set the paper down just as I finished my food. "Were you able to find out more about the girl who was almost kidnapped?" he asked.

"Not much. I only got the physical description that I texted you Friday night, and then yesterday Emma told me a few more things...but nothing to tip us off on whether it was a random kidnapping or an attempt to find Emma." I nodded toward the paper Jason was holding. "Do they know who tried to kidnap her?"

Jason set his finger on the article he'd been reading. "No, it said the girl could only describe the kidnappers as males wearing ski masks. She said there was something familiar about one of them, but she didn't know why."

"That's not much for the police to go on. Do you think the kidnappers could be working for Fenris and thought they'd found Emma?"

"I don't know," Jason answered. "If girls Emma's age are the target, it may not be a coincidence—especially since their names are so similar."

"Looks like we better keep an even closer eye on Emma now." I would have to find ways to spend more time with her. I'd never forgive myself if something happened to her while she was supposed to be under my protection...and for the first time, it wasn't just because it was my job.

20

EMMA

"I HAVE A PROBLEM," I said into the phone Sunday morning. "I think I like Arie. I mean I think I *really* like Arie."

"Are you serious?" Maya said on the other line. "When did this happen?"

"I think it's been slowly coming on since I met him. I tried to push it away at first because of what happened with Nick, plus I thought you might like him. But after this weekend I don't know what to do."

"I say you go for it!"

Go for it? Just like that? It couldn't be that simple. I still didn't know whether I was ready to trust a guy again. Plus, why would Arie be interested in me? I was about as plain Jane as they came.

"What if he doesn't feel the same way?" I whined. "We've become really good friends. I don't want to mess it up."

"Hmm, it is kind of a sticky situation," Maya allowed. The line was silent for a moment. "Has he done anything to show he might be interested in you?"

"I don't know. He flirts, but he might be like that with lots of girls. I mean, doesn't he flirt with you?" I hadn't seen him around other girls besides my friends, so I had no idea what he was like with them.

"Not really," she said. "When he first moved here, I flirted with him a lot, and he played along, but I could tell he didn't want to encourage me too much."

"I don't know what to think, then." I raised my free hand into the air as I paced along the plush carpet in my bedroom. "Maybe he's playing along with me, too, like he did with you." I sighed. "I wish I could read his mind."

"Hey, I'll tell you what. I'll watch him more closely at school and see if I can tell whether he likes you or not."

"I guess that sounds like a good idea." I stopped my pacing and sat down on my bed. Having an extra set of eyes to figure Arie out might be helpful.

"Isn't crushing on a guy so fun?" Maya asked. "How was your choir trip, anyway?"

"It was amazing." I smiled at the memory of hanging out with Arie. "We had some downtime, so that was nice. I hung out with Kathryn for part of it, but she was with Conner Thursday night, so I ended up hanging out alone with Arie."

"Lucky for you he's new and doesn't have any other close friends in choir."

"I know. It was fun being with him," I said. "He saved me a spot on the bus the first day, and we sat together the rest of the time."

"That's something, isn't it?" Maya asked.

"Yeah. And on the bus ride home, he offered to let me lean against him to rest." I tried not to sound too excited. It had been nice being close to him for so long. The ride had taken four hours, and I had slept most of the time. When I'd woken up, Arie had covered me with his jacket—which was so sweet to me, for some reason. Not wanting to move away, I had pretended to sleep awhile longer.

"Oooooh." Maya made her voice go up and down as she said it.

"He was just being nice."

"I don't know about that," she said. "A guy doesn't invite a girl to cuddle up with him unless he's interested."

"Maybe." A flicker of hope blossomed in my chest. "I sure hope he's interested." I realized I had no idea what she'd done last week while Kathryn and I were gone, so I asked her.

"Landon and Derek invited me to go to a party at Derek's house Saturday night."

"Did you go?" I lay back on my bed, still holding the phone to my ear. I could relax now we were done talking about my new crush on Arie.

"Yeah."

"How was the party?" I was a little surprised she'd want to hang out with Derek since he seemed to drive her nuts at school.

"It was fun." Then she hurried to add, "Of course, it would've been much better with you and Kathryn there."

"You're just saying that so I don't feel bad," I teased.

"Fine, it was super fun, even without you." She giggled. "Derek was actually a great host and made sure I was comfortable, since he knew I'd come by myself."

"Wow...that's surprising."

"Tell me about it." Her voice took on a serious tone. "Speaking of surprising, isn't it so crazy about Emmy almost getting kidnapped?"

"I know. I hope she's okay. I don't think I would ever feel safe going out alone at night again if I were her." She was such a nice girl at school it was weird to think someone would try to kidnap her.

My parents sure seemed shaken up by it. They'd lectured me all during breakfast about ways to be safe, warning me about going places alone when it's dark. "I don't think I'll be allowed to go to football games anymore after the way my parents reacted."

"I know what you mean. My parents freaked out, too."

The next Wednesday, I went to the annual Maplebridge Halloween Festival with my parents. My mom used to be an event planner, and because she was going through withdrawal, she'd volunteered to be in charge of the whole thing this year. Since she and Dad had to stay late to clean up, I ended up walking down the street to my work around nine. My parents said they'd come pick me up at work as soon as they were finished.

I had cleaned all the offices and was coming in from emptying the trash when the sound of male voices drifted down the hall from the lobby. I froze where I was and strained to listen. I could only make out a few words.

Who is here at this hour?

Then I heard one of them say clearly in a hushed voice, "I'll go in and look. You stay here and keep an eye on the door."

I peeked around the corner as a dark, bulky figure crept down another hall. My stomach dropped, and I went cold with fear. Thoughts of the almost kidnapping last week came to my mind. Could these be the same guys?

My heart pounded in my ears as I shakily tiptoed toward the back door. Had they seen or heard me? Should I call the police? What were they doing here?

Footsteps sounded around the corner. *Crap!* Where the heck was I supposed to hide? Just a few feet ahead was the dark stairwell. My breath came in short bursts as I dashed toward it, barely making it around the corner before the guy could see me. My pulse thrummed in my chest as I tried to formulate a plan. I didn't have a car outside to assist me in a quick getaway, so I was stuck until my parents came. But I needed to get out of the building before the guys found me. I peeked my head around the corner to see how far the back exit was. About five feet. I could make it if the coast was clear. I glanced down the other way only to yank my head back. A tall, lanky guy with a baseball cap stood at the end of the hall. I leaned my back flat against the wall, placing a hand over my chest.

I waited and listened for movement. After a few, long minutes, I peeked around the corner again. He was gone. I rushed to the back exit and slipped outside.

The door creaked loudly as it closed. I clamped a hand over my mouth to hold in a scream as I ran, knowing the guy keeping watch probably heard the noise. I scrambled toward the dumpster at the side of the building and crouched down behind it.

When no one came to inspect the noise, I pulled my phone out of my back pocket with a trembling hand. My parents should have been done by now. But knowing them, they'd probably lost track of time and ended up gabbing with their friends. My mom was famous for talking anyone's ear off if given the chance.

I called my parents, but it went straight to voice mail. Why did they always have their cell phones turned off?

Maybe I could walk back to the community center. I tried to step back, but my legs were paralyzed. I couldn't move them if I wanted to. It wouldn't be good to be seen walking alone in the dark anyway. It would be all too easy for someone to kidnap a lone girl walking this late at night.

Arie. I could call Arie. I dialed his number, and relief washed over me when he picked up after two rings.

"Hello?" He sounded surprised.

"H-hey, Arie," I tried to whisper with my shaky voice. "I-I'm sorry to bother you so late, but I need help."

"What's wrong?"

"Could you pick me up from work? I can't reach my parents, and I'm creeped out right now. I don't think I can wait any longer for them to show up."

"What's going on? Are you okay? Are you in danger?" His voice wavered, like he was running, and I heard his truck door open and slam shut.

"I can't talk right now," I whispered back. "I'm at work, and the address is 337 South Main Str—"

The back door creaked open.

I hung up on Arie, hoping the guy hadn't heard me whispering or seen the light from my phone.

"D?" the guy called quietly. "Are you out here?"

Silence.

I pressed myself against the dumpster, not caring what kind of grossness might be smeared all over my clothes.

My phone made a deafening ring, a discordant echo that shook every cell in my body, putting my pulse on hold. I muffled the sound against my stomach, before finding the button to silence it completely.

My heart banged against my rib cage as I waited for the guy to approach my hiding spot. But I couldn't hear any movement.

The door creaked shut again.

I sank to the ground with relief as my fingers fumbled to turn the ringer on my phone off. I glanced down and saw I had a missed call from Arie.

A car door slammed in the parking lot, and an engine hummed to life. I released a breath. After a moment, I poked my head up and saw a dark car parked out front with the base-ball-cap guy sitting in the driver's seat. The bulkier man soon came out of the office, striding toward the dark car with a handful of papers. His face turned in my direction as he scanned the area. I dropped down again before he could see me. It was too dark to get a good look at his face.

A moment later, I heard the car pull out of the parking lot, leaving me alone behind the dumpster.

Soon headlights beamed from the parking lot again.

Had they come back?

I peeked around the dumpster and recognized Arie's truck. My blood pumped through my veins as I rushed to the passenger side of the vehicle and jumped in as fast as I could.

"What's going on? Are you okay?" Arie's brow was puckered, and he sounded out of breath.

"I'll tell you about it in a sec," I said, breathing heavily. "Let's get out of here."

I fumbled with my seatbelt. My hands and arms shook so badly I couldn't hold steady enough to latch it. Arie noticed me struggling and leaned over, placing his hands over mine.

"Let me do it." He took the seatbelt from me and snapped it into the buckle.

"Thanks."

He sat up straight again, switched the truck into gear, and turned onto Main Street. He must've sensed how desperate I was to get away from there, because he didn't ask until we were safely parked in front of my house.

He turned the engine off and stared at me, concern written in his eyes. "What happened, Emma? Are you hurt?" His voice was rough with worry.

"No, I'm not hurt, just freaked out."

"What happened?" He leaned closer and studied me, as if trying to make sure I truly hadn't been hurt.

I drew in a shaky breath and told him everything. I let out a big sigh when I finished, hoping Arie didn't think I was scared over nothing. "I probably sound ridiculous getting so worked up about this."

"No, not at all." He undid his seatbelt and scooted closer to me on the bench seat. I didn't need any more encouragement than that to undo my seatbelt and lean against him, wrapping my arms around his torso. I didn't like feeling this way, like a little girl scared out of her wits as the big bad wolf circled around her.

"Sorry I'm acting so weird," I said after a minute, still clinging to Arie.

He put his arms around me and gave me a reassuring squeeze. "Don't be sorry. I know guys are supposed to be fearless and all, but even *my* heart was pounding as I drove to pick you up."

I sat up again and looked at his face. He gave me an understanding smile. "Thanks, you're sweet." I wiped at a tear threatening to escape.

"I'm being honest."

"Do you think I should tell someone what I saw?"

Arie rubbed the back of his neck. "I think so. I mean, if not the cops, then at least the people you work for."

I swallowed. "Do you think it could have been those kidnappers?"

Arie frowned. "I don't know. It could be."

My phone rang, startling me.

It was my mom.

I lifted the phone to my ear. "Hey, Mom." I tried to speak in as bright and cheery a voice as I could.

"Emma! Where are you?"

"I'm home. I couldn't get a hold of you guys, and something happened at work, so I asked Arie to come pick me up."

"Something happened at work?" My mom's voice raised an octave.

"It's okay now. I'll tell you when you get home." I tried to sound calm so she wouldn't be worried all the way home. I knew my attempt was futile—she'd been worried all week about the attempted kidnapping. I'd be put on lockdown for sure once she heard about tonight.

"We're on our way now."

"Okay, bye." I turned to Arie. "Would you mind waiting with me until my parents get home?"

"I wouldn't leave even if you told me to." His tone was light, but there was something in his eyes that made me think he wasn't speaking lightly at all.

"Thanks."

"In fact, if you ever end up working late again and wanted someone there with you, I'd be happy to come. You know, in case something like this happens again."

Did he really care that much about my safety?

I cleared my throat. "I might take you up on that. I hate being there alone so late."

"Please do. I don't want anything like this to happen again." He paused and lowered his voice. "I thought something terrible had happened after you hung up on me. And when you didn't answer my call right after..." He sighed and shook his head.

Dizziness swept over me at the thought of Arie actually caring enough to want to keep me safe. I studied him in the dimly lit truck. The look in his eyes really was sincere.

He scooted closer. "I'm really glad you called me."

"Me too," I whispered, the dizzy feeling growing as I gazed at him. His eyes were still intense, but there was something else in them, too. Apprehension? Nervousness? He glanced down at my lips and inched closer.

The truck flooded with light. I broke out of my daze as my parents pulled into the driveway. They opened the doors, jumped out, and sprinted toward Arie's truck.

"I better go." I turned in my seat, feeling my cheeks burn. "I-I'll see you tomorrow at school."

I was about to get out when my mom ripped open the door.

"What happened?" she cried, hugging me as my feet touched the pavement. "You had us worried sick."

Once I wriggled out of her tight hug, I told her everything that had happened at work and how Arie had rescued me. When I was done, my mom looked past me into Arie's truck.

"Thank you so much for helping Emma out tonight." She drew in a deep breath, put an arm around my torso, and pulled me to her side.

"You're welcome. I'm happy I could help."

My mom nodded. "You must come to dinner with us on Friday night so we can thank you properly."

"You don't need to do that. I was doing my..." He shook his head. "I was helping a friend in need."

"No, I insist." Mom leaned into the cab of Arie's truck. "It's Emma's birthday dinner anyway, and it would be fun to get to know one of her friends better."

Arie's gaze wandered to me briefly. "Okay. If it's her birthday, then I would love to come help you celebrate."

"Great. We'll see you then."

21

ARIE

I DROVE to the other end of the street to watch Emma's house while I called Jason to find out where he'd been. He should've been at the office watching her tonight. If he'd been there, we could have caught those guys and found out what they were doing and who they worked for.

Jason answered his phone after a few rings. "Hi, Arie, what's up?"

"That's what I'd like to know." I knew I sounded angry. I couldn't help it. Emma had been left alone tonight, without protection, and it was the one night she'd needed it. Him not being there was unacceptable. "Where the heck were you tonight? I just dropped Emma off at her house after a close call at the office."

"I-I lost track of her." He sounded defensive. "I was watching the parking lot at the community center, waiting for her family to leave, and after a couple of hours her parents left without her. She must've slipped out a side door and walked to the office while her parents stayed behind."

"It looks like you need to pay closer attention in the future,"

I said through clenched teeth. Jason was getting older and had been doing this job for a long time. Maybe he was becoming lax in his duties.

"I'm pulling up to her house now," Jason said. I glanced down the street and saw his headlights approaching. "What happened at the office?"

"Emma said there were a couple of guys searching the building when she was about to go home. She had to run out and hide behind the dumpster and wait for them to leave." Jason parked his car in front of Bruce's house, across the street from Emma's. "When she called me, she was terrified. The guys didn't see her, but that doesn't mean they won't try coming back."

"Are you serious?" I could imagine the confused look on Jason's face as he spoke.

"I know. I'm starting to worry that the guys working for Fenris may have figured out where she's been all these years." I pinched the bridge of my nose and squeezed my eyes shut for a moment, trying to relieve some of the tension I felt. "I'll try to get Emma to let me come to work with her from now on. Those guys may come back, and we'll need more than just one guard watching from outside to protect her."

We finished our conversation, and I pulled out from the spot I'd parked in. I waved to Jason as I drove past his car, still frustrated with him for making such a huge mistake.

22

EMMA

THE NEXT MORNING, I called the office to let them know what I had witnessed the night before. They didn't know of a guy nicknamed "D" who worked in the building, so they said they'd report the incident. They appreciated the call but said I shouldn't worry about it any further.

I had a lot of other things to think about, anyway, so I pushed the incident from my mind. Today was my birthday, and Arie was coming to dinner with us.

Eighteen. I couldn't believe it.

At six sharp, Arie arrived at my house, looking way too good in his gray V-neck shirt. Once I had discreetly checked him out, we headed to the best Mexican restaurant in town, La Casa Garcia, with my parents. It was a family-owned restaurant, in a quaint old house on Main Street that desperately needed a facelift. The stucco exterior was chipped and discolored, and the interior needed a fresh coat of paint as well, but the food was authentic and delicious. I had actually applied for a job there last year, just so I could learn the secret recipe for the salsa. Sadly, I never got the job or the recipe.

"It's a good thing you and your siblings were cute when you were little. If you hadn't been, you probably wouldn't have survived after all the mischief you got yourselves into," Mom said as we ate. Instead of tonight being a nice relaxing dinner with my parents getting to know Arie better, they'd decided to turn it into an exposé on all the embarrassing things I'd done growing up. Apparently, I'd been quite the tornado when I was two, and my parents wanted to make sure Arie knew every detail there was to know.

"What other things did Emma do?" Arie asked as he cut into his pork burrito. "Sounds like she kept you busy." He winked at me, obviously loving all the stories.

"I think we've heard enough for one night," I said, hoping to end the humiliation.

My mom patted my arm. "It's okay, sweetie. I just have one more." She looked at Arie. "It's really cute, actually."

"Oh yeah?" Arie grinned.

"When Emma was a baby, she loved her binky so much she had to have it with her all the time. It got so bad that we finally decided to cut her off from it, cold turkey. We told her how there was a binky fairy who was gonna take her pacifier to give it to new babies.

"One night, we showed her a picture of the new baby who was getting her binky." Mom stifled a giggle. Ugh, why were my parents so embarrassing? "Let me tell you, Emma wasn't happy at all. She went around saying, 'I no wike dat baby,' all night. It was hilarious!"

Both my parents were laughing now.

"Oh, come on, honey," Dad said to me. "You were so cute when you were mad."

Arie's smile ran from ear to ear. He was *so* planning to tease me later; I could see it in his eyes. But my parents weren't done yet. Mom looked at me pointedly and said, "You were quite the little drama queen. I'm glad you grew out of that phase, or I'd be completely gray by now. Possibly in a mental institution."

Dad cracked up. I rolled my eyes at them. "Yeah, yeah."

My dad reached across the table to squeeze my arm. "I can't believe our baby girl is an adult now. Soon you'll be off to college and then getting married. The years have gone by so quickly."

My mom sniffled and dabbed at her eyes. I started to feel a little sentimental myself and drew in a deep breath to calm my emotions. I couldn't have Arie see us all become a blubbering mess.

Dad removed the glasses from his face, looked at them, and then wiped them clean with the tail end of his shirt. "You've certainly matured over the years, and we're proud of the beautiful, bright daughter you turned out to be."

Wow, this was getting over the top. It was just my birthday dinner. It's not like I was leaving the house or anything. No need to get all mushy. "Thanks. I think I turned out okay." Then for added measure, I said, "All thanks to your awesome parenting." I might as well try and earn a few brownie points while I was at it.

As if I had said the magic words, Mom set a silver gift bag on the table in front of me. "Your father and I got you this for your birthday."

"Thanks!" I gazed at the bag, trying to guess what it was. I'd hinted before that I would like a car for my birthday, but I knew there was a fat chance of that happening. My parents didn't believe in buying their children vehicles. That was something I would have to save up for on my own.

I reached inside and found the latest electronic tablet sitting at the bottom of the bag. "This. Is. Awesome!" I turned it over in my hands.

"We hoped you'd like it," Dad said, glancing at my mom.

"We thought it would be a good thing for you to have for college next year."

My mom pointed to the bag. "There's something else in there."

I reached in the bag again and felt around for a moment before my fingers found a small aerosol can. Pepper spray. I furrowed my brow.

"And that's to give your father and me peace of mind," my mom said, noticing my confusion. "After what happened at work on Wednesday night, we wanted to make sure you had some sort of protection with you."

I gave my parents an appreciative smile. "These gifts are perfect. I can't wait to use them—well, at least the tablet, that is." I held up the pepper spray. "Hopefully I won't be needing this anytime soon."

"We hope so, too." Mom glanced at Dad, then back to me. "Did you have anything planned with your friends after this? Is there a basketball game tonight?"

"Uh-huh. Maya and Kathryn wanted us to meet them at the game after this, and then we were gonna drag Arie to the discount theater to see a chick flick."

My parents smiled at Arie, who smiled back in a way that made me think they were all keeping something from me.

23

EMMA

IT WAS ALMOST seven thirty by the time we arrived home from dinner, which meant Arie and I were late to the basketball game. As soon as we walked through the door, the lights flicked on and we were greeted with a loud, "Surprise!"

My jaw dropped as I scanned the living room. Maya, Kathryn, and about fifteen other friends from school stood in my living room. There were bright balloons and hot pink streamers, and a large ice-cream cake on the coffee table. A huge smile crept across my face.

"Wow!" I said, setting my gift bag on the coffee table. "Talk about a surprise! How'd you guys keep this secret from me?"

"We're awesome, that's how." Maya shrugged when I hugged her. Everyone else in the room grinned and nodded, Arie included. The sneaky smile he'd shared with my parents at dinner made sense now.

After I finished my round of hugging and thanking everyone for coming, Kathryn called out, "I think the birthday girl deserves a special song, don't you?"

Mom lit the candles on the ice-cream cake, and the group

sang happy birthday to me. When the song was over, I made a wish and blew out the candles.

I followed my mom into the kitchen to help serve the cake to my friends, but Kathryn grabbed my arm and stopped me. "Oh no you don't, Birthday Girl. *We* will be serving *you* today. Not the other way around."

I stayed behind, glancing around the room for a place to sit. The only seat left was a chair next to my wizarding friend, Brian. Nope, better to stay standing. But Brian caught me looking in his direction and motioned for me to sit by him. So I did, not wanting to be rude.

Since our date, I had avoided Brian pretty well. The times I had talked to him, he'd given the impression that he liked me more than I wanted. At school, I'd always gotten away before he could ask me out on a second date.

"Hey, Birthday Girl," Brian said.

"Oh, hey." I wondered how he'd ended up being invited to the party. I didn't think Maya would go out of her way to invite him. "How long have you known about this?"

"A few days. Kathryn was drawing up some party plans before school when I stopped to talk to her." He pushed his glasses up higher on the bridge of his nose. "I asked her what she was doing, and she ended up inviting me."

So that was it. Kathryn was too nice sometimes. But I couldn't be mad at her, because I'm pretty sure I would have done the same in that situation.

"I even helped with some of the plans," he went on. "They didn't use all my ideas, but I'm sure you would've loved them."

"Really? What were some of your ideas?" I couldn't begin to imagine the things he'd come up with for a party. Maya came over at that moment and served us our ice-cream cake. I stabbed it with my fork and took a bite of the chocolate ice cream.

"One idea I knew you'd love was to have a wizard-themed

party. I remembered how much you enjoyed using the wands on our date, and I thought it would be fun to continue." I almost choked on my cake. "I even offered to let them borrow my collection of wands to decorate with. Maya didn't like the idea for some reason. I guess she doesn't know you as well as I do."

I cleared my throat. "Uh, that's an interesting idea. Nice that you even offered up some of your wands. I know how special they are to you." I crammed the last bit of my cake into my mouth, excused myself, and escaped to the kitchen.

"What's next?" I asked Maya, who was eating her cake at the counter.

"What? You want more?" Maya asked sarcastically. "Isn't this enough?"

"What I meant was, are we going to be hanging out here for a while or going to the last half of the game?"

In between bites, she said, "I was thinking we could hang around here tonight. We could get the karaoke machine out downstairs, pull out some other games, or watch a movie. Maybe have a few things going on at once for people to choose from."

"Sounds fun."

A sudden spark came into her eyes. "Hey, maybe we could even get Arie to serenade the birthday girl with that sexy voice of his."

"Shhh." I peeked behind me to make sure no one had overheard Maya's suggestion. Thankfully, no one else was near the kitchen.

She laughed. "Oh come on, I'm sure I could get him to do it for you."

"Ha-ha, yeah. There's nothing more uncomfortable than being serenaded in front of fifteen other people. I mean, you of all people should know. Didn't you get, like, three singing valentines last year?"

"It's not so bad once you get used to it." She leaned against the granite counter.

"Please don't ask him to do it," I said. "I don't want everyone to know that I like him."

"Fine, I won't."

A little later, Maya and I ushered our friends downstairs. We got the karaoke machine going, which was popular with the girls. It was fun to listen to some and painful to listen to others. After a lot of begging, a few of the girls were able to persuade Arie to sing a song with them. It was cute to watch him get all self-conscious in front of the group. He really had nothing to worry about, though, because he totally rocked it. After karaoke, the group broke up—some started watching a movie while others went upstairs to play party games in the living room.

Exhaustion started to creep over me, and I yawned. I hadn't slept well since Wednesday night and wanted to lie down and rest for a minute. But I couldn't do that with everyone at my house.

Instead, I decided to go out back, hoping the cool night air would wake me up. I went upstairs, grabbed a thick jacket, and went out on the deck.

My breath swirled in the air as I walked to the porch swing. I loved rocking back and forth on the swing. The motion had a calming effect and was a place I always came to when I needed to think.

My mind wandered back to Wednesday night. I hadn't heard anything back from the office or police, so maybe I'd freaked out over nothing? It certainly hadn't seemed like nothing as I'd cowered behind that dirty old dumpster.

I startled when the door opened behind me. *Hopefully, it's not Brian again.* My stomach flip-flopped when Arie stepped out, wearing his jacket. Was he headed home and coming out to say goodbye before he left? My heart sank at the thought.

He zipped up his jacket and put his hands in its pockets as he strolled over to the porch swing. "I saw you come out here all alone and wanted to make sure everything was all right." His brow furrowed.

I was flattered he'd noticed my absence. "I'm fine. I was feeling tired. I'm sure I'll perk up again in a minute." I didn't mention how having him come outside to find me had already brightened my spirits.

"It does feel nice out here." He took a deep breath, gazing into the night sky. "Do you mind if I sit with you?"

"Of course not." I slowed the swing.

We began swinging back and forth, sitting in silence for a few minutes, just enjoying the peaceful evening atmosphere—well, at least I *pretended* to be serenely enjoying the clear night with stars twinkling high above us. I was actually freaking out on the inside at being alone with him again.

"Have you had a good birthday?" Arie asked after a while.

I nodded. "It's been good, and definitely full of surprises." I turned in my seat to face him, putting my back against the armrest, and tucking one leg beneath me on the seat. "I had no idea everyone would be here when we got back from dinner."

He smiled his signature dazzling smile that made my heart pick up its pace. "Maya threatened us with our lives if we so much as mentioned that your birthday was coming up."

"I'm glad no one lost their life because I turned eighteen."

"*Eighteen.*" Arie said the number as if it had some special significance. He ran a hand through his tousled hair that looked almost black in the moonlight. "You're old enough to date older men like Mr. Rochester now." He winked.

I scrunched up my face. "Ew. Just because you're old enough to do something, doesn't mean you should."

"Oh yes, yes. I remember. You have those rules of yours. No one over, let's see," he made a show of counting on his fingers, "eighteen, nineteen, twenty, twenty-one...and since you said a few years, which most people translate into three or four, that means twenty-two-year-olds are also included in that list."

"I don't think I'm quite ready for that." The eighteen-year-old in front of me was all I could think about at the moment.

"Come on." He smiled. "Older guys are cool, too."

"Is that what you say to all those fourteen-year-olds you've been trying to pick up?"

He scowled. "Now that's just not cool, Emma. You know I wasn't talking about dating middle schoolers."

"I know. But if you think you can tease me about dating older men, then you better be able to take what you're dishing out."

"Okay, okay." He held his hands in front of him. "I was just reminding you of the significance of this birthday. You being eighteen changes *everything*."

"Everything?" I challenged. "How?"

He opened his mouth to say something when the door burst open.

"Emma. Are you out here?" Maya called out.

"Yeah, over here on the swing...*with Arie*." I hoped she'd take the hint and leave us alone. I really, *really* wanted to see where this conversation was headed.

She didn't take the hint. Her shoes clomped on the wooden deck as she hurried toward us.

"I've been looking *everywhere* for you." She placed a hand

on her chest as she tried to catch her breath. "I need to warn you before Brian finds you."

"Warn me?"

Arie sat up straight and scanned my backyard.

Weird.

Maya eyed Arie, seeming to notice his change in behavior, too. She said, "I just overheard Brian and Troy talking about the Winter Ball. Brian says he's planning on asking you tonight!"

The blood drained from my face. "Are you sure you heard right?" The Winter Ball was the boy's choice dance coming up in two weeks. It always had a theme to it, and this year's was a masquerade. I loved the idea of a masquerade and hoped to get asked...just not by Brian. I actually hoped Arie would ask me, but I wasn't about to blurt that out right here and now.

"Yes, I'm sure. He said he's asking *the birthday girl* tonight." Maya made air quotes with her hands. "You're the only birthday girl here that I know of."

"Oh no! What am I gonna do?" I jumped up from the swing, wanting to run and hide.

Arie just relaxed in his seat and laughed.

"He was looking all over for you. I'm amazed I found you before he did," she said. "We better think of something fast."

I started bouncing up and down, shaking my hands at my sides. "Umm..." I tried to think.

"Hey, I got it!" Maya said. "Sit down next to Arie." I sat where I'd been earlier. "No, closer." Maya motioned with her hands as she spoke. She turned her head to look at Arie. "Now, Arie, if you wouldn't mind placing your arm across Emma's shoulder."

Arie smiled and draped his arm around me. "Like this?"

"Yes, just like that. Now Emma, you'll need to cuddle up a little closer." I did as she said, feeling my face heat up and heart rate increase. I hoped Maya wasn't just playing some kind of sick joke on us. "Okay. Perfect. I don't think Brian would dare ask you after seeing you all cozied up with Arie."

I hoped this would work, because I didn't have any other ideas of what to do.

We all turned our heads when the back door opened again. To my dismay, it was Brian. Maya was still standing in front of Arie and me, so we pretended to be talking as he came to stand by her.

He studied Arie and me on the swing. There was no way he'd continue with his plans after seeing such a display.

"Hey, guys," he said.

"Hi, Brian," Maya answered for us all.

Silence.

"Soooo." Brian rocked back on his heels with his hands behind his back. Was he trying to think of some other reason to be out here? After giving Arie a cold look, he took a deep breath and looked straight at me. "Emma, as you know, the Winter Ball is coming up in a few weeks. Since we had such a great time on our last date, I was wondering if you wanted to go with me to the dance?"

My mouth went slack. What could I say to that? Even though I wasn't interested in going on a second date, I didn't have the heart to turn him down, not when he had an audience and I didn't already have a date.

Maya shook her head at me, probably knowing I was about to cave.

I couldn't help it, though. It was scary to ask someone out on a date, and rejection felt horrible. I opened my mouth to respond, but then Arie cleared his throat.

"Sorry, but I just asked Emma to the dance." He scooted even closer to me. "She already said yes."

I couldn't believe my ears. *Was he serious?* He squeezed my shoulder, answering my unspoken question. I focused on Brian again and answered, somewhat hesitantly, "Yeah, Arie and I already made plans to go together. Sorry."

Brian looked down at his shoes. "Well…I hope you have a great time together at the dance."

"Thanks," I said. "I hope you find someone to go with soon."

Brian checked the time on his phone. "It's getting late." It was only nine thirty. "I better get home. I forgot I needed to walk my dog tonight. Happy birthday, Emma. I hope you enjoy the rest of your evening." His voice sounded dead.

"Thanks for coming. I'll see you at school on Monday." I tried to sound cheerful, but I really just pitied him. Maybe I should have said yes before Arie spoke. It was awesome of Arie to help me out, but I felt bad for Brian. I could've endured a few more hours at a dance with him. I hated hurting people's feelings.

Brian left, his shoulders slumped.

"Whew! That was close," Maya said after the door closed behind Brian. "Quick thinking there, Arie." She took a few steps toward the door. "I'll just leave you two to discuss your plans for the Winter Ball. It's so nice you guys are going together." She winked, then headed back inside.

"Thanks, Maya. I'll be inside in a sec," I called before she shut the door.

Arie and I were alone again, still cuddled up on the swing. I didn't know whether I should move back to the end of the swing where I'd been before or stay put. I didn't want to move. He was warm, and strong, and smelled amazing. Maybe I would just stay put for now. I'd move if he acted like he wanted me to.

"Thanks for saving me there. I kind of froze and didn't

know what to do." I played with the sleeves of my jacket. "I didn't think he'd ask, not after seeing us like this together."

"No problem," he said, his breath in my hair. "I could tell you didn't know what to do."

"I feel so bad, though. It's scary to ask someone out. I'd die if someone turned me down in front of others."

"We'll just have to really go to the dance together, so he won't know he was being rejected for real."

I liked that idea. I probably liked that idea a little more than was healthy. I tried to sound cool about it, but I was bursting with excitement inside. "If you don't mind." Then, just in case, I added, "But if you were planning to ask someone else, we could stage a fight in front of Brian or something. I don't want to ruin your plans." I turned to read his face.

His lips twitched like he was fighting a smile. "No, I hadn't planned on asking anyone else. Really, I don't mind." Then he paused before saying, "Unless *you* were hoping to go with someone else."

I shook my head. "No, there's no one else."

Definitely not!

24

ARIE

I WAS glad I'd been outside with Emma when Brian came out to ask her to the dance. I'd heard about the dance coming up, and the thought of asking her had crossed my mind—especially since she was eighteen now. I'd decided against asking her initially because it wouldn't have been appropriate under the circumstances. But the opportunity had presented itself, so I was more than happy to take advantage of my luck.

If Jason or Sophie had a problem with it, I'd tell them I was doing my job of staying close to her. They couldn't argue with that. Plus, hadn't Jason suggested I ask her out when we went to Salt Lake anyway?

"Has anything out of the ordinary happened since Wednesday night?" I asked Emma as we sat, still close together on the swing. I hadn't had a chance to talk with her about it since dropping her off in front of her house that night.

"No, but I'm kind of nervous about going to work again." She sighed. "I need the money for college, so I can't just stop cleaning the office."

"My offer still stands," I said. "I'd be more than happy to go with you to work. I could help keep an eye out."

She thought about it for a moment. "If you're sure...then that would be great." She turned and placed her hand on my bicep. My pulse quickened. "I mean, who'd want to mess with these guns." She giggled.

I knew I was in good shape, but Emma had never seemed to notice before. I didn't know whether I should be flattered or embarrassed. I decided to go with flattered. "Let's hope it doesn't come to that," I said.

"Does Emma know anything more about those guys from Wednesday night?" Sophie asked me at breakfast the next morning.

"Not really. What about you and Jason?"

"We talked to the different businesses in the building. The only one who noticed anything was the girl who works at the front desk of the adoption agency. She said the front door was unlocked when she got there Thursday morning."

"What? That can't be good."

Sophie shook her head. "We can't know for sure, but it's possible the men were searching for certain records from eighteen years ago."

I went to work with Emma that afternoon. At first, I sat on a chair in the office she was cleaning at the time and flipped through a magazine. That got boring fast, so to make the time pass by, I grabbed a rag and started dusting things around the office. Emma tried to stop me, but I insisted that I wanted to do it. After all, cleaning was much better than hiding behind a dumpster for a couple of hours. She relented, and we were able to finish in about half the time it usually took her.

We hung out at my house the rest of the day. It was a nice evening and the weather wasn't too cold, so I suggested I just walk Emma home when it was time for her to go.

It was relaxing, walking down the sidewalk with Emma. Her hand was only inches from mine, and I was almost certain she'd let me hold it if I tried. All it would take was a brush of the hand. I forced those thoughts away and instead focused on how the slight breeze blew leaves down the sidewalk, swirling them around for a moment before pushing them farther along the path. Emma started telling me about some of the interesting vacations her family had taken when she was a child. Apparently, her dad was super outdoorsy and had once made her family go on a week-long camping trip where they had to live off the land and catch their dinner in the lake.

"Thankfully, Mom went behind Dad's back and packed a cooler with food. My dad was thankful for that since we all ended up being much worse fishermen than he'd thought." Emma peeked up at me and smiled.

Hearing Emma talk about her father made me think about my own father. He was definitely a different kind of man than her father seemed to be. And hearing her talk about the fun things they did as a family made me realize all the more how many things I had missed out on.

My heart still clenched each time I thought of him, but the fear no longer crippled me as it had when I was younger.

"Sorry to talk so much about my dad; I forgot for a moment that your dad passed away a few years ago," Emma said, probably because I'd been too quiet.

"It's okay," I said. "Don't be sorry. You were telling me about your life. There's nothing wrong with that."

She nodded, then spoke in a quiet voice. "Can you tell me what happened to him?"

My family and my past wasn't something I ever cared to

talk about with people. But for some reason I *wanted* to tell her. I needed someone else to understand and maybe even tell me it was okay to feel the way I did.

"Well." I cleared my throat and looked down the dimly lit street, not really seeing anything but my memories from six years ago. "He died in a car accident." That's what I usually told people, leaving it at that. But I needed to be more transparent with Emma. I had lied to her about so many things already I wanted to be fully honest in this at least. So I stopped walking. She noticed my sudden halt and turned back. "Actually, he drove himself off a cliff."

Emma's light-blue eyes grew big, and she covered her mouth with her hand. "An accident?"

I shook my head. "We'll never know for sure, but I don't think it was an accident."

"I'm so sorry. That's...that must have been so hard!"

I nodded, remembering the details of that evening long ago and the way I'd felt when I heard the news. "At first I was shocked, too numb to really feel anything at all. We all were— my mom, my sister, and me. But after the initial shock wore off, all I felt was...*relief.*"

I surveyed Emma with careful eyes, anxious to see her reaction, worried about what she'd think of me for being relieved my dad was dead. I always felt so guilty for feeling that way. I had to be super twisted and messed up to be like this. But Emma didn't look like she was passing judgment; she simply waited for me to explain.

"Things were hard at first, as we tried to figure out how we would pay the bills now that my dad was gone. But after my mom found a job, life got easier. I no longer had to worry about whether my dad had a good or a bad day at work. I didn't have to listen to him yell at my mom anymore. I didn't have to constantly be ready to jump in and protect her from his swinging fists." It was so ironic that my dad was a judge who had sent people to jail every day for doing the very things he'd done at home. But no one in the community would have believed us if we'd told them what he was really like. He'd practically been turned into a saint after the crash.

"Did he hit you, too?" Emma asked after a beat.

I bit my lip and nodded. "My last memory of my dad is of him chasing after me with a baseball bat." I'd never been more terrified in my life than that day when I was fifteen. "I was so grateful my mom and sister weren't home then, because I was able to jump our back fence into the neighbor's yard and escape, instead of sticking around to take the brunt of my dad's anger in order to protect them.

"I came home hours later to find he'd taken his anger out on our dog. It was horrible digging Brutus's grave, but I was also thankful it hadn't been me in his place." We didn't find out until the next day that my dad's car had been found at the bottom of a cliff. We never found out whether it was an accident or suicide. Given the circumstances of that night, I've always leaned toward suicide—thinking his guilt over everything he'd done to our family through the years had finally gotten to him."

"I'm so sorry." Emma stepped closer and squeezed my arm. It was such a sweet gesture, and for some reason, it did make me feel better. "I can't imagine going through that and how confusing it must have been when he died."

I swallowed, trying to stifle the wave of emotion attempting to come over me. In all the years since that time, I never imagined I would receive this reaction. Emma didn't think I was a monster. "I was pretty messed up for a while and had my time of rebellion for a few years."

She stepped back and gazed at my face, looking beautiful in the moonlight. "You'd never even know it." She smiled, as if she found something amusing. "I still can't believe you were some troubled teen who was sent away to be reformed by his aunt and uncle."

She looped her arm through mine, and we resumed our walk. "I'll take that as a compliment." If only I could tell her the truth, that I hadn't been sent here for that reason. Sure, it was true I'd gotten into some trouble after my father passed, but I'd turned things around years ago.

We walked the rest of the way to her house in comfortable silence. I had so many thoughts running through my mind. When I took this job, dating someone was nowhere in my plans. I hadn't thought I would ever open up to anyone the way I'd opened up to Emma tonight. And now that I knew she wasn't easily scared off, I ached to tell her more.

What did she think of me? Did she want to kiss me as much as I wanted to kiss her? Was she wondering why I hadn't? I hoped so, but at the same time knew I shouldn't. I needed to keep my distance if I wanted to keep my job.

Sometimes living this lie was so confusing.

25

EMMA

IT WAS PRETTY CRAZY, what Arie had told me about his dad. No wonder he was so built. He'd probably needed that extra muscle when defending himself. It was so hard to believe a father could treat his family like that. How did anyone go off and beat up his wife and kids? I couldn't imagine doing that to someone I hated, let alone the family I was supposed to love and cherish.

I knew he had worried about telling me about his past. That was probably why he'd always gotten a little weird around me when I asked him personal questions. I hoped he would feel comfortable enough to confide in me whenever he needed. I was finally to where I could trust someone again, and I wanted to be trusted as well. That was really the most important thing in any relationship. If you couldn't be honest with each other about everything, then you were doomed.

The Saturday before the Winter Ball, I went dress shopping with Maya and Kathryn. Kathryn, of course, was going with Conner to the dance, and weirdly enough, Maya had been asked by Derek. Even weirder was she'd said yes. I always thought they hated each other, but apparently, it was one of those love/hate relationships.

It didn't take long for me to find the perfect dress. It was practically love at first sight. A lavender, floor-length formal with beaded flowers on the bodice and skirt. I loved the lace-up back, which reminded me of the corsets women used to wear long ago.

After we found our dresses, we drove to a costume shop to look for masquerade masks. In the display case was the perfect silver Venetian mask. It had to have been laser cut because it was so intricately designed.

While we shopped, my phone beeped with another text message from a blocked number. It read, **"Why would you want to go to the dance with a stalker and a liar?"**

My brow furrowed. *What the heck?* Who was sending me these texts?

"What is it?" Kathryn asked.

"I've been getting these weird texts lately," I said, handing her my phone.

She read the text as Maya came over to see what we were doing.

"What's up?" Maya asked, slipping between Kathryn and me to look at my phone. Her eyes scanned the message. She turned to me. "Who sent that?"

I shrugged. "I have no idea. This isn't the first text they've sent, either."

"Someone's harassing you?" Maya said a little too loudly before realizing she was drawing attention to us. She cleared her throat and spoke in a quieter voice. "Did you tell your parents?"

"No. I figured someone was playing a prank."

Kathryn shook her head as she handed me back my phone.

"It sounds like whoever is sending you these isn't a big fan of Arie."

I took my phone from her outstretched hand. "That's what it sounds like, but Arie isn't a stalker. Sure we've been spending more time together, but it isn't considered stalking when you *want* the person to be hanging around you."

I shook my head as I deleted the text from my phone. These texts were so ridiculous it was annoying. The first text I'd received had scared me because I was already suspicious of Arie and his possible player-type behavior. But now that I knew him better, he was not like that at all. He was a cool, normal guy who would never lie to anyone. Joke around, of course. But purposely deceive with the intent to hurt? No way.

I got ready at Maya's house the night of the Winter Ball, since my parents were out of town for my grandpa's eighty-fifth birthday party. Anticipation bubbled in my stomach the whole time Maya curled my hair, and by the time the doorbell rang I was so sick with nerves I didn't know whether I'd be able to make it through the night.

Maya opened the door and Arie stepped through the threshold with a corsage in hand. I was careful to make sure my jaw didn't drop as I looked at him. He looked incredible. He wore a black tuxedo with a purple vest and a purple tie around his neck—matching the color of my dress precisely. It was almost as if he'd watched me buy it.

He stopped a few feet short of me, and a crooked smile crept up his lips as he studied me. "You look stunning, Emma."

My cheeks heated at his compliment. "Thanks. You look very handsome yourself." I noticed he didn't seem to have his mask with him and wondered whether he'd forgotten this was a masquerade ball. I didn't want to wear a mask if he wasn't; that would be weird. "Where's your mask?"

"It's in the truck. I didn't know if I should wear it now or wait until the dance." He held a corsage out to me. "I, uh, brought you a corsage, though. Do girls even wear these things nowadays? Sophie told me they did."

"Yeah." I reached out my arm, and he placed the corsage on me. "It's beautiful! Thank you!" I gave him a brief hug, then studied the corsage. It was made with a single, large purple rose and was unlike any corsage I'd ever seen. It had little jewels on it that resembled little leaves with plastic stems and the band was an actual purple bracelet that I could wear long after the flower dried up. I loved it!

Maya walked over to admire the corsage. "That *is* pretty! You have good taste, Arie."

I stepped to the mantle and grabbed the boutonniere I had for Arie. "I got you this."

"Nice." Arie smiled and held out the lapel of his jacket for me to pin it onto. "I think this is the right side for it."

"It is." My fingers trembled as I attempted to pin the white rose to his jacket. After fumbling for a minute, I got it secured.

Maya picked up the camera her mom had set on the couch. "Let's get a couple of pictures of you two. I promised your mom I'd take a few since she couldn't be here this evening."

Arie held out his arm and I placed my hand in the crook of it as we posed for a few pictures. I always felt awkward taking pictures for dances. I smiled and hoped it looked like a normal smile. I was so nervous that my facial muscles quivered as I tried to turn the corners of my mouth up. I hoped Arie didn't notice.

I knew I shouldn't be so anxious since I'd spent plenty of time alone with Arie. I think I was just nervous because this was an actual date.

The lights were turned down low, and music filled the air as Arie and I walked into the university's ballroom where the Winter Ball was being held. I glanced around at our surroundings. The dance floor took up most of the space, and there were tall columns along the outer edge, wrapped with twinkling lights, which held up the second story balcony. The dance committee had outdone themselves this time. It was breathtaking.

I spotted Kathryn and Conner dancing close by and waved to them.

Arie led me to the middle of the crowded dance floor. Peering at me through his black Venetian mask, he asked, "Would you like to dance?"

"I'd love to." I took a few steps to close the gap between us. Arie placed his arms around my waist, and I wrapped mine behind his neck as we swayed to the music.

Nearby, Maya and Derek were dancing, too. Maya smiled at him, and he looked like he was over the moon. I was surprised at how different Derek appeared all dressed up—more mature and dapper in his tuxedo. Maybe Maya really was right about him being sweet and charming, instead of cocky and argumentative like I'd always thought. I never would've predicted them ending up together, but after seeing it, I could believe almost anything.

After a few dances, Arie took my hand and led me to one of the tables for some refreshments. He pulled out a chair for me and then said next to my ear, "I'll be right back with your water. Is there anything else you'd like?"

I wouldn't mind a few minutes alone with you in some secluded alcove. "Umm, whatever you're getting is fine," I said instead.

I watched Arie as he walked to the refreshment table. He had a confident walk, almost a swagger. I don't know whether he moved that way consciously, but he looked good doing it. I studied his broad shoulders and the strong lines of his body, feeling lucky to be at the dance with the best looking guy at school.

It wasn't just his looks I was attracted to, though. Yes, he was gorgeous, but there was more to him than that. He was such a gentleman, and he always made me feel special. He was smart, always ready with a witty remark, trustworthy, patient, caring, and he also had the most amazing voice I'd ever heard.

Arie returned with water and a plate of goodies in hand—brownies and chocolate-dipped strawberries. "I recall you liked brownies."

"Thanks. I'm surprised you remembered." I took a small bite.

He winked at me. "I have a good memory, what can I say."

"Oh yeah? What other things do you remember?"

"I remember the first time we met."

"Oh no! Not that, please!" I briefly covered my eyes with my hand. "I've never been so embarrassed in my life! I think you need to find some way to wipe that from your memory."

"Why?" He leaned closer, his eyes dancing with delight. "It's okay to have accidents every now and then." He paused. "Unless, of course, you weren't paying attention to where you were going."

He knew! He'd known all along that I thought he was so unbearably attractive and hadn't been able to think straight when he was around.

"You weren't distracted by anything now, were you?" He took a small bite from his strawberry.

"I might have been the *teensiest* bit distracted by something."

"Really?" he asked, feigning surprise.

"Come on. Like you don't know the effect you have on women." I couldn't meet his gaze. I might as well admit to it since he knew anyway. "The only reason I crashed my cart was because I had to catch one last glance at the cute guy I just walked by."

"You thought I was cute then?"

"Didn't I say that?"

"I wanted to hear you say it again." He smiled wickedly at me.

"And what did you think of me the first time we met? Did you think I was a complete ditz?" I asked.

"Not a *complete* ditz." When he saw me scowl, he added, "Come on, I'm kidding. No, I didn't think you were a ditz. I thought you were a sweet damsel in distress who needed some assistance from the dashing new guy in town." He crumpled his napkin into a ball and tossed it on the table.

"Okay, that's better." I nudged him in the side. "As long as you thought I was sweet."

When a slow song started, Arie pointed to the balcony above us and asked, "Do you want to go up there for this song?"

I nodded. I had hoped for a secluded alcove earlier, but a balcony would do. Arie placed a hand on my lower back as he guided me past the chaperones and climbed the staircase at the back of the room. When we made it to the top, I saw the balcony was empty. No one else had thought of sneaking up there yet.

Perfect.

If we stood near the edge of the balcony, we would be able to see everyone dancing below, but if we stayed closer to the wall of windows, it would almost be as if we were the only couple at the dance.

We opted for the more private area, away from the railing.

Arie pulled me into his arms, holding me so my body was pressed against his as we danced.

He looked down at me with a coy smile on his lips and said, "Is this the time where I'm supposed to whisper sweet nothings in your ear?"

I smiled and nodded, curious about what he'd do next.

Arie moved his mouth next to my ear. His warm breath sent chills down my spine as he whispered, "Sweet nothings, sweet nothings, sweet nothings."

I giggled and slapped his chest. "Oh, Arie, you are smooth. Is that what you say to all your dates?"

"No, just the ones I like." He winked.

I tried to catch my breath, hoping he wouldn't hear the sudden pounding in my chest. I'd hoped for so long that Arie would like me, and now that he'd said as much, I was tongue-tied and didn't know what to say or do. Somehow, with all that was going on in my head, I managed to dance without tripping over my own feet.

The song had reached the final chorus when Arie started singing the words to the song, his warm breath causing goose bumps to rush along my neck and arms.

He was serenading me! I hugged him closer as he sang, not wanting the song to ever end. It felt amazing to be so close to him, held tight against his muscular body as we danced. But the song ended, and I reluctantly let go of him as he loosened his arms, which had been wrapped around my waist.

He removed the mask from his face, placing it on top of his head, and then he touched the mask on my face. "Do you mind?" he asked, as he peeled the mask off.

"No, I don't mind." Anticipation filled me.

"There, that's much better." He smiled, setting the masks to the floor. Another slow song started, and we resumed our dancing position, only he held me a little closer now. "I'm glad you decided to come with me to the dance. I wanted to ask you long before the whole thing with Brian happened at your party."

"Really?" My voice squeaked.

He dipped his chin down. "When Maya came to warn you about Brian, I thought I missed my chance."

I was dumbfounded but managed to say, "I'm glad to be here with you, too."

Our faces were so close. I only needed to move slightly to close the distance between our lips. My stomach muscles tightened at the thought.

I let my eyes linger on his lips. They were so perfect. I wanted to reach out and touch them, to trace the outline of his mouth and feel the smoothness under my fingertips.

But I pulled my gaze away from his lips and stared into his deep blue eyes instead. Our eyes locked, and something of a spark reflected in his.

Could he be thinking about kissing me, too?

We stood there, staring at each other for a long moment with something growing between us, like an invisible electric charge that kept building and building as the seconds ticked by. When I didn't think I could take it anymore, a half smile spread across Arie's lips, and he broke eye contact.

My chest deflated.

Another moment lost.

Arie started singing along with the music again, his lips close to my ear. I contented myself with wrapping my arms more tightly behind his neck as I listened to his velvety baritone voice. When the song was almost over, Arie's lips pressed against the spot below my ear. A rush of blood flowed through me, goose bumps prickling my skin, and my heart skipped three beats. He nuzzled into my neck, kissing me there again before pulling back. When he looked at me, his eyes were different. They were full of desire, scorching my insides.

He seemed to forget all about dancing as he placed four fingers behind my neck, his thumb caressing the skin along my jaw. A path of fire followed his touch, and then he leaned his face closer. His lips brushed against mine ever so lightly, his lips softer than anything I ever felt before. He gave me a series of slow kisses that left me breathless. He took his time, tasting each kiss, measuring each breath, causing a tidal wave of bliss to pour over me.

"Are you okay with this?" He mumbled against my mouth, his breathing shallow.

"Yes," I gasped. And his lips moved with mine again.

I clung to him as he kissed me, thinking for sure I would faint. Thankfully, I didn't, but I could barely breathe in my tight dress as his arms wound around me, pressing me against him.

I'm finally kissing Arie Blackwell! I'd dreamed of this moment so many times, but all my imaginings had fallen so short of the real thing. It was overwhelming! His mouth was warm, his kisses addicting.

I was pulling him even closer when one of our phones buzzed in Arie's tuxedo pocket.

Arie pulled back. "Sorry, I have to check that. It could be my aunt." He reached into his pocket and pulled out his phone.

Couldn't his aunt wait? I tried not to feel annoyed that our moment had been interrupted.

"It wasn't my phone," he said after checking. He stuffed his phone back in the pocket and pulled out mine, handing it to me.

It was the blocked number again.

I can't believe you still came with Arie after getting my texts. He's been following you around

for weeks. You should have said yes to me when I gave you the chance.

I gasped and covered my mouth with my hand. Brian had sent those?

"What is it?" Arie leaned closer, a concerned expression on his face.

I showed him the message.

Arie clenched his jaw. "Brian's been harassing you?"

I nodded. "I didn't know they were from him until now. My phone always said they were from a blocked number."

"Why didn't you tell me?" Arie asked, almost impatient.

I shrugged. "I didn't know you'd care so much."

"Well, I do." Arie stuffed my phone back in his pocket, grabbed my hand, and rushed me down the stairs. When we were on the dance floor again, Arie scanned the crowd. His eyes narrowed when he spotted Brian.

"I'll just be a minute. Don't go anywhere," he said before leaving me alone on the dance floor. Arie headed toward Brian, who was talking to one of the chaperones for the dance, Mr. Lund. He pulled Brian aside to a corner of the room.

The fast song that had been playing soon ended, and a slow song started. I felt awkward standing in the middle of the room by myself while all the couples slow danced together, so I decided to find a bathroom to freshen up in.

When I walked out of the ballroom, the hall was empty, save for Mr. Lund who was stuffing his phone into his pocket.

"Where's your date, Emma? Didn't you come with Arie?" Mr. Lund asked as I got closer.

"Yeah, he had to talk to Brian about something. Figured I might as well get some air while he was busy."

He tilted his head forward and spoke in a hushed voice. "Didn't want to stand alone during a slow song?" He smiled as if he understood completely.

I nodded. "Guilty as charged." I looked around the lobby. "Do you know where the nearest restroom is? I always get turned around in big places like this."

He pointed behind him. "Just go around this corner, and then take the second left."

"Okay, thanks." I smiled and then headed in the direction he pointed. The hall was dimly lit, and I didn't see any obvious signs of a restroom. Had I heard his instructions wrong?

After making it to the end of the corridor and finding no restroom, I turned to head back the way I came. But I barreled right into Mr. Lund's chest.

"Oh, sorry, Mr. Lund," I said, fighting the urge to scream as I jumped back. "I-I didn't know you were behind me."

"That was the plan," he said before grabbing me around the waist, hoisting me over his shoulder, and running out the back exit.

26

ARIE

WHERE HAD EMMA GONE? I looked back to where I'd left her but didn't see her.

I bolted out the ballroom doors and ran down the main hall, scanning my eyes around frantically.

She wasn't anywhere!

My head pounded as I ran into the parking lot just in time to see two men stuffing Emma in the back of a white van and driving away.

No!

I sprinted to my truck thirty yards away and started it with a shaky hand. I couldn't let that van out of my sight.

I shouldn't have left Emma alone for a minute. This was all my fault!

What kind of an agent was I? I had one person to keep track of, *one*, and I hadn't done that. Who knew what her kidnappers planned to do with her? I had no idea what Fenris's plans were.

All kinds of terrible thoughts forced themselves into my

mind as I chased after the white van. I pulled the phone from my pocket and called Jason.

He picked up after the first ring. "Hello?"

"They took Emma," I said, breathing hard.

"What?" He barked. "Who? Do you know where they went?"

"I don't know who. I'm following them."

"Where are you? Sophie and I will try to head them off."

"We just turned on Highway 56, headed west."

"We're on our way. Don't do anything stupid," Jason said. "We'll get her back."

"I'll never forgive myself if anything happens to her."

I hung up the phone and concentrated on my driving, gripping the steering wheel so hard my knuckles turned white. This road wouldn't meet another city for miles, and I didn't have a full tank of gas. The chase couldn't go on forever.

I pulled my gun from its clip in back of my tuxedo pants. All I needed to do was close the distance between us to get a good shot at the tires.

I rolled down my window, and a cool breeze whipped at my face. I pushed the gas pedal to the floor, praying the freshly fallen snow wouldn't cause me to spin out of control and lose the chance I had at catching them.

27

EMMA

CHEST TIGHT, I tried to breathe inside the pillowcase, but I couldn't get much oxygen in. It was like trying to suck air through a straw. If I didn't draw in a deep breath soon I would pass out.

The van made a quick turn, causing me to slide to one side. With my hands tied behind my back, I couldn't keep myself from sliding all over the floor as the van turned with the bends in the road. My stomach turned sour, and my mind started whirling around in circles. I knew my stomach wouldn't hold up much longer once my ears began pounding and my face flashed with heat.

Bang! Bang!

I screamed. Were they shooting at me? Or was someone shooting the van? I couldn't tell. I ducked down in an effort to avoid being hit by a bullet. My body jerked with each shot until the van spun out of control and I crashed into a wall of hard metal.

28

ARIE

MY HEART FROZE for a moment and then pounded with a burst of adrenaline. It worked! I'd blown out the tires, but it sent the van flying into a ditch. I held my breath, worried I might have gotten Emma hurt. I pulled my truck over to the side of the road and jumped out, gun in hand. I ran to the front of the van and stumbled when I recognized my Psychology teacher in the passenger's seat. He was unconscious, with blood running down his face. The other guy was a mammoth of a man, and he seemed dazed as he struggled to open the crushed door. I wanted to do something about them. But my first priority was Emma, and I needed to get her out of there before the big guy found a way out of the van.

I ran to the back and opened the doors to find Emma's body crumpled in a heap before me. My stomach jumped to my throat when I realized she wasn't moving at all.

Was she dead?

I ripped the pillowcase off her head, and my stomach churned. Emma had blood oozing out of a large gash on the back of her head. I reached for her neck to feel for a pulse.

Thump thump. Thump thump.

Relief washed over me when I felt her heart beating. I pulled a knife from my pocket and cut the zip ties that bound her wrists and ankles. Then I scooped her out of the van and ran with her to my truck.

Her arm was hanging crookedly. It had to be broken. Emma needed medical attention immediately. She appeared to have lost an awful lot of blood from the gaping cut on her head.

I laid her down on the seat of my truck, then shrugged out of my tuxedo jacket, throwing it on the floor. Then I ripped off my shirt and tore a long strip from it. I balled up the rest of my shirt and pushed it onto the head wound, and then I tied the strip around her head to secure the makeshift bandage. It should help slow the bleeding.

I jumped into the driver's seat. There was more movement in the front seat of the van up ahead.

I wanted to run back and take care of the guys and make sure they couldn't find Emma again. But Emma was slowly waking up—I needed to get her to a hospital before she lost any more blood.

I sped toward the Maplebridge hospital, calling 9-1-1 on my way. I could only pray the police or Jason and Sophie would get to Mr. Lund and the big guy before they had the chance to wander off into the woods.

29

EMMA

"HOW ARE YOU DOING?" Arie came into my hospital room after the police finished asking me questions about my kidnapping. They'd been nice enough to wait until after the hospital had taken care of me. But I probably hadn't answered their questions well in my shocked state.

Arie sat in a chair next to me. I smiled weakly at him, knowing I looked terrible. I was propped up in a hospital bed, my left arm in a sling and wrapped in a bandage. My right hand had an IV stuck in it, I had stitches in my head, and there were machines beeping all around me.

"H-how did you find me, anyway?" I remembered waking up as he drove me to the hospital, but with all the craziness I hadn't gotten a straight answer, at least not one I was coherent enough for.

"I'll start from the beginning." Arie cleared his throat. He told me how after he'd talked to Brian, he'd noticed I was gone. He'd run out into the parking lot in time to see me being stuffed into the back of a van. When he spoke about chasing the van and shooting out the tires, I was confused about why he'd be carrying a gun in the first place. Maybe his uncle kept a gun in the truck or something?

"Have you heard about whether they caught Mr. Lund and his friend yet?" I'd been so nervous when talking to the police that I hadn't dared ask them any questions.

Arie frowned. "When Jason and Sophie arrived at the scene, the van was empty. Mr. Lund and the other guy were moving around as I drove away with you and must have run off somewhere. The police are searching for them, but as far as I know, they haven't had any luck yet."

"So they might still come back for me?" I heard the hysteria in my own voice. I glanced at the wall of curtains, expecting Mr. Lund to part the sea of green fabric at any moment.

Arie placed his hand over mine. "I won't let anything happen to you."

Tears brimmed in my eyes. I wiped at them, desperate to stay in control. What was going on? Why did a teacher and his friend try to kidnap me? And would they try it again?

My tears soon turned to a flood of water streaming down my face as I thought about how I might never feel safe again. All I wanted was to go somewhere safe with my parents, but when I talked to them earlier they'd told me they were stuck in a blizzard at my grandparents' house. I was all alone, and my parents were worried sick.

Arie leaned over my bed and wrapped his arms around me. I clung to him and sobbed into his shirt. "You'll be okay," he said, lips against my hair. "I won't let you out of my sight again."

It was nice of him to say that, but what could a senior in high school do to protect me from two kidnappers?

His voice was soothing, and after a while my tears slowed. I looked at him again and realized he was wearing a T-shirt with the hospital logo instead of his tuxedo. "Did you get hurt, too?" I asked between sniffles, pointing at his shirt.

He looked down. "No. Don't you remember that awesome shirt bandage you had tied around your head when we got here? I think the nurses felt bad for me sitting around like a hobo without a shirt, so they gave me this a while ago."

"Oh, good," I said and lay back on my pillows. "I'm glad that you're okay."

He placed his hand on my unbroken arm. "If I could trade places with you, I would. I hate seeing you like this."

I nodded. "When can we get out of here?" My kidnappers were probably hiding close by. This had to be the most obvious place for someone to come looking for me after that accident.

"I asked the nurse a while ago, and she said they'd discharge you after you spoke to the police."

The doctor came in a little while later.

"Your arm will be in a splint for a few more days," the doctor said, glancing down at his tablet for his notes. "Once the swelling is down, you'll need a cast. And I'm worried you may have a mild concussion. Nothing showed up on your CT scan, but I'd like someone to monitor you for the next twenty-four hours, as a precaution."

At the mention of being monitored, I thought of my parents again. Would I have to stay at my house alone tonight? Even if the weather did improve, it would take over ten hours for my parents to drive back from Colorado.

After the doctor told me how to take care of my stitches, he left. A nurse came in a minute later to help me change back into my formal dress, since I didn't have anything else to wear. She was sweet and even commented on what a beautiful dress it was as she laced up the back.

I signed the discharge papers, and then Arie wheeled me out to his truck with the nurse at our side. Arie had to help me buckle in, since my gimpy arm was no help. Having a broken arm would complicate things. How would I do simple things on my own, like shower or get dressed?

"Do you want to stay at my house tonight?" He glanced at me as he drove. "There's no way I'll let you stay at your home alone."

Relief washed over me. I didn't know what I would do if I was on my own tonight. "Are you sure your aunt and uncle won't mind?"

He chuckled at my comment, though I couldn't imagine what was so funny. "I'm almost certain they'd insist on it."

Arie parked his truck in the garage, pressed a bunch of buttons on some fancy security system, and then led the way into his dark house. "It looks like Jason and Sophie are still out," he said, shouldering much of my weight as we walked. Every step I took caused pain to shoot through my body, and I had to make a conscious effort not to moan as we made our way up the stairs. It felt like I'd been bulldozed over. I probably had bruises all over my face and body.

The nurse had cleaned up what she could at the hospital, but my hair still felt grimy. I wasn't supposed to get my stitches wet, but I had to at least try to wash around them. "Is there any way I can take a shower before going to bed?"

"Of course. Let me get a bag to put over your arm to keep it dry." He left me standing in a long, carpeted hallway while he ran downstairs. He soon returned with a garbage bag and some rubber bands. After handing me those, he went to get a T-shirt and pajama bottoms from his bedroom.

"I'm sure this is quite a step down from what you're

wearing now." He handed me the clothes. "You looked beautiful in that dress, by the way."

"Thanks." I didn't mention that I sort of liked the idea of wearing his clothes. "You wouldn't happen to have an extra toothbrush, would you?"

"We should. Sophie always keeps a few extras on hand." He took a few steps down the hall and retrieved one from the linen closet. "You can use my bathroom, if you like." He gestured to the door behind me. "All the usual stuff is in the shower. Towels are in the cupboard on the left, and toothpaste in the top drawer on the right."

I took the toothbrush from his hand. "Thanks again. For everything. I don't know what I would've done without you."

I shut the bathroom door, set my things on the counter, and then stood there for a moment, trying to figure out how to get out of my dress and into the shower. I moved my good arm to the laces at my back and tried to undo them. I was able to untie the bow at the bottom but couldn't unlace anything else. Pain shot through me as I tried again. After struggling a few minutes more, I gave up and admitted to myself that I needed help.

I took a deep breath and peeked out the door. "Arie?" My throat was thick. "Can you come here a sec?"

"Yes?"

"Umm." I looked at the ground. "I can't seem to get out of my dress." My cheeks burned. Why couldn't his aunt be here to help instead? "If you could loosen the laces in the back and unzip it, I'm sure I can do the rest."

He hesitated and then cleared his throat. "Uh, sure." He shuffled closer.

I turned away from him, pulling my hair off my back. I held my breath and looked at the ceiling as he unlaced my dress. Had my dress gotten tighter? I couldn't draw in a decent breath. He pulled the fabric out of each loop so slowly and carefully. Once the back was finally unlaced, his fingers gently grazed the skin above the back of my dress and lingered there, causing goose bumps to rise along my skin. His fingers stopped at the zipper. Could his heart be pounding as hard as mine was? He only hesitated a moment before one hand crept over my shoulder and the other tugged the zipper down inch by inch until it was low enough for me to reach.

As soon as he was done, I let go of my hair so it covered my now bare upper back and turned around. My heart was galloping as I dared a glance at his face.

His cheeks were more pink than usual, and on him the flushed color looked way more attractive than was safe right now.

We were alone.

In his house.

Definitely not safe.

I needed to make good decisions right now.

"Thank you." I stepped back into the bathroom, and grabbed hold of the door to shut it.

He stuffed his hands in his pockets. "No problem."

Showering was difficult and took much longer than usual, especially with my stitches, but at least I was able to do it. Getting dressed also took quite some time, but I wasn't about to ask Arie to help me with that, too.

Once done, I went back into the hall, carrying my phone and dress in my good arm. Arie was in his room, wearing a pair of gym shorts and a T-shirt, lying on his bed with his arm over his eyes.

I felt bad for keeping him up so late. He must be exhausted.

He got up when he heard me and gestured to his bed. "You can sleep in here tonight. I'll sleep on the couch downstairs."

"I couldn't make you sleep on the couch. I don't want to keep you up all night *and* steal your bed."

"No, it's fine. You'll sleep better in here. I grabbed a few pillows for you to elevate your arm." He pointed to the stack of pillows on his bed. "And lucky for you, I changed the sheets this morning."

It was a generous offer, but the thought of sleeping in a room all by myself terrified me. I couldn't help imagining Mr. Lund sneaking in through Arie's window and snatching me away into the dark night. I almost wanted to ask Arie to let me sleep on another couch in the living room near him.

I bit my lip, trying to decide what to do.

"Come on," Arie said, reaching for my hand and pulling me through the door. I glanced around his bedroom, which was pretty bare. There was a queen-size bed in the middle and a dresser and desk along the wall.

I plodded to his bedside, dreading the moment I would be left alone with my imagination working overtime to scare me. Arie took the dress from my arm and put it on a hanger in his closet, next to what was left of his tuxedo. When he turned around, he frowned—he must have noticed my apprehension.

"Are you all right?" He raised an eyebrow as he studied my face. He shook his head. "Stupid question. Of course you're not all right. You were kidnapped tonight *and* got in a car accident because of me." He stepped closer and pulled me into a hug. "I'm so sorry."

I leaned against his chest. "I-I'm scared to be alone right now."

"Would it make you feel better if I stayed with you until you fell asleep?" He took a step back, his brow furrowed with concern.

I breathed a relieved breath. "Would you mind? I'm sure you're exhausted."

"You know what? I'll sleep on the floor, if that's okay."

I nodded.

He left for a moment but returned with a sleeping bag and a sleeping pad. He set them up on the floor next to the bed and then reached for one of the pillows.

I grabbed his wrist to stop him. "No, let me sleep on the floor. It's your bed after all."

He looked back at me. "No, you sleep in the bed. You'll be uncomfortable enough with your broken arm already. I won't allow you to make it any worse."

"Okay...if you say so." I let go of his wrist and then pulled the covers back on the bed and climbed in. I propped the extra pillows under my arm in order to keep it elevated. There was an ice pack on the nightstand, and I smiled at Arie's thoughtfulness. I hoped the swelling would go down before long.

Once I was situated, I called my parents and told them where I was staying the night. My mom was still debating whether to risk the storm and drive through the night, but I told her I was okay. It wouldn't do any good if they got in an accident as well. It took some convincing, but my mom finally relented and said good night.

The tension in my body released when I finally lay against the pillows. Arie's bed was so comfortable. When he saw I was ready for bed, Arie turned out the light and climbed into his sleeping bag on the floor.

Today had been such a long day, and with the intense last few hours, I was dead tired.

"Good night, Arie," I said, trying to stifle a yawn. "Thanks for everything. I don't know how I'll ever repay you for saving my life."

Arie yawned as well. "Don't worry about it. I'm glad I was able to get you back."

"Me too." I paused for a moment, remembering back to the dance. "Oh, and thanks for taking me to the dance. It was fun."

"Was that only tonight? It can't still be the same day, can it?" He yawned again and I heard him turn on the floor, his sleeping bag making a rustling sound as he moved. "What would your friends say if they knew you were sleeping in my bed tonight?" I could hear a smile in his voice. "What gossip that would cause."

Before I could stop myself, I answered, "I'm pretty sure they'd be shocked, actually."

"Why do you say that?"

My face flushed with heat. "Um, no reason." I couldn't tell him. That would be *so* awkward.

"Just tell me. I can take it." I heard him exhale loudly. "Why would it be so hard to believe that you'd end up here tonight?"

Now he thinks I'm not into him like that. "It's not what you're thinking." I stared at the ceiling. "My friends would only be surprised because they know I'm waiting to have that kind of a relationship until I'm married." I was glad it was dark and he couldn't see my face. I was sure to be as red as a rose after admitting to the very guy I liked that I was a virgin.

His voice was quiet when he answered. "Oh, I see."

Had I just blown my chances with him? Is he totally weirded out right now?

It was silent for a moment as I tried to muster the courage to ask him something. I took a deep breath and went for it. "Is that weird for you?" Thank goodness my voice didn't squeak.

He rolled onto his side to face me. I could barely make out his features in the moonlit room. "Honestly, I think we feel the same way about that particular subject."

What? Had I heard him right?

He continued, "You're not the only virgin in the room."

A huge smile spread across my face then. "For real?"

"Yep. My mom raised me right."

"That's good to know. Not many guys would admit to that."

"I'm not like other guys, am I?"

Oh no, you are too good to be true! I didn't say my thoughts out loud, though. Instead, I said, "I guess not."

30

ARIE

I STARTLED awake when I heard Emma whimper. She was probably still asleep, but I should check on her anyway.

I rubbed my eyes and sat up, my back cracking with the movement. Sleeping on the floor wasn't quite as comfortable as I remembered. I must be getting old. I crept on my knees over to Emma. Still asleep. I tiptoed to the window and looked for Bruce's car. After making sure he was still watching the house, I went back to Emma's bedside and studied her for a moment. She looked so sweet as she slept, her worries wiped off her face. Her nose had a slight bump at its bridge, and her cheeks looked soft in the moonlight. My eyes then lingered on her soft pink lips, making me wish I could kiss her again.

I'd crossed into dangerous territory by kissing her earlier tonight. I realized deep inside I shouldn't have done it, but the moment our lips touched, I knew I could kiss her for hours and never get enough.

I shook my head. I shouldn't be thinking about that. Jason said we'd most likely be moving on to plan B tomorrow. My stomach churned at the thought of what might happen when she found out the truth. Would she understand? Would she hate me?

Emma's eyes popped open and she screamed. I almost jumped out of my skin. I reached over to try and calm her, but she struggled away from my hand at her shoulder. Her panicked eyes gaped at me.

"Shhh, it's me, Arie." I put my hand on her cheek. Slowly her wild eyes relaxed as she took in my face.

"S-sorry," she said. "I-I thought you were Mr. Lund, coming for me again."

"No," I tried to speak in a soothing voice. "It's just me. I was checking on you."

"I'm a little out of it. Sorry." Her voice trembled.

"No, it was my fault." I reached up and brushed away the hair that had fallen in her eyes. As I ran my fingers down the side of her face, I felt moisture on her cheeks.

She was crying.

Soon her crying had elevated to sobbing. My heart squeezed in my chest when I realized how frightened she must be. I climbed on the bed next to her and gathered her to me, careful not to touch her broken arm.

Emma clung to me as she cried. I knew she needed me to help her feel safe again, but what could I do?

The only thing that came to mind was to hold her until she calmed down. I moved to sit against my headboard, then pulled her onto my lap. I whispered, "It's okay. You're safe with me now."

After a time, she rested her head against my chest, drew in a deep breath, and moved her good arm behind my back.

She turned her face up to me. "Thank you," was all she said.

I nodded and squeezed her tighter.

A minute later, her eyes grew heavy, and I knew she would

soon be asleep in my arms. I pressed a kiss to her forehead and watched as she drifted off to sleep.

I sat holding her close for a few minutes until exhaustion crept over me again. I wanted to just lie down in my bed with her close by. But I didn't. I kissed her cheek and then scooted to the edge of the bed, gently laying her head back on the pillow. I crawled back to my sleeping bag on the floor.

31

EMMA

I WOKE in the morning to the sound of someone knocking.

"Emma? Are you awake?" called an accented female voice from behind the door.

"Yeah." I awkwardly sat up in bed, noticing Arie was not in the room with me. I checked the clock—it was twelve thirty in the afternoon.

"Can I come in? I brought you lunch."

I combed my fingers through my hair, careful to avoid the bump at the back of my head. "Come in."

"I thought you might be hungry," Arie's aunt Sophie said as she entered with a tray holding a plate of bread and a bowl of soup. She set it in front of me and then sat on the edge of the bed. "How are you feeling today?" She studied my face with a look of real concern.

"I'm doing okay. I hope Arie's not in trouble for letting me sleep over."

"Not at all. You're welcome any time," she said. "Your parents called a few hours ago. I would have told you sooner, but I figured you needed your sleep after last night." She offered me a warm smile. "Your mom said they are on their way and should be here by six if the weather cooperates."

I nodded as I eyed the food before me. "This looks and smells delicious."

"My mother always made it for me when I wasn't feeling well." Sophie lowered her voice to a whisper and gave me a wry grin. "She always said it had magical healing powers."

"Well, if that's the case, I may need to eat the whole pot." I felt a little better than I had last night, not quite as sore, but my head and arm still throbbed. I noticed my pain pills also sat on the tray and decided to start my meal with those.

The food was as delicious as it looked and had such a different taste to it than what I was used to. It was spicy yet sweet at the same time.

"What is this?" I asked after eating a few bites. "It's amazing. I bet my mom would love the recipe."

She shrugged. "It is a recipe from my homeland," she answered.

"Where's that?" I always wondered where her slight accent originated.

A guarded look crossed her face, and it took her a moment to answer. "I moved here from Russia almost twenty years ago."

"Wow. Russia. That's really cool." Something told me this was a major revelation for her for some reason, but when she didn't say anything more I just felt awkward.

She got up a minute later. Before she left, she peeked out the window, which only reminded me of how much danger I could be in. I was opening my mouth to ask whether she'd heard any more details on my kidnapping when Arie walked through the door carrying an ice pack.

I heard Sophie mumble something to Arie as they passed each other, something about moving forward with plans.

Arie nodded at her. He plopped down next to me on the

bed. "I've been talking with Jason and Sophie about last night." He rested the ice pack carefully on my arm. "They said the police weren't able to find your kidnappers. They checked their apartment, and it was completely cleaned out. Apparently, they hadn't planned on sticking around town at all after taking you last night."

"They're still out there?" My voice raised a few notches.

"For now." He placed a hand on my knee. "But we won't stop searching. We know what they look like, and they have a whole file on Mr. Lund from the school, so they can't hide forever."

Why *had* Mr. Lund kidnapped me? It didn't make any sense. He didn't even know me. Not really.

Why did my parents have to be so far away when this was happening? All I wanted was for my mom to hold me and make me feel safe again.

"You know what I think you need right now?" Arie smiled. "You need something to take your mind off things. How about we go downstairs and watch movies until your parents get here? It won't do you any good to sit here in my bed, worrying all day long."

32

ARIE

I DIDN'T KNOW how tired I was until I woke up and the movie was over.

"Tired much?" Emma asked.

I rubbed my eyes and looked at her, finding her smiling at me with an arched eyebrow.

"Yeah, sorry." I tried to shake the sleep fog away and ran the back of my hand across my mouth. It came away slightly wet. I'd been drooling.

I cleared my throat a couple of times and worked myself back up into a sitting position. "How was the movie?"

"It was fine, though I could barely hear what was going on over your snoring."

"I was snoring?" *Smooth, Arie. Real smooth.*

She laughed. "No. But if you were, I probably wouldn't tell you anyway."

"Great." The movie seemed to have done something, at least. She wasn't nearly as anxious as she had been earlier. If my drooling and snoring had anything to do with that, then I guess it was worth it. "Do you want to watch another movie?" There were still a couple of hours before her parents should arrive.

"Sure," she said.

We went through the movie options on TV, eventually deciding on a romantic comedy. Not my first choice, but this was for her.

"Are you still thinking about last night?" I asked when I noticed her fidgeting as the movie started.

"Yeah." She sighed. "I mean, movies are a good distraction, but...you know." She shrugged.

I did know. I needed to see whether I could help her relax. She was safe now. Now that we knew she'd been discovered, we would make sure she wouldn't be taken again. Only a couple more hours and Fenris would have no idea where she was.

"Here, lean against me." I tugged on her arm, and she let me pull her into my side. I wrapped my arms around her. "You're safe here with me."

She breathed in deeply as she tucked her good arm behind my back, and I felt the tension release from her body as she melted against me.

As we watched the movie, with her head resting on my chest, thoughts of last night's kiss flashed through my mind. It had been incredible. My best first kiss, hands down. And if we hadn't been in such a public place, I probably would have tried to kiss her all night.

Her lips on mine. Her body so close.

My heart started banging thinking about it.

She gazed up at me.

"Checking to see if I'm still awake?" I asked, hoping to play off my escalating attraction.

A slight smile played at her lips. "Your heart is beating so fast."

"Heard that, did you?"

She nodded. She knew she was the reason for it.

"I-I like listening to it. It's so strong." She rested her head against my chest again.

I had no idea what went on in the movie after that. All I could do was study her. Her silky brown hair, her beautiful blue eyes, and her heart-shaped lips. I wanted to kiss those lips again. But as much as I wanted to kiss her, I knew I should wait. Jason and Sophie were arranging everything for plan B tonight. Which meant I only had a few short hours before Emma would know everything.

"Do you have any idea what's going on?" she asked, turning her head up again.

Was she talking about the movie? Or was she talking about my high chances of having a heart attack?

"Not a clue," I breathed.

"Me neither," she whispered, nuzzling into my chest again. I kissed the top of her head, breathing in the sweet scent of her hair when she tilted her head back to look at me. Her eyes told me she wanted more than a kiss on the head. There was a tightness in my chest as I tried to decide what I should do. Jason and Sophie were upstairs, busy with plans for tonight, so they wouldn't walk in on us. But I shouldn't kiss her again with this secret hovering between us. That wouldn't be right.

But the signal didn't transfer from my brain to my lips.

Instead of stopping the kiss before it got started, I cradled her head in my hand and pulled her lips to mine. I tried to keep my lips soft and careful, deliberate and unhurried, but the moment our lips connected, it was...fire. I wound my arms behind her back and held her tightly against me, mindful of her broken arm.

Her lips met mine in a long, slow kiss, and I knew she wanted me. She cared about me. The thought that she might feel the same way about me as I felt about her caused my stomach muscles to tighten. I slowly traced a path along her spine until my fingers gently stroked her hair. It was as soft as I remembered. And she smelled amazing.

When I felt her relax against me, I knew I needed to stop. It took all my willpower to push her away.

"Wow," I sighed.

"Yeah," she said as she smoothed her hair.

"Maybe we should go back upstairs for some hot chocolate." My voice came out much rougher than I wanted, but I couldn't breathe anymore. "I think I could use a little fresh air." I stood and reached for her hand, then helped her up next to me. "I have to admit," I whispered in her ear, feeling more vulnerable than I'd let myself feel in a long time. "I've wanted to kiss you like that for months."

Her eyes widened, and her face filled with desire mixed with something else. *Apprehension?*

"So why did you stop?" she asked in a quiet voice. And I knew it had taken a lot for her to say those words. She wasn't usually so bold. The fact that she said that to me melted my insides, and I had to kiss this girl again.

I grasped her waist in my hands and walked her back against the wall. It felt so good to hold her in my arms. She wrapped her good arm behind me, pulling me closer, like she was inviting me into her heart.

I shouldn't be kissing her like this. Not before she knew the truth. But I wasn't thinking clearly—her kisses had taken me to a detached, light-headed place that pushed aside my usual caution.

I wanted to tell her everything. I wanted to know everything there was to know about her. She—in such a short amount of time—had somehow become the most important person in my life, and the fact that our whole relationship was built on lies gnawed at my conscience worse than ever before.

33

EMMA

KISSING ARIE WAS nothing short of magical. I could stay in his arms all day.

But just as I was thinking I could kiss him forever and never get enough, I sensed him pulling away. First it was slow, drawing his lips back, and then seeming to change his mind and kissing me again for a minute. Then pulling back again and letting his lips linger next to mine with the lightest of kisses. I opened my eyes to see whether I could read his face. His eyes were pinched shut, his face etched with anguish—like he was having some sort of internal battle.

Then he groaned and pushed himself away from me completely, taking a step back.

"I shouldn't have done that." He pinched the bridge of his nose. "I *really* shouldn't have done that."

He regretted kissing me.

My face burned.

"Sorry," I said, barely able to meet his gaze.

"Don't be, I'm the one who should be apologizing." He

lifted a hand to tuck some hair behind my ear. "I don't want you to think I'm trying to take advantage of you."

I dared glance at him. "Why would I think that?"

His face turned serious again. "There are things you don't know about me, and I can't keep it secret any longer."

"What?" I drew in a quick breath. "What do you mean?"

"I need to tell you something, Emma." He took a couple of steps back from me, his shoulders slumped.

What's going on?

"There are things about your past that you need to know." He covered his eyes with his hand and then rubbed his forehead. "I worry you won't see me in the same way after you hear what I have to say."

34

ARIE

EMMA and I sat down on the couch. How would I even begin to tell her everything that had been kept secret from her these past eighteen years? How did you tell someone their whole life was a lie? How did you tell someone you cared about that you weren't who they thought you were? I was crazy about Emma and dreaded what she might think about me after hearing why I had come into her life. Would she think I was a complete fraud? Would she feel betrayed?

I looked into her eyes, and took a deep breath. "I don't know how to tell you what I need to say. So I'm just going to start by telling you a story."

"Okay." She frowned.

I launched into the story I'd rehearsed many times in my mind. "Before you were born, there was a wealthy man named Cormac who lived in Russia. Cormac had two sons, Grayson and Fenris. When Fenris was in his early twenties, he became involved with a terrorist group and fell out with the family. Because of this, his father changed his will, leaving Fenris only a small portion of the family fortune." I studied Emma's face for a sign that any of this sounded familiar, but nothing seemed to ring a bell. "Fenris didn't know about this change in his inheritance. He didn't find out that all the money was willed to Grayson until *after* the terrorist group killed Cormac. This, of course, did not sit well with Fenris and his group. Within a few days of his father's passing, Grayson was in a fatal hit-and-run accident, leaving all the money to his wife."

Emma leaned back into the couch and frowned. "What does that have to do with us?"

"Just listen, that's only the beginning of the story." I sighed. "You see, Grayson and his wife, Adelle, were expecting their first child at the time of his death. And when both her husband and father-in-law died, Adelle worried she and her baby would be next."

Emma nodded as if it made sense.

"So Adelle quickly drew up a will of her own, setting up a trust fund for her unborn child to inherit once she turned eighteen. In the will, she also allocated a portion of her estate to her closest friend, Sophie, to pay for the protection of her daughter in case anything were to happen to Adelle. Once that was taken care of, Adelle fled to the United States. She told no one where she was going and slipped away in the dark of the night with Sophie to keep her company."

Emma's eyebrows furrowed. "Are you talking about Sophie your aunt?"

I nodded. "Adelle gave birth to a baby girl a month later, and shortly after that, an attempt was made on Adelle's life. Adelle knew she needed to disappear, so she did the only thing she could think of to keep her daughter safe. She found a young couple to adopt her baby, requesting they never tell their daughter she was adopted. She told them that having people think she was their biological child would help keep the girl safe from possible danger. They agreed, of course, with the understanding that after the girl graduated from high school they should expect a lawyer to show up at their door with a letter explaining everything. Once her daughter was taken care of, Adelle asked Sophie to keep tabs on her baby, and then Adelle disappeared. But it wasn't long before Fenris found her, too."

Emma's eyes widened as I said this, so I continued on carefully. "The couple took that baby into their home and raised her as their own, never telling her she was adopted. The girl grew up never knowing she was an heiress with a target on her back."

"No...it can't..." Emma placed her head in her hands.

"The girl was watched over the years by bodyguards that Sophie hired as a precaution."

I swallowed the lump forming in my throat. I was almost to the end of my story, and she would soon know everything.

"The girl was never threatened and had never needed the secret bodyguards to protect her. Not until a couple of months ago, that is. When Fenris was about to be released from prison, Sophie decided to tighten security and have a young bodyguard pose as a fellow student, in order to keep a closer watch over the heiress."

Emma turned to look at me. Her eyes narrowed—she was connecting the dots in her head. My stomach turned sour and my heart thumped out of control, so loud I was sure she could hear it, too. After I fumbled my way through my next sentence, I knew she would hate me.

I took a deep breath and looked into her sapphire eyes. "You see, I'm that bodyguard...and *you* are the hidden heiress."

35

EMMA

"YOU'RE JOKING, RIGHT?" Please, please, *please* let this be some kind of twisted prank. It couldn't be true! There's no way I was adopted, and there was definitely no way I was some rich heiress.

Arie's face was solemn as he shook his head. "No, Emma. It's all true."

I felt the blood drain from my face, my pulse pounding through my whole body. He wasn't joking. He believed what he'd said.

"There has to be some sort of misunderstanding. Somehow I've been confused with some other girl. There's no way I could've been adopted at birth. It doesn't make sense."

Arie shook his head.

I sat there in silence for quite some time, trying to process what Arie had said, my mind whirling, my heart pounding, my anxiety overflowing. This couldn't be real. I couldn't believe it.

"So you're saying there is a guy named Fenris who wants me dead?"

"Yes, that's why you were kidnapped last night."

Tears welled up behind my eyes. "Can't I just give him the money, then? Won't he leave me alone if I give him what he wants?"

"You could, but the whole reason Adelle gave you the money in the first place was because she didn't want Fenris to have it. She knew he would use it to fund his terrorist group. Plus, we think he would probably kill you anyway." Arie leaned forward and reached out to touch my hand. "That's why I won't let you out of my sight again."

"Then why not kill me last night? If that's what they're going to do anyway?"

Arie grimaced. "Only you can access the money. Fenris needs you to transfer everything to him first."

"How much money are we talking about here? Several hundred thousand?"

Arie shook his head slowly. "More like eighty-nine million."

"What?" I shrieked. "Eighty-nine million dollars?" I said the number slowly as I tried to wrap my mind around it. That was an insane amount of money. I couldn't even fathom what that much money looked like. How in the world would I hide with that much money?

This could not be happening.

"Where would this Cormac guy even get that kind of money from?" He had to have done something illegal, too.

"Sophie said he was an oil tycoon or something."

I stiffened as another thought occurred to me. If all this was true, then it meant that Arie was only my friend because it was his job. The reason he'd spent so much time with me was because he *had* to. I thought of the amazing moments I'd just spent kissing him and felt so stupid for thinking he cared about me the way I cared about him. He'd just been doing his job and playing the part he was paid to play—probably paid extremely well at that.

My face grew red hot with humiliation. I didn't want to believe it. I didn't want to believe that I'd been tricked *again* by someone I had grown to care so much about.

I'd been lied to my entire life! What other things were fake? Who else had been put in my life to watch over me? Who else had deceived me? Were my friends really my friends, or were they paid to hang out with me like Arie had been? Dizziness flooded through me. I was going to throw up.

"So you're like some glorified babysitter for me?" I yanked my hand away from his.

"I prefer agent, but yes, that's what I came here to do." His eyes were cautious. He knew I was upset and that he was walking on thin ice.

"Did you get some kind of bonus pay for kissing me?" I spat the words at him, using anger to keep my tears at bay.

Hurt reflected in his eyes. "Of course not. You know I wouldn't do that." He reached out, but I jerked away from him.

"Apparently, I don't know anything about you. I bet you had a good laugh with your fellow agents, making fun of how I fell for it all. How I thought you might like me."

He held me by my shoulders, making me face him. "No, Emma, that's not it at all. I do care for you." Why did he still sound so sincere? He must be a professional actor as well as a bodyguard.

"Sure you do. Just as you would care about any other person you were paid to protect," I scoffed. "I can't believe I fell for it! I should have trusted my gut feeling from the first time I met you. I can't believe I was so stupid to fall for such a charade." I poked a finger into his chest. "Y-you lied to me!" My voice quivered, coming out quiet and tortured. He knew I had been hurt so badly last year; how could he have done the exact same thing to me? Did I mean so little to him that he could disregard my very real feelings in order to keep up his facade?

I broke away from him and stood, feeling my eyes burn with tears threatening to escape. There was no way I would let him see how hard I'd fallen for him, so I ran up the stairs to get away. Arie called after me, but I ignored him and continued to flee.

When I reached the top of the stairs, I realized I didn't have anywhere to hide. I was at *his* house after all. And even if I did run off I'd probably just get kidnapped again. Who were Jason and Sophie anyway? Were they agents like Arie? I was sure they weren't his aunt and uncle now.

And how old was Arie?

So many questions ran through my mind. Questions for my parents. Questions for Arie. Questions for Sophie. I wasn't in any mood to talk, though, so I went to Arie's bathroom for some privacy.

I slammed the door shut before locking it, and then I finally let a sob escape. My whole body heaved as emotions poured out. How was I going to hold it all together and try to resume a normal life? I didn't even know whether I could trust *anyone* anymore. My parents had lied to me my entire life! They were supposed to be the people I could go to, no matter what. I was sure Maya and Kathryn were still trustworthy, but I couldn't tell them about all this. Not while I was still in danger. The more people who knew the truth, the higher the chance that word would get out. And if word got out, I would be found all the more easily.

I buried my head in my hands when I realized that Brian was right about Arie after all. How had he figured this out, when I was so blind? I'd pegged him as a crazy stalker, when he was actually the only one telling me the truth.

Not knowing what else to do, I sank onto the hard tile floor, spiraling down, down, down, hugging myself to keep from breaking apart.

A few minutes later, there was a knock on the door. "Emma. Please talk to me."

It was Arie.

I didn't respond.

"Emma..." he said. "It wasn't like that...not for me..."

I imagined him leaning his forehead against the door, arms above his head with his hands in fists. That's what an excellent actor would do, anyway.

"Please, Emma. Let me explain." Pause. His voice broke. "Please, don't hate me..."

He waited by the door, but I wasn't about to let him in to work his charms on me again. After a while, his footsteps retreated down the hall.

Sophie tried to get me to come out later, as well, but I told her I needed to be alone.

The doorbell rang. It had to be my parents, coming to pick me up. I didn't want to talk to them, either, so I stayed hidden in the bathroom.

Half an hour later, there was another knock.

"Emma, please open the door." It was my *mother*.

I stood and studied myself in the mirror. My eyes were red and swollen from all the crying I had done. My nose was pink, too.

I opened the door to face the woman who had deceived me for the past eighteen years. I scrutinized her blonde hair and petite form and finally understood why we'd never looked alike. When I looked at her, I wanted to be angry. I wanted to punish her for not telling me that I was adopted.

But I couldn't.

Instead of yelling at her like I imagined, I collapsed in her outstretched arms and sobbed.

"Mom, tell me it's not true," I cried. "Tell me this is some kind of horrible nightmare that I ended up in."

"Oh, honey." She sighed, rubbing my back with her hands. "I can't tell you how much I wish it were. Jason, Sophie, and Arie told your father and me everything. I'm as shocked as you are."

When my crying slowed, I pulled back from her to look in her eyes. I needed to see whether she was telling me the truth.

Her green eyes were wet with tears. "Did you really not know who I was?" I was desperate to feel like she hadn't been a complete fraud.

"Honestly, Emma, I only knew you were a beautiful gift. Adelle said you'd be safer not knowing you weren't biologically ours. That's the only reason we kept it a secret." She grasped my shoulders and held me at arm's length. "Believe me when I say that if it hadn't been to protect you from danger, I never would've kept it from you."

I saw truth in my mother's eyes and was somewhat relieved. I wiped the tears from my cheeks, drawing in a shaky breath. "I believe you."

We were quiet for a few moments before my mom murmured, "At least Arie seems to be conscious of the fact that he's far too old to have pursued a relationship with you. I always thought he looked older than eighteen."

I sniffled and nodded, not about to mention that we'd made out this afternoon.

"Come on, let's go downstairs. We have a lot of things to talk about." My mother slipped an arm around my shoulder, and we walked down.

We found everyone sitting in the living room. My dad gave me a tight hug, careful to avoid hurting my arm. "Hey, Em, I'm so glad you're okay. We were so worried." He stood back. "How's your arm? Arie told us it was a pretty bad break."

"It's okay." My eyes wandered to the three people sitting behind him. "It seems to be the least of my worries right now."

My father nodded. "Yes, I suppose that's true."

We all sat down to discuss what would happen from here on out. I sat between my mom and dad, which seemed like the best option, until I locked eyes with Arie, who sat across from me. His eyes were sad, and it looked like he wanted to say something to me. I crossed my arms and stared out the window behind him instead. I wouldn't be able to look at him again without feeling humiliated.

Sophie broke the awkward silence first. "As you might have guessed, after what Arie told you this afternoon, Jason and I aren't Arie's aunt and uncle like we pretended. We are also agents and have been watching over you for many years."

I nodded, setting my jaw tight so I wouldn't start crying again.

Sophie continued, "We know this is a lot for you to take in all at once, but after what happened last night we no longer feel comfortable with you staying in Maplebridge. It is just too dangerous now that Fenris knows who you are."

"What? No! I can't move. I'm graduating in a few months."

Jason set a hand on Sophie's knee. "It isn't safe. You can still take classes online. You can still graduate."

"But I'm supposed to graduate here, with my friends. I can't just pick up and leave everything behind." I looked to my mom and dad for backup.

"I think they're right, honey," Mom said, carefully. "We can't take the risk. You're too precious to us."

"Dad?" I pleaded. Surely he would stand up for me.

But he just shrugged. "I'm sorry, Em. But they're right. They explained everything while you were upstairs. We need to keep you safe."

"Can't I just put on a disguise or something and change my name for the last six months of school? The police know what Mr. Lund looks like. He doesn't stand a chance of getting close to me again. I mean, isn't that what you hired Arie for anyway? You can hire more people. I'll even do online school from home. Just don't make me move!"

"Those are all great ideas, Emma," Sophie said. "But Fenris can always hire someone new, and you can't blend in here like you can in a big city."

A big city?

"Where?"

"We have a safe house in Philadelphia for you, Jason, Arie, and me to move into. We bought it a few years ago just in case something like this happened. The rest of your family will move to Louisiana."

I put my head in my hands. I was going to be moving all the way across the country to a place I'd never been, living with a bunch of strangers? And my family was moving, too? It was too much. Tears pricked at my eyes.

I hated Fenris! I hated that he had the power to change my life completely. I didn't even know him!

"We fly to Philadelphia tonight," Sophie continued. "And our other agent, Bruce, will go home with your parents while they pack their things. We're arranging for your sister and brother to join them in Louisiana as well. Fenris will use anything he can to get to you. He won't hesitate to hurt your family."

The guilt that piled on was so thick it was suffocating. I was ruining everyone's lives.

No, *Fenris* was ruining everyone's lives.

"We have other agents out there, trying to track Fenris down," Jason added. "But we don't know how soon it will be."

"That could take forever! I can't hide for the rest of my life!"

"We're doing everything we can," Sophie said.

They went over the rest of the details of the move. I wasn't allowed to say goodbye to my friends and other family members. No one would be informed that I was leaving tonight, in case that information somehow ended up in the wrong hands. We didn't know how many people Fenris had on the prowl.

Before we left, Dad pulled Arie aside for a few minutes. His lips were pressed together, his jaw set as they walked into Jason's office.

When they rejoined us in the entryway a few minutes later, they both stood stiffly, and Arie's face was even more solemn than it had been throughout the past hour.

A moment later, my guards had their suitcases waiting at the door, indicating that the time had come for us to leave.

Saying goodbye to my parents was the hardest thing I had ever had to do, especially since I didn't know when I would see them again or even get to talk to them. After many, many tears were shed, I left all that I had ever known: my family, my friends, my home, my school, my town. Everything. I left without a single thing besides the clothes on my back—which weren't even mine.

36

EMMA

I HAD NEVER FLOWN first class before and probably would've enjoyed it more if I hadn't been so depressed at the moment. The seats were in rows of two, so I was stuck sitting next to Arie, while Jason and Sophie sat across the aisle from us.

I hadn't spoken to Arie since he'd told me everything in the basement earlier, and I wasn't ready to start now. It couldn't be that hard to give him the silent treatment for the next three hours. I would be living in the same house as him for who knows how long, so I might as well start practicing.

Sure, if I were to be reasonable right now, I might admit that he'd probably tried to maintain a professional relationship with me, like my mom thought. But when I fell for him, he'd had to go along with what I wanted because it was his job to stay close to me. If he'd pushed me away before now, I wouldn't have wanted to hang out with him anymore, and that would have defeated the whole purpose of why he'd started going to school with me in the first place.

But I didn't want to be reasonable. I was hurt and embarrassed, and I hated that I couldn't get away from him for even two minutes. The universe must really hate me. My future was not only this big, ambiguous cloud but I was also stuck with the one person in the world that I never wanted to speak to again.

37

ARIE

EMMA BELIEVED I'd been acting the whole time. She had no idea that I truly *wanted* to kiss her. That I was so close to being in love with her, and that thoughts of her were what consumed my mind most of the time.

"Emma, I..." I began after the plane took off.

She crossed her arms and turned to me. "What, Arie?" She sounded so annoyed.

"I need to explain myself. I wasn't—"

"It's okay," she interrupted. "I understand why you did what you did."

"No, it's not that. I—" I tried to spit my confession out, but she interrupted me again.

"It's fine. Really." She sighed and shook her head. "I don't want to talk about it anymore. It's been a long day, and I need to get some sleep." From the look on her face, I could tell it wasn't okay. None of this was. But if she didn't want to talk about it right now, I wouldn't press her.

Plus, her dad had made his feelings extremely clear on the subject when he pulled me aside earlier. He didn't want me to so much as lay a finger on her while we were away. We would be living in the same house for who knows how long, and it would be inappropriate for me, a bodyguard, to attempt to have a relationship with her.

I promised to keep our relationship professional so he wouldn't have to voice his concerns to Sophie and get me fired. And I suppose that with Emma's apparent disinterest in me now, it would be much easier to keep that promise to her father.

I studied Emma out of the corner of my eye after she shifted away from me. She looked exhausted and vulnerable, slumped in her seat. Her shoulders shuddered slightly, and I heard her sobbing quietly.

Instinctively, I reached a hand to her arm. "Emma—"

"Please"—she tensed under my touch almost like I'd burned her—"don't touch me. I can't..." But she didn't finish. I saw a tear trickle down her cheek before she turned away completely.

"I just—" But there was nothing I could say to take away her pain, so I simply said, "I'm sorry," and let my hand drop from her arm, trying not to feel the sting of rejection.

Rejection coursed through me anyway.

38

EMMA

THE NEXT FEW weeks inched by as I acclimated to a new life and a new home, and figured out my new online school. Philadelphia was much bigger than Maplebridge, so that was something I had to adjust to.

We moved into a three-bedroom condo in the center of the city. The master bedroom was on the main floor, which Jason and Sophie used. My bedroom was upstairs, across the hall from Arie's room. There was only one bathroom upstairs, so I had to share that with Arie. It was awkward sharing the bathroom with a guy, especially one I'd had a crush on, but I had to make do. I didn't know Jason and Sophie very well, so living with strangers was uncomfortable the whole way around.

I learned that Sophie was in charge of everything regarding my protection, and that Jason was like a supervisor for Arie. Apparently, Sophie had hired Jason shortly after my parents adopted me, and it had only taken a few months for them to fall in love and get married. They'd been watching me together ever since.

When we first arrived in Philadelphia, I'd found out the

bracelet Arie had given me with my corsage doubled as a tracking device. So even though that night might not be one I wanted to remember for forever, I was stuck wearing a memento from it.

Along with the bracelet, Sophie insisted on some other precautions to change my appearance somewhat. I got my hair cut to where it sat just below my shoulders, and I added a lot of blonde highlights. I supposed I looked quite different from behind, but if anyone got a good look at my face, I would still be recognizable; it's not like I could tack on a mustache or beard without drawing even more attention to myself.

As the weeks passed, I went through the motions of completing my schoolwork and keeping up with the basics, but I didn't have the energy to do anything else. I missed my family and friends so much it hurt. My appetite was gone, and anything I did eat didn't always stay down, thanks to my nerves. I usually studied all morning, took a nap in the afternoon, and then helped Sophie cook dinner before holing myself up in my room for the rest of the evening. Christmas was especially hard. Sophie tried to make it special, but without my family it almost didn't even seem worth celebrating.

One thing I anticipated was having my cast taken off in a few weeks. I'd had a fiberglass cast put on a few days after arriving in our new town, and it was driving me nuts! They said it would be better than the old plaster casts, more waterproof and less itchy. But it was still super annoying and made normal things so much more difficult than they used to be. I guess it was good I went to online school now, because at least I could get away with wearing a ponytail every day and not worry about looking cute.

"You look like them, you know," Sophie said to me as we made dinner one evening.

"Like who?" I asked as I chopped carrots for the salad.

"Adelle and Grayson." Sophie covered a casserole dish with aluminum foil and placed it in the oven to bake. "You have Adelle's dark hair and blue eyes, but your beautiful complexion and cheekbones come from Grayson." Sophie smiled, her eyes looking off, lost in a memory. "Adelle would be so jealous."

"What were they like?" I still missed my parents like crazy, but I couldn't help wondering what it would have been like to grow up in another country with different parents.

"They were wonderful. Adelle and I had been friends since we were children. She was spunky and outgoing—always getting into some sort of mischief. And Grayson was the more serious type who liked order and for everything to be in its place—which I've noticed he seemed to have passed on to you."

"Sounds like they were very different. Were they happy?"

"They balanced each other out well. They were so in love." Sophie sighed and looked to the side. "I only wish you could have met them. Adelle would have been a great mother."

I nodded. I'd finished making the salad, so I washed my hands and pulled some glasses out of the cupboard.

"Would you like to see a picture of them?" Sophie asked. "I have one if you'd like to see."

My heart skipped a beat at the thought of actually seeing the people I'd come from. "Yes."

Sophie disappeared down the hall and was back in less than a minute, holding out an old photograph.

I saw the mother and the father I would never know, captured in the photo as a young couple on the beach at sunset. They were so young and vibrant looking, only a few years older than I was now. Grayson, who seemed to be quite tall next to his short wife, had his arm around Adelle, his hand resting on her slightly rounded belly. All my life I'd wished I resembled my parents more, and I could finally see that I did. I looked like Grayson and Adelle.

"They looked so happy," I said.

Sophie nodded. "This was taken about a month before Grayson died. They were so excited to be parents." Her eyes glistened with moisture. "They were my best friends, such great people. I wish you could have met them."

I felt a pang in my chest. "Me too." Even though I loved my parents, I still somehow felt a loss at never meeting these people Sophie spoke so highly of. It was a strange sensation, missing someone you never met.

I wiped at my eye and held the photo out for Sophie to take back. But she shook her head and said, "No, you keep it. I have other copies of that at home."

I pressed the picture to my chest. "Thank you."

I looked at the photo a little longer before taking it upstairs and putting it in my journal for safekeeping.

Sophie was placing plates around the table when I returned. "Are you liking your online classes?" she asked.

I was happy for the subject change. School was a safe topic.

"They're fine, but I miss being with my friends." It was sad that we wouldn't be graduating together. We'd been looking forward to that moment for years, and now that it was so close, it was heartbreaking that we wouldn't be able to pass that milestone together.

She glanced at me. "I get that. But what about that nice girl next door? We checked everything out on her; she should be safe to hang out with."

I shrugged. "Tenley is nice, but it's not the same. Plus, it kind of seems pointless to make new friends since we could pick up and move at any time." Tenley had invited Arie and me to hang out with her and her friends a few times. But we still hadn't done anything with her yet, because I was an antisocial bum these days. Plus, it seemed like she only really wanted to hang out with Arie.

Sophie put a hand on my shoulder. "I know it's hard adjusting to a new place, but things will get better. My men will find him soon."

"I hope so."

———

After dinner, I decided to stay at the table to do my homework instead of hiding in my room. Because of my hermitlike tendencies, I was an even better student than I'd been before. Thank you, Fenris, for getting me a better scholarship...Oh yeah, wait. I couldn't go to Maplebridge University, now that I was in hiding.

I was in the middle of my chemistry assignment when Arie sat across the table from me with his laptop. I darted my eyes around the room to see whether Sophie or Jason were in clear view. I couldn't see them, but I did hear the faint sound of the TV coming from the other room. *Dang it.* We were on our own. This hadn't really happened since we'd moved here. Whenever we'd been left alone in the same room before, I'd quickly made an exit to my bedroom. But I couldn't stand the idea of spending the rest of the night in my room again. I'd already been in there most of the day and was starting to go stir-crazy.

I peeked at him when his gaze was focused on his computer. What was he doing? Was he trying to intimidate me and send me back to my room?

I wasn't about to let him win. I'd stay here all night if I had to. I wouldn't even leave to take a bathroom break.

We worked silently across from each other for a while. His fingers clicked away on the keys, so he must have been working on something, not scrolling aimlessly through social media. I noticed him glance up at me a few times. *Was he typing up something about me?* For all I knew he could be typing up an exposé about his days following around a secretly rich girl and how she was so clueless that she had no idea she was being stalked at all. He probably had all sorts of juicy gossip. I'd spent the last few weeks wondering what all he'd seen when I hadn't thought anyone was watching me.

I tried to ignore him, but the thought had already been planted, and I had to know.

"What are you working on?" I asked, hoping it came out casually disinterested.

He looked at me carefully, probably surprised I was speaking to him. When he did speak, his eyes were cautious. "I'm applying for a law-enforcement training program."

What? "Why are you doing that?" I blurted out.

"My internship will be over next fall, and this is the next step," he said, sounding matter of fact, like it was old news.

"Internship?" His job was only a year-long thing?

"You didn't know my position was temporary?" He lowered the screen on his computer. "I'm trying to get into the law-enforcement program so I can eventually get into the Special Agent training program near Washington, DC. My end goal is to get into the Secret Service."

My mouth fell open as the reality of him not following me around forever hit. I'd figured it would be me, Sophie, Jason, and Arie until the end of time. And for some reason, this new information bothered me. I might have been mad at him for lying to me for months, but that didn't mean I wanted him to totally disappear from my life. The thought of never seeing him again in a few months made my throat close up.

"Isn't being in the Secret Service dangerous?"

"Yes, of course, but then, so is protecting an heiress."

He had a point there.

"Does your mom know what kind of dangerous career path you've chosen?"

He shook his head once. "Nope. She still thinks I'm doing an internship for a senator."

I'd assumed as much after accidentally eavesdropping on his phone conversations with his mom. It's not my fault that our shared bedroom wall was paper-thin. It sounded like she thought he was still in Utah right now. Which was probably hard for him, since Philadelphia wasn't that far from New York. He could take a couple of days off and easily go home for a visit if he wanted, but I guess he was grown-up enough that he didn't miss his family as much as I missed mine.

My heart ached for my family. A couple of days after we left, my mom had a scare. She was getting into her car after grocery shopping in their new town when a man tried to grab her. Luckily, she was carrying her pepper spray and was able to get away. While he was disabled, she jumped in her car, slamming her attacker's hand in the car door when he tried to grab at her again.

When my parents talked to the police, they realized they were not as safe in Louisiana as they'd thought. It was obvious that Fenris had found them somehow, so my parents and siblings had all had to go to another safe house in Montana. I felt so guilty that their lives were so messed up now, all because of me.

"What are you thinking about?" Arie asked in a soft voice.

"I'm thinking about my family," I answered, picking my pencil up from the table and doodling a flower in the margin of my notebook paper. "It's hard being away from everyone."

"I'm sure it is. Please remember you're not alone in this." He looked down, then back at me again. "I hope you know you'll always have me for a friend."

Yep. Sure. "Haven't you just been doing your job all along?"

He flinched. "Yes, I have been doing my job, but our friend-ship was real. At least it was for me."

"You honestly enjoyed hanging out with a bunch of high school kids who were so much younger than you?" I asked.

"I never thought I'd enjoy hanging out with you guys so much, but I did."

"I'm glad. I'd hate to think you'd been miserable the whole time."

"Far from it. If I had done my job better, instead of enjoying myself at that dance, I never would've been so care-less, and you wouldn't have this broken arm today." He reached out and touched my arm.

Though I knew it was stupid and weak of me, I wished I could feel his hand through my cast. I missed having physical contact with anyone. My child development teacher had told us last fall about an article she'd read that said humans needed ten touches a day. Hugs, pats on back, handshakes, whatever—we thrive better when we feel connected to others.

And I was feeling starved for those ten touches these days. I didn't have my mom or dad around to hug me, or Maya nudging me when she said something embarrassing, and I definitely didn't have Arie cuddling with me anymore.

"Don't blame yourself." I stared at his hand that I couldn't feel. "If it hadn't been for you, I could've been dead."

"ARE you looking forward to Matt's party tonight?" I asked Emma after breakfast one morning. The neighbor girl, Tenley, had come over yesterday to invite us to her friend Matt's party. I was shocked when Emma said she wanted to go since she hadn't been in the partying mood before.

The first few weeks after moving here, I'd sat with my back against the wall separating our bedrooms, listening to her cry for hours when she thought no one could hear. My heart broke each night for her, but I felt helpless. I wasn't sure what she was comfortable doing with me now that she knew I was her bodyguard. I wanted to take her out and away from the condo but hadn't been allowed to until Jason and Sophie trusted that things were safe here in Philadelphia. Finally they decided we were safe. It didn't seem like Fenris had any clues to where we were hiding, so Emma was free to leave the condo as long as she had one of us with her.

Emma's face lit up a little at my mention of the party. "It'll be nice to act normal again and get out for a change."

"It will. I know moving away from everything you've ever

known with a bunch of strangers had to be tough." I turned to finish loading the dishwasher with the breakfast dishes.

"I'd hardly call you a stranger, Arie." She handed me her cereal bowl and then leaned against the counter beside me. She was cute in the mornings, wearing a fluffy pink bathrobe over her pajamas, her hair falling out of a braid. "But yes, I'll be the first to admit that it wasn't the way I'd planned for my life to pan out."

"I wish things didn't have to be this way for you." I wiped my hands on a dishtowel. "I miss the days when you were this carefree girl I got to hang out with."

She shrugged. "We still hang out all the time, but now I know you're my bodyguard."

I hated how she saw me as her bodyguard now, not her friend. Of course, I knew she thought of me as a friend as well, but our relationship wasn't as effortless as it had been in Maplebridge. There was a strain that hadn't been there before. The fact that I was sent to watch over her hung in the back of her mind. "Yes, but it isn't the same. Now it's as if you have the weight of the world on your shoulders."

"Maybe not the whole world. It's not like I'm carrying around a ton of bricks or anything." Her shoulders hunched.

Did she feel that weighed down?

"I know I can't take your circumstances away from you." I cautiously placed my hands on her shoulders, touching her for the first time since moving. She startled. "But I'm here to help you out in any way I can."

"Thanks." She stepped to the side as if to leave, forcing me to drop my hands. A surge of rejection pulsed through me. She still couldn't stand my touch.

Instead of leaving, she looked at me thoughtfully. "Do you think you could teach me some self-defense skills? I mean, if I have people trying to kill me, I should probably be more prepared to protect myself."

"Of course. I don't know why I didn't think of that before. When should we start?"

"How about today? I need to shower first, but after that, I'm free until the party."

"Sounds good. I'll be ready whenever."

40

EMMA

I WENT DOWNSTAIRS to meet Arie in the living room. He had pushed the furniture to the sides of the room, making space for us to move around on the plush carpet.

"Are you ready to go?" He stood and walked over to me, all professional. This was Arie in work mode.

"I guess so." I pulled my hair up in a ponytail.

"Great. First, I want to teach you about the target areas you should go for if someone were to attack you." He clasped his hands in front of him. "It's normal to assume a smaller person couldn't get away from a bigger attacker, but that's not always true. There are soft targets on everyone's bodies, and if you were to attack those targets, you could cause enough pain to get away."

I nodded, listening.

"Those places are eyes, ears, mouth, and nose." Arie gestured to each spot as he spoke. "Neck, groin, fingers, and toes." He rested his hands on his hips. "Can you repeat that?"

I nodded and repeated what he'd said.

"Very good," he said. "To attack the eyes, you can use the thumb gouge." He placed his hands on the sides of my head, his thumbs in front of my eyes. "Like this, except you'd dig in with your thumbs. You could also use the spear-hand." He straightened his hand and pointed the tips of his fingers straight at my eyes. "Or the leopard's fist punch." He pointed the ridge of his knuckles right at my eyes. "Remember, accuracy is critical. You need to get the right spot." He stepped back from me. "Okay, now you try it on me."

"Okay." I straightened up a little. "So first there is the thumb gouge. Is that right?"

"Uh-huh."

We then went through all the moves he'd shown me, which were somewhat difficult with my cast, but I think I did okay.

"Awesome," he said, after I demonstrated the techniques.

Arie then showed me the other self-defense techniques for the soft targets on someone's face. I demonstrated them back to him with ease. "I know those are all well and good, but is it likely that someone will attack me from the front? What if I'm grabbed from behind?"

"Good question. If someone were to grab you from behind, what would you do?" He spun me around so my back was to him. Then he wrapped his arms around my shoulders in a bear hug.

My mind went blank. "Um, I don't know." It was hard to think clearly with his body next to mine. We hadn't been this close since we'd kissed in his basement over a month ago, and my body seemed to forget it shouldn't be reacting to him like it was.

"Think about it for a sec," he said, his voice close to my ear. "Of all the soft targets we talked about, which ones could you attack right now?"

I thought about it. "I could get your toes, maybe fingers if I move my hands a little, and your, um, groin if I step to the side."

"That's exactly right. Let me show you." He let go of me and stepped in front. "Okay, now put your arms around me like I did to you."

I did as he said, somewhat reluctantly.

"Something you could do is grab an attacker's fingers like this and pull back." He demonstrated this as he spoke, though not pulling back with the force necessary to hurt me, of course. "As you can see, whatever way your fingers are pulled, your arm wants to follow in order to avoid pain."

He was right. As he pulled my fingers backward, my arms released the hold I had on him. "Wow, I would never even think to do that," I said, impressed.

He looked at me over his shoulder and smiled. "Now it's your turn."

We switched places. His hands were positioned near my rib cage, and when I tried to pry his fingers away, it worked.

"That's crazy! If I'd known all these things earlier, I might not have this stupid cast." I lifted my left arm encased in pink. "Then again, I could always use this as a club or something—it is pretty hard," I joked, trying to push down the attraction growing inside me. Being close to Arie was still as intoxicating as it had been a month ago. And the tight black shirt he wore accentuated his muscles with every movement, making it extremely difficult to concentrate on what he was teaching.

"True." He chuckled. "I don't think I'd risk being punched in the nose with that thing."

"What else could I do if I were attacked again?"

Arie showed me a few more things, having me practice each new technique a few times before moving on to the next. He was an excellent teacher, and I learned a lot in the short training session.

We reviewed everything once more before calling it a day.

"Thank you so much for helping me." Before I could think better of it, I reached up to give him a quick hug. It felt wonderful to be more confident in my ability to defend myself against an attacker.

He returned my embrace, folding me into his strong arms. "My pleasure. I just hope you won't ever have to use those new skills of yours."

It was nice to be held close to him again, even if it was just for a brief hug between friends. He still felt good. When he didn't pull away immediately, I wondered what was going through his mind. He stood there for a time, resting his face close to my neck as he held me tight.

His warm breath was on my hair and I became conscious of my own quickened breathing, the flash of heat rushing along my body, and the aching in my heart. Though my mind knew better, my body wanted this. It craved his touch, like a chocoholic on a diet.

He moved his head slowly, resting his cheek against mine. The stubble on his jaw felt rough against my skin. I swallowed, fantasizing about how easy it would be to turn my head and press my lips to his—forgetting why we'd been brought together. I wanted him to brush his lips across mine and tell me he hadn't been pretending before, that he wanted me.

He held me a moment longer before stepping away. I imagined I saw the same longing in his eyes that I felt, but it was gone almost as soon as it had appeared, so I couldn't be sure whether it had been there at all.

"Thanks again." I tucked a strand of hair behind my ear.

It was embarrassing that he knew how I had felt about him back in Maplebridge. He knew I'd kissed him because I wanted to—there hadn't been a reason for me to fake that. But why had he kissed me? Had he just been trying to keep his cover all along, or had he actually liked me back? I wanted to straight-up ask Arie those questions, but I was too scared of what his answer might be. I didn't think I could take any more rejection when I had to see him every day and sleep across the hall from him each night.

41

EMMA

"I'M glad you could make it tonight," Tenley yelled to me over the loud music blasting through the speakers. We were at Matt's party, in his parents' exquisite colonial home. Even though the house was huge, it was still packed with teens. When Arie and I arrived, I'd expected a little get-together with maybe ten people, like the parties I attended in Maplebridge. This was so different from that. It was hard to walk around the huge house without bumping into someone or knocking someone's drink to the ground. So instead of checking the house out, I stood with Arie, Tenley, and a few other friends of hers in a tight circle as the music blasted through the speakers.

"Is this what you guys do on a regular basis here in Philadelphia?" I asked Tenley, trying to be heard over the music.

She nodded as she bounced to the beat. "Pretty much. Isn't it great?"

I wasn't so sure how I felt about it—it was actually quite overwhelming after weeks of isolation—but I said, "Sure."

Tenley danced closer and gave me a hip bump. "So is Asher really your brother? You don't look related."

For safety purposes, Arie and I had changed our names when we moved here. I was now known as Peyton, and Arie went by Asher. It was weird to go by a false name, and I hoped I wouldn't slip up tonight.

"Umm, yeah, stepbrother," I said, hoping she didn't notice the anxiety creeping up my face at the lie. I didn't like lying to her, but it was kind of a necessary evil in my situation. Was this how Arie had felt back in Maplebridge?

"Man, that's gotta be hard. He is sooo hot! I'd have a hard time keeping my hands off him if I were you. Stepbrother or not." She bit her lip as she eyed Arie, who was across the circle from us. "Is he dating anyone?"

I fought the twinge of jealousy attempting to show on my face. "No, he isn't dating anyone. At least, not that I know of." *He is pretty good at keeping secrets, though.*

"Ooh, so he's free game." A satisfied smile spread across her face as she nodded. "Good to know."

"He doesn't get out much, though." Which was code for, *Back off.*

She must not have understood my code because she said, "We'll see if I can change that." She winked, then walked across the circle in his direction. Once she was at his side, she asked him a question I couldn't hear. She batted her eyelashes and sent him a seductive smile. Okay, maybe it was her regular smile, but she was the kind of girl that could get any guy she wanted...therefore, everything about her had a come-hither sort of look.

Arie stepped from side to side to the music, looking uncomfortable with the situation. He answered her back, but I still couldn't hear what they were saying. He did smile, though, which made me think he liked what she was saying.

"I'm going to get a glass of water," I called to them and stepped away from the group.

"I'll come with you." Arie caught up to me, grabbing my arm. He was about to follow me when Tenley grabbed his bicep and pulled him back next to her.

"Hey, I know you have this protective-brother thing going on, but she'll be fine," Tenley told him. She waved me away with that sultry smile on her face. "*We* should dance. This is my favorite song."

Arie looked back at me, a torn look on his face.

I nodded, smothering my jealousy. "It's okay, you guys dance. I'll be fine."

That settled it. Arie stayed with Tenley, and I went to find something to do that didn't involve watching them.

I walked into the kitchen, which was connected to the large room, and got myself a cup of water from the tap. I'd already seen a few guys huddled around the punch bowl earlier, refilling their cups after drunkenly spilling them on the table and laughing. I wasn't about to take my chances with any of the drinks at this party.

I glanced over at Tenley and Arie, who were now dancing. I tried to hold back a grimace when Tenley wrapped her arms around his neck. Part of me wished I could dance with him right then, but of course I couldn't. Even if I wasn't still trying to keep my distance, everyone here thought we were brother and sister.

I stood there, watching them for a while. Arie seemed to be having a good time. Maybe he thought Tenley was cute. I already knew what Tenley thought of him.

I should be a good person and be happy he was having a good time...but I wasn't that selfless. Instead, I thought of ways to get Arie away from Tenley. I could walk over there with a glass of punch and *accidentally* trip and spill my drink all over Tenley. Or I could get close by and suddenly have an allergy attack and sneeze all over them.

I shook the ridiculous ideas out of my head. That would make me look like some sort of jealous ex.

"Do you want to dance?"

I startled before noticing that someone was standing next to me. A tall guy with chocolate-brown eyes. Matt. The guy whose party this was. He was asking me to dance?

It took me a moment to come fully to my senses. "Umm," I said, trying to figure out how to answer him. I wasn't really in the mood to dance with anyone tonight, especially with a bunch of people I didn't know. My eyes darted back to Arie and Tenley, who were still dancing. Tenley was smiling brilliantly as she grabbed his hands and pulled him closer.

I looked back at Matt, who was thankfully not looking like he regretted asking me yet. "I'd love to dance." Two could play at this game. There's nothing a guy wants more than a girl he can't have, and tonight I wanted to be that girl.

As Matt and I walked, I scanned the room and saw all eyes were on us. I hoped I could pull this off with an audience; my ego needed to make this look good. I stood close to Matt, put my arms on his shoulders, and gave it everything I had. He seemed all too happy to go along with my plan, which made it better. I may have been dancing with Matt, but every move, every smile, and every twist of my hips was for Arie.

Arie stood a few feet away, watching me with a frown of disapproval.

Well, he could frown at me all he liked. If he didn't like what he saw, he could keep dancing with Tenley or some other girl for all I cared.

Dancing with Matt was strangely invigorating. I felt powerful! *I'm not broken anymore,* I thought while looking at Arie. *I'm done pining for a guy who only sees me as a pathetic helpless girl.*

Matt and I danced to a few more songs. He turned out to be

a pretty good dancer. It was fun letting loose again, being a regular teenager for a time. I'd been so weighed down with wondering whether I'd ever be safe again, and worrying about my family and friends, that I'd forgotten I still needed to live along the way. I decided then and there that I wasn't going to play the victim anymore. I was going to take charge of my life again!

42

ARIE

I KEPT a close eye on Emma after she left me with Tenley. As I watched her dancing with Matt, I found myself debating how badly our cover would be blown if I yanked him off my supposed-to-be sister. He shouldn't be dancing with her like that, so close there was barely any space between them. His hands shouldn't be on her hips, or his chest pressed to her back as they swayed to the music. How could she be okay with that? They'd just met.

If anything, *I* should be the one with her in my arms.

Knowing it shouldn't look like I cared, I was careful how I watched them, guarding my face of any emotion. It would be bad if others noticed my jealousy, since they all thought I was her stepbrother.

"Is something wrong, Asher?" Tenley asked, dancing beside me.

I broke my gaze from the spectacle before me. "No. Everything's fine."

My eyes wandered back to Emma when the song changed. Matt started introducing her to a few of his friends. Content that Matt didn't have his hands all over Emma for a moment, I stopped ignoring Tenley, feigning enthusiasm when she told me her story about taking her dog to the vet the day before.

A few minutes later, one of the guys at the party let out a loud wail just as a song was ending. "What the heck, Stacey?" his voice boomed.

Everyone whirled around to see what happened. In the center of the room was a guy crouched over in a lot of pain. Emma stood in front of him, her eyes wide, looking around as if she didn't know what to do.

"Stacey? Who's Stacey?" she asked the boy.

"Stacey is my girlfriend," he said through clenched teeth. "I thought you were her."

Understanding washed over Emma's face. "I'm so sorry!" She held her hands out, about to pat the guy on the shoulder. Instead of touching him, she returned her hands to her sides. "I had no idea. I thought you were trying to attack me or something."

"What? Why would you think that?"

"I don't know. It was stupid." She searched the room with desperate eyes, as the spectators held up their phones, catching the embarrassing moment on camera.

I rushed to where she was and grabbed her elbow to pull her away from the staring crowd. "Come on, Peyton. Let's get you home." We grabbed our coats and headed for the door.

———

A frigid breeze whipped at our faces as Emma and I stepped into the bitter cold night. The loud music faded as we walked down the path until the only sound to be heard was our feet crunching on the thick layer of frozen snow that blanketed the ground. After we climbed into the car, I turned the defrost on high to melt the thin sheet of frost covering the windshield and waited for the car to warm up.

"Thanks for getting me out of there," Emma said as she shivered.

I nodded. "What happened? That guy sounded ticked."

She inspected her hands, not meeting my eyes. "You know how you taught me some self-defense stuff today?" She peeked up at me, a guilty expression on her face. "I think I may have unnecessarily put those skills to good use tonight."

"What?"

"I was standing there, talking to some people, when I felt a guy's arms wrap around me," she explained. "Instead of thinking, I went into defensive mode and stepped to the side. Then I may have rammed my fist backward in a hammer punch to that guy's um, you know, man parts."

"You did *what?*"

Concern etched her features. "I think I hurt him pretty bad."

"You think so?" I barked out a laugh. "I guess our little training session sank in, then."

"I'd say so." She was fighting the giggles, and I could see her wiping tears from her eyes. "I don't think anyone is going to invite me to another party now. I mean, first I'm the hermit girl who doesn't go anywhere, and now I'm the girl who hurts anyone who tries to show her the least bit of affection."

"Hey, at least they'll remember you."

"I guess I needed to make a lasting impression somehow."

I nodded. It wasn't likely anyone would soon forget Emma's hammer punch to a guy's groin. *Ouch!* I winced at the thought. I wondered which arm she'd used. Was it the one in the cast, or the other arm? I hoped, for the guy's sake, it wasn't the arm with the cast.

The windshield was clear enough now, so I switched on the

heater and pulled onto the street.

"How did you like the party?" I asked.

"It was so fun!" She answered a little more enthusiastically than was normal for her.

"I saw you hanging out with Matt a lot. What did you think of him?" I gripped the steering wheel a little tighter as I waited for her response.

"Matt's so nice, and such a great dancer!" Was that a mischievous smile playing at her lips?

"He does seem like a nice guy," I allowed, feeling a twinge of jealousy resurface at her comment. I thought back to watching her dance with Matt this evening. She'd seemed like she'd had the time of her life, smiling from ear to ear while dancing way too close to a guy she barely knew.

I reminded myself that it was good she was making friends. It's not like I could expect her to be happy hanging out with my fellow agents and me all the time, even though that was exactly what I wanted. I wanted to be the one she wanted to hang out with. I wanted to be the one she was excited to see each day. I wanted to be the one she danced with all night.

When we arrived at the condo, I followed Emma up the stairs after locking the front door, checking all the windows, and making sure the security system was on since Jason and Sophie had probably gone to sleep hours ago.

Before going to bed, I knocked on Emma's door.

"Come in," she called from inside her room.

She was sitting on her bed in her pajamas, writing in what looked like a journal.

"I wanted to say good night," I mumbled. She looked up, sucking on the end of her pen. "What are you writing?"

"Oh, just about my embarrassing experience tonight. I'm sure my grandkids will love to hear about all the stupid things I do."

"Do you write in your journal often?"

"Usually once a week, sometimes twice. It depends on what's going on in my life at the time."

"That's cool." What else had she found worthy to write about? "Has my name ever appeared in your journal?"

"Maybe." I loved the way her cheeks got all pink and flushed at my question. It was beautiful, and I'd forgotten how much I'd missed seeing it.

"I hope your grandkids will have reason to think I was an okay guy."

She gave a noncommittal shrug.

When I sat next to her on her bed, she clapped her journal shut and held it against her chest under her cast.

"Why the secrecy?" I asked. "Were you writing bad things about me after all?"

She shook her head. "No, of course not! What bad things would there be to say about you?"

"Oh, I don't know." I raised my hand in the air. "Maybe that I'm a strange guy you can't get rid of."

"I wouldn't write that about you." She shook her head, her silky hair begging me to run my fingers through it. "You're just doing your job," she mumbled, almost grudgingly. This would not do. We needed to get over this tiptoeing around each other. We needed to start having fun again.

"Then why not let me take a peek." I reached over to touch her journal, hoping she'd loosen up for a change.

"Uh-uh." She stood up, transferred her journal to her good hand, and held it behind her back.

"Do you think holding your journal behind your back could keep me from getting it if I wanted?" I paused for a second, remembering how she'd hurt that poor guy tonight. "Then again, maybe I should worry about what you might do to me."

"Yes, you better watch out, Arie." A reluctant smile snuck up her lips. "I'm practically a master in self-defense now."

"Oh yeah?" I challenged, happy to have earned a smile. "And what would you do to me if I did this?" I stood and walked over to her, trying to reach behind her back to grab the journal.

"Not so fast," she said as she darted away from me.

"There must be some dang interesting stuff in there if you don't want me reading it this badly."

"I don't know. I've only had this journal since we got here, and nothing too interesting has happened since then. My journal in Maplebridge, on the other hand, now that one..." She stopped mid-sentence and covered her mouth with her casted hand.

I smiled. Had she written about me in her journal back then? "What kinds of things did you write about in Maplebridge?"

"Nothing." She avoided my eyes.

"Come on, you can tell me."

"Like you don't know," she said, as if it were obvious.

I didn't want to assume anything, so I prodded. "I'm not a mind reader, so I can't pretend to know." I reached around her again, snatching the journal from her hand and holding it high above my head. She started jumping, trying to reach it with her good arm. It was a cute attempt but useless. I was too tall for her.

"Come on, please give it back," she begged.

I shook my head with a grin and lowered my arm to hold the journal behind my back. She tried to reach around me again, but I seized her about the waist with my free hand.

Caught off guard at our unexpected closeness, she stepped

away. Emma tried to get her journal back a few more times without success.

"Okay," she said, giving up. "If you must know, I wrote about how great you were and how I loved hanging out with you." She looked down. "You know, those kinds of things. Can I please have my journal back now?"

"Did you really think those things about me?" I asked in a low voice.

"Yes, I did," she whispered. She raised her beautiful blue eyes to look at me, her face a few inches from mine. "I still think those things, even though I probably shouldn't."

My body flooded with warmth when she spoke those words. I wanted to tell her how I felt. Even more, I wanted to lean in and *show* her how I felt. I took a step closer, trapping her in the corner. There was vulnerability in her eyes, like she was waiting for me to make my move. That look brought emotions I'd tried to suppress for so long right back up to the surface, and my breath caught in my throat.

I dropped her journal onto the chair beside us and then placed one hand on the wall beside her head while the other caressed her cheek. Emma's eyes widened, and she lifted a trembling hand to my chest. At first I thought she was going to push me away, but she didn't. Instead, she bunched the fabric of my shirt in her fingers. I looked at her lips and then at her eyes again—they were filled with the same desire I felt crashing over me. So I tilted my head down, moving my face closer to hers.

"What's going on in here?" Jason barged into the room, dressed in Scooby-Doo pajamas, and holding a Glock.

I stumbled back from where I had cornered Emma, feeling my cheeks burn as I bit down. "Nothing, everything's fine. I was saying good night to Emma." This didn't look good.

He lowered his gun and looked away, visibly trying to calm

himself in front of Emma. "I heard shuffling up here and thought Emma was in danger."

Emma stood wide-eyed, wringing her hands. "We were playing a game of keep away. I-I'm sorry to have alarmed you. Everything's fine up here."

Jason waved her away. "Don't worry about it. I'm glad everything is all right." He nodded at me and left the room.

That was my cue to leave as well. Our moment had passed, and it was probably for the best. I'd told her dad I'd stay away, after all. So I picked up the journal from the chair and held it out to Emma. "I better get to bed as well."

Ask me not to go.

Emma took the journal from my outstretched hand. "See you tomorrow." My heart fell when she followed me to the door and closed it behind me.

I walked across the hall to my room. Jason was waiting for me in there. His face was stern, and I had a sinking feeling I knew why.

"Close the door and take a seat." Jason started pacing about my room.

I obeyed and sat on the edge of my bed.

Jason cleared his throat before beginning. "I can't pretend not to understand what I walked in on a minute ago."

I winced.

"Is there something going on between you and Emma? Romantically, that is?"

It looked as bad as I thought.

"No. Nothing's going on. Nothing happened." Which was true...Jason's sudden appearance had stopped me from kissing her.

Jason narrowed his eyes. "It didn't look like *nothing* from where I stood." I was going to be fired for sure now.

"I know what it looked like." It looked like I had trapped Emma in the corner and was about to have my way with her. "But nothing happened."

Jason held up a finger. "Because I came in at the right moment." He blew out a breath. "Arie, you are Emma's bodyguard! She's in serious danger and needs people watching out for her, not falling in love with her!"

I threw my hands in the air. "Don't you think I know that!" I stopped, realizing Emma would hear me at this volume. I brought my voice down a few notches and whispered, "I've tried to keep my distance this whole time we've been living in Philadelphia. It's not like I *want* to get fired. You of all people should understand that." He'd fallen in love with his boss, after all.

"I know, I know. But that was different." Jason stopped his pacing and stood in front of me, his expression softer. "And I assume the feelings are mutual, by the way Emma was looking at you. But you can't act on your feelings, Arie. Emma is in real danger right now. We have no idea where Fenris is...but we know he won't stop looking for her until he has what he wants. Until we find him, I need you to stay focused on the task at hand. And if you can't, we will have to replace you."

"I know." I studied the carpet. The last thing I wanted was to lose my focus and have her stripped away from me again. "I'll keep my hands off Emma."

"Hands *and* lips?"

I looked up. He had a hint of a smile on his face.

I sighed. "Yes, hands *and* lips."

"Good." Before he left my room, he glanced back at me. "It'll all turn out, Arie. This can't go on forever."

43

EMMA

I DIDN'T KNOW what I'd been thinking when I almost kissed Arie. The fact was, I hadn't been thinking at all, because if I had, I never would have been in that situation. Apparently, my mind was still having a hard time controlling my body and my emotions when it came to him.

Thankfully, he never brought up the almost kiss, either. Instead, we continued on as almost friends. We talked, but the conversations weren't very deep anymore. It was like we were dancing around each other, afraid to let down the walls we'd manufactured out of unspoken conversations and guarded emotions.

"How does it feel to finally have the cast off?" Arie asked when Sophie and I came home after my appointment with the doctor.

"Wonderful." I sat on the other end of the couch Arie was on. "The doctor said my arm healed well, but I'll need to exercise it to slowly build back the muscle I lost."

"I'm sure you'll be back to normal in no time." Sophie

squeezed my shoulder and smiled before moving toward the kitchen.

Once Sophie was out of the room, I turned my attention back to Arie. "Did Jason find out anything new while I was gone?"

Arie rested his arm along the back of the couch, and a huge smile crept up his face. "He did. They know where Fenris is. The police are on their way as we speak. And it sounds like Fenris still has no idea where you disappeared to."

I let out a breath I hadn't realized I'd been holding, my chest feeling lighter than it had in so long. "So it's almost over?"

"Yes." Arie's smile broadened further—something I hadn't seen him do so freely before. "We still need to be careful because he still has his guys out there. But things are looking up."

My arms tingled, and I almost jumped out of my seat with joy. I'd get to go home with my family soon. This nightmare was almost over.

———

A little while later, I was on the couch with my nose in a book when the phone rang. Since I wasn't allowed to answer the phone, I waited for Arie to get it. He did, and a moment later I was holding the phone to my ear talking to Matt.

"Hi, Peyton," he said calling me by my false name.

"Hey, Matt." I marked my spot in my book and shut it around my finger. "How's it going?"

"Good." He cleared his throat. "Are you doing anything Friday night?"

"I don't have any plans yet," I answered, though I was hoping I'd be packing my bags by then.

"I was wondering if you wanted to go on a date with me."

He wanted to go on a date? After watching me ninja-chop his friend's crotch? I hadn't been out on a date since moving to Philadelphia. Maybe it would be a nice way to celebrate the end of my lockdown. And it would be fun to go out with Matt—he seemed really cool at his party a couple of weeks ago.

There was just one problem: even if things were looking up right now, I was still supposed to have a guard with me at all times. How was I supposed to manage that on a date? It's not like I could say I could go as long as one of my babysitters could tag along to make sure I didn't get killed.

I racked my brain, trying to think of a solution to my dilemma without giving Matt the impression I didn't like him. Then it came to me.

"I'd love to!"

"Great..."

I interrupted him before he could say anything else. "But my parents have this rule that they need to know where I'm going to be when I go on dates. You could say they're slightly overprotective." I smiled even though he couldn't see it. "Let me know where we'll be going in advance so I can tell them, and I'm sure they won't have any problem with it."

"Wow, that's strict."

"Tell me about it."

The line was quiet for a second.

"Do you like bowling?"

"I love bowling!" Bowling would be perfect! I could have one of my secret agents stationed there, and Matt would never even have to know we were being watched.

"Good. So I'll pick you up at seven?"

"I'm looking forward to it." Well, at least part of me was—I'd try to ignore the other part of me while we were out.

I gave him my address, said goodbye to Matt, and hung up.

Arie walked back into the room once he saw my call was finished.

"What did Matt want?"

"He asked me on a date for Friday night." I carefully watched his face to gauge his reaction.

His eyes narrowed, and he didn't look too pleased to be hearing my news. "Even though we found Fenris, you do realize that either Jason, Sophie, or I still need to be near you at all times, don't you?"

I smiled at him. "Don't worry. I've already thought about that. Matt said we're going bowling. I figured the bowling alley's a crowded-enough place that he wouldn't notice one of you following me around."

"I see." His mouth was set in a firm line.

44

EMMA

THE POLICE WEREN'T able to get Fenris. Somehow he'd been warned, or something, and he'd disappeared from his apartment before they could get to him.

So we were back to living in Philadelphia until the end of time.

At least I had gone ahead and agreed to that date with Matt, I guess. Even though I was super depressed, I managed to pull myself out of it a little bit by doing some retail therapy and getting a makeover.

I figured that if I was an heiress, I might as well look like one. Thankfully, Sophie had the foresight to make my tracking bracelet cute enough to match my new wardrobe.

The doorbell rang, and I heard Arie answer the door below. A moment later, he called my name from the bottom of the stairs. I grabbed my jacket and walked downstairs. I first noticed Arie.

Why was he already wearing his jacket? Wasn't he supposed to wait to follow us a few minutes after Matt and I left? He looked my way as I made it to the bottom step. I imagined something like admiration flash in his eyes.

I walked past him to where Matt was standing near the front door. Matt gave me an approving smile. "Hey, Peyton. You look great!"

I smiled at his compliment and said, "Thank you!" I hoped Arie noticed Matt's reaction.

"Shall we go?" Matt asked.

I nodded.

Matt said to Arie, "Hey, Asher, were you planning to ride with us, or are you taking your own car?"

What the heck was he talking about?

Arie stepped closer to me. "If you wouldn't mind, I'd like to ride with you guys.

Matt shrugged. "Fine with me."

I looked back and forth between the two guys, hoping one of them would enlighten me.

Arie spoke next. "Didn't I tell you, sis?" He winked. "When I heard about you and Matt going on a date, I talked to him about how I've been wanting to try out the dating scene in Philly myself, so he said he'd hook me up with someone cool that he knew."

Date? Arie was going on a date with someone else? My heart shrunk in my chest, but I forced a smile on my face. "What a great idea." I turned to Matt. "That's so nice of you to let my sweet brother tag along. He doesn't get out much." If Arie wanted to tag along on my date, I was going to make him regret it. I was going to show him that I had moved on and I didn't envy his date at all.

Arie placed his arm around my shoulder in a brotherly way. "Oh, Peyton. I'm so glad you're not mad."

"Of course not," I said, shoving his arm off my shoulders.

"It's not every day you get to go on a double date with your brother."

Matt's car only had two doors, so I had to let Arie climb in through my door before getting in myself. Two-door vehicles were such a hassle when you had to use the back seats.

As we drove, I wondered what kind of girl Matt would set Arie up with. It didn't sound like it was Tenley, which was somewhat relieving, but with my luck I'd probably end up watching him put the moves on some other supermodel-type girl at the bowling alley.

We stopped in front of a red brick house a few minutes later. I climbed out and held the door open for Arie to get out. He stood close to me and whispered in my ear before passing by. "You look beautiful tonight."

I blushed furiously at his comment because his quiet voice had made the words sound so sincere. My cheeks continued to burn as Arie walked up the sidewalk and I was left behind, wondering whether I imagined him saying those words that caused my heart to flutter.

The sounds of bowling balls crashing into pins and people laughing filled my ears as we entered. It was disco night, so the main lights were turned down, leaving the colorful neon lights to set the fun atmosphere. Matt was friends with the guy working the desk tonight, so he was able to get us a lane relatively fast, saving us from waiting long on the busy night.

Arie's date ended up being Matt's cousin, Sydney. She was cute, and average height with short auburn hair. She seemed like a sweet girl, but she didn't talk much. I tried to be courteous to her, though deep down I was hoping she'd fall on her face...twice...and get a bloody nose, both times. Okay, maybe that was going too far.

Obviously, I was still mad that Arie had intruded on my date. Having him there kept him fresh on my mind, making it hard to concentrate on Matt and any possible connection we might have.

We all grabbed our shoes and made our way to lane seventeen. I found myself a bowling ball and came back to discover that Arie had already typed our names into the computer. I read the names on the screen: Matt, Peytie-poo, Asher, and Sydney. *Peytie-poo?*

I put my hands on my hips and walked over to him. "'Peytie-poo?' Why in the world did you put that for my name?"

Arie looked at me with an innocent expression. "I thought brothers were supposed to have nicknames for their little sisters."

"When you're little. I'm eighteen."

"Oh, sorry." He shrugged, not looking sorry at all. "I thought since I didn't know you when you were younger, I might as well try to catch up on all we missed." He winked, then smiled wickedly at me. Apparently, he was going to play the part of annoying stepbrother all night long.

I tried to scowl. If he'd been a plain-looking guy pretending to be my stepbrother, I could play the part of annoyed stepsister much better. But no, he was the cutest stepbrother a girl could ever pretend to have. Frustrated, I turned away from him and gave my attention to Matt.

Matt nodded at the screen. "I didn't know you preferred being called 'Peytie-poo.'" He snickered.

I sighed, exasperated. "I don't. My sweet stepbrother thought it would be fun to give me a nickname." I turned my head and glared at Arie, resisting the urge to stick out my tongue. He chuckled and turned to talk to his date.

Once we were all ready to begin, Matt said, "Why don't we play in teams to make it more interesting?"

"Like me and Sydney against you and Peyton?" Arie clarified.

"Exactly," Matt answered. A competitive glint formed in his eyes.

A look of anxiety crossed Sydney's face. "I don't know if that's such a great idea, Matt. You know I'm not good at bowling. I'll be lucky if I get ten pins all night."

"You can't be that bad," Arie said.

She shook her head. "No, really. I am."

"Don't worry about it. It's just a game, and we're here to have fun." He raised his eyebrows at Matt as if to make a point.

Matt rubbed his hands together. "Yes, it is a game. A game I intend to win."

My palms started to sweat at the thought of having to bowl well. I thought we were here to have a good time, but it sounded like Matt meant business. I knew he was athletic and played football and baseball at his school, but I didn't think he'd take bowling this seriously.

I turned to him and said, "I hope *you're* good, because I'm afraid my bowling skills are rusty."

"Watch the pro and learn." He winked. Matt picked up his bowling ball, then flung it down the lane as fast as lightning. I watched in amazement as his ball struck every single pin down. It looked like he meant business.

I was up next. I picked up my pink bowling ball, swung my arm back, and let go. It didn't fall into the gutter, knocking seven pins down. I felt pretty good about that and turned around to retrieve my ball. Arie and Sydney were both clapping for me.

Matt gave me a high five and said, "Better luck next time."

"Thanks?"

Arie bowled after me and ended up getting a spare. As Arie walked past us, Matt said, "Too bad you couldn't get that one down the first time." I gaped, surprised he'd say that. I thought a spare was something to be proud of, but apparently, Matt wasn't impressed so easily.

Arie just smiled, getting a congratulatory high five from Sydney.

Sydney was up next. She walked up and sort of flung the bowling ball at the pins, without looking like she was trying to aim at all. The ball immediately found its way into the gutter. She turned around, and her face was completely red. Arie was a gentleman, though, and encouraged her, telling her it was fine.

I wondered whether Matt would be so understanding if I ended up with a gutter ball.

The game continued on in much the same way. Matt got strikes or spares almost every time. It made me wonder whether he had a bowling alley in the basement of that great big house of his.

I bowled okay. Matt gave me a few pointers, which helped a little. I even tried to flirt by asking him to help me get in the right position, which he was happy to help me with. He put his hands on my shoulders to guide me to the correct stance. I didn't like him getting so familiar with me, letting his hands trace their way down my arms, but I went along with it for Arie's benefit. When I glanced back at Arie to catch his reaction, I was disappointed to find he wasn't even looking at us. He was busy talking to Sydney.

All this flirting with Matt, and Arie didn't even seem fazed by it. He didn't even notice.

As bad as I was at bowling, Sydney was much worse. Arie

tried to give her a few suggestions to help her game, but her ball still ended up in the gutter almost every time. Arie was sweet, though, and threw the game himself. He walked up to the lane with the bowling ball in both hands. He bent over, lifted the ball between his legs, and then rolled it down at a snail's pace. It seemed to take forever to make it to the end, where it knocked over a grand total of three pins.

"Come on, Grandpa, you've got to have something better than that in you," Matt called to Arie.

Arie shuffled over to us with his hand on his back. "Nope, sorry, my arthritis seems to be acting up tonight."

I could tell Matt was frustrated that Arie wasn't taking the game as seriously as he was. Arie had turned it into something fun instead and was making his date more comfortable. He ended up flinging the ball down the lane in all kinds of ridiculous ways the rest of the night.

Matt and I were so far ahead of Arie and Sydney that I thought Matt might decide to loosen up and enjoy the game, but he didn't. Instead, he stayed intense, getting most of the pins down each frame. I continued to feel pressure from him to do well, and it made me bowl worse and worse.

After one particularly bad frame, I turned around to find a look of frustration on Matt's face. He didn't even offer a *nice try* or a high five. I took my seat between him and Sydney in silence, ready for this date to be over with.

My attempts to make Arie jealous of my date had backfired, and the opposite had occurred. *I* was the one who was jealous of *his* date with Sydney. They were losing horribly, but they were still having a blast. I gave up trying to appear like I was enjoying myself and slumped on the seat with my arms crossed. Matt had turned out to be way too competitive for me.

When Sydney got up to bowl again, Arie scooted next to me and leaned close, speaking next to my ear. "Are you okay?"

I gave him a curt nod. I wasn't about to let him know how lousy I felt.

I excused myself and went to the bathroom. I needed a few minutes alone if I was going to be able to fake my way through the rest of this date.

I washed my hands and looked in the mirror above the sink. Why did I always have to have the worst luck with guys? Was I ever going to find a decent guy who didn't end up being a jerk?

I dried my hands under one of those stupid hand dryers before growing impatient and wiping my hands on my jeans instead. Outside the ladies' room, Arie was leaning against the row of orange lockers along the wall.

I rolled my eyes and released an annoyed sigh. "You really didn't need to follow me to the bathroom, Arie. I didn't spot any thugs here."

"I know." He shoved his hands in his pockets. "I wanted to make sure you were all right. Matt's not the most charming of dates."

"It's fine." I took a few steps toward our lane where Matt and Sydney were waiting. Matt was probably annoyed I was holding up the game.

Arie grasped my arm, making me turn back to face him. "It's not fine with me. You deserve to be treated better than that."

"I know I do, but apparently, the only guys I attract are jerks." I raised my eyebrows, daring him to contradict me.

He pointed a finger at me. "That's not true. I'd dare to say you attract many more guys than you know." He dropped his hand from my arm. "The reason why it's the jerks that you end up going out with is because they're the only ones cocky enough to think they have a chance. The rest of us know you're too far out of our league."

45

EMMA

AFTER BOWLING, Matt suggested we go out for ice cream. I faked a headache and asked whether he could take me home instead. When we got to the condo, I waited in my seat for a moment to see whether Matt would come around the car to let me out or walk me to the door—trying to give him one last chance to prove he could be a gentleman. He stayed in his seat, so I thanked him for the date and opened the door for Arie and me to climb out.

I shook my head all the way up the walk to the front door. That date had definitely gone in a direction I hadn't foreseen. Before tonight I'd thought Matt was a cool guy, but obviously, good sportsmanship was not a quality he was blessed with.

Once inside, I turned on a lamp and sank into the couch.

"Well, *that* was fun." I sighed.

Arie came over to sit by me. "I'm sorry you didn't have a good time. I hope your head feels better soon."

"I don't have a headache. I wanted to get away from Matt."

He gave me a half smile. "I figured."

"Sorry to make you end your date early," I said. "It looked like you and Sydney were having a fun time."

Arie nodded. "It was fun, but I still feel bad you got stuck with Mr. Competitive. Matt was *way* too serious about bowling tonight."

"I know, right?" I turned in my seat to see Arie's face better in the dimly lit room. "It's like he thought we were bowling for our lives or something!" I thought back to how Arie had handled the situation. "That was cool of you to make a joke out of it all for Sydney's sake."

He waved the thought away as if it was nothing. "That's the way it's supposed to be, isn't it? Dating is supposed to be a fun thing."

"It should be. I just haven't had much luck in that area lately." I remembered back to my more recent dating experiences. First there was Nick, who had cheated on me for most of the time we were dating. Then there was that date-auction evening with Brian, where we had ended up acting like a couple of weirdo wizards in his backyard.

"We had a good time at the Winter Ball, didn't we?" He peered at me with careful eyes.

"It was great," I said. "Right up until the time I got kidnapped, broke my arm, then found out you were my bodyguard."

A look of regret passed across his face. "I'm sure things will turn up for you in the future. A guy would have to be blind not to like you, Emma."

If that was the case, then wouldn't you want me? I didn't say it out loud, but that's the way I felt. Arie was saying those things to be nice. "No, I think I've decided to be one of those crazy cat ladies."

"Now that's an idea." He laughed at my attempt to be funny. "But I doubt you'll be single for long." He looked at me with those deep-blue eyes of his. "I'm sure some other million-aire will sweep you off your feet one day." The tone of his voice was serious, and he sounded somewhat disappointed.

Why do you want some other guy to sweep me off my feet?

I shook my head. "I don't want a millionaire. All I want is to go back to being regular, ordinary Emma, who didn't have to worry about anything more than what to major in next year."

Arie scooted closer to me on the couch and brushed a stray hair behind my ear.

I froze.

"You could take away all the money, but you would still never be ordinary."

I didn't know what to say, so I just sat there, trapped in his gaze. I had the impression that if I were to lean into him, things might change between us. But I didn't know whether it would be a good change or not. If I leaned in and he moved away, I would know once and for all that he didn't want me. There would be no questioning it anymore. But if I leaned closer and he accepted my advance, I would know he did care for me.

I didn't know whether I was brave enough to take that chance. I didn't want to risk losing the closest friend I had. So I held still, balanced between the possibility of something and nothing.

Arie held still, too, as if waiting for me to decide which path to take. His eyes were full of some emotion, like he longed for me to do *something*. My heart quickened when I thought about that possibility. I moved my gaze from his eyes down to his lips, hoping to escape his intense stare. That was a mistake, because when I looked at his lips, I had the urge to take his gorgeous face between my hands and pull his lips to my own.

I stood from the couch, feeling awkward. "I need a drink of water." I wiped perspiration from my brow as I stepped toward the kitchen.

I drained a glass of water, then stayed by the sink, looking out the dark window, not seeing anything.

Arie came behind me, his chest pressed against my back. "It is true, you know," he said, his voice low against my ear.

"What's true?" My mind went blank. What had we been talking about in the other room?

"You aren't ordinary, Emma." He put his hands on my shoulders and turned me to face him. "You are amazing."

I couldn't look at him. "Thanks for saying that, but I don't see it." I took a breath and mustered the courage to say my next words. The words I'd bitten back since moving here. "If I'm so amazing, why don't *you* want me?"

There. I said it. I finally said it.

"But I do." He looked at me with a piercing gaze. "You are the most beautiful girl I've ever seen." He lifted a hand and caressed my cheek with his fingers, making me tremble. "From the moment we met in the store, I knew I was in trouble." The corners of his mouth quirked up into a smile. "How was I supposed to maintain a professional relationship when the mere sight of you caused my pulse to race? And it's not just your beauty that captivated me." He ran his hands down my arms to hold my hands in his. "I've never had more fun than when I'm hanging out with you. I love all your witty remarks and your ability to make me laugh. You amaze me every day with how brave and selfless you are. You make me hope I can become a better man, so I can somehow deserve you." He paused, giving me a chance to catch my breath.

"What are you saying?" My heart practically beat out of my chest, and I felt lightheaded.

"I'm saying I've never wanted anyone more than I want *you,* Emma." He drew in a deep breath, his voice full of emotion when he spoke. "I've been fighting with myself over what my heart wanted and what I thought was the right thing to do. I never should have let you think I'd only been around you because it was my job." He ran his thumbs along the back of my hands. "Even if it weren't my job, I'd still follow you around all the time."

I tried to find words but was left utterly speechless. Never in my wildest dreams had I expected he would truly feel that way about me.

"Say something, please." He swallowed, his Adam's apple shifting. His face showed a vulnerability I hadn't seen before.

I took a deep breath and smiled at him, stepping closer. "You don't know how many times I wished you would say those things. For months, I've been trying to get over you, but it's been impossible, Arie. *Impossible.* It has tortured me to see my dream guy right in front of me and not feel like I was ever going to have him. I—"

I was about to say more when Arie grasped my shoulders and whispered, "Then let's stop torturing ourselves, Emma. Who cares what Jason and your dad say? It's insane to keep living this way." His face was intense as he backed me against the counter. "If they don't want us to be together, then that's their problem. I, for one, am going to start living my life without regret, and I know if I don't kiss you now I'll be kicking myself for the rest of my life."

Before I could do anything, Arie had his hands tangled in my hair and he was kissing me. He kissed me again and again, and I kissed him back. Months of misunderstanding, heartache, longing, and pain unraveled as we kissed.

He moved his hands from my hair and traced his way down to my waist, pulling me even closer to him. My heart raced as I ran my fingers across his shoulders, feeling his tightly corded muscles and loving the feel of his strong body next to mine.

Our kiss slowed and deepened. Arie's lips became gentle,

tasting of salt and desire. He kissed me until chills coursed through my body and fire burned in my veins.

His kiss had a way of speaking to me, letting me perceive the depth of his feelings. I knew he wanted me as much as I wanted him, and that he had silently suffered as much as I had these past few months.

Arie rested his forehead against mine, his breathing ragged. I moved my hands to his chest and felt his heart beating as erratically as mine. When I gazed into his eyes, I couldn't help but smile.

I studied his rugged face, his strong jaw, his blue eyes. I inhaled the scent of his oh-so-familiar cologne. He was all I wanted right then, all I wanted for my future, and he was looking at me with such admiration it melted my heart.

He spoke in a husky voice. "I think I'm in love with you, Emma."

My heart stuttered in my chest.

"I think I love you, too." My voice broke, and a happy tear escaped down my cheek as I whispered, "I think I've loved you this whole time."

His lips found mine again. His hands were at my waist, lost in my hair, and then caressing my cheeks. He kissed me slowly one moment and then playfully the next. I was intoxicated by him and by the knowledge that he loved me. He crushed my body to his as if he couldn't get enough, as if he needed to get rid of every space that separated us.

I don't know how long we were there in the kitchen, but when the storm of emotions had calmed, we just stood there with our foreheads pressed together.

"We better get to bed before Jason and Sophie find us kissing. I really don't want to get fired right now."

I raised my eyebrow and smirked. "We better get to bed?"

Arie gave me a half smile. "You know what I meant."

"Just checking."

Arie reached for my hand and led me upstairs. His shirt lifted slightly over where his gun clip sat in the back of his pants. I smiled. There was just something so sexy about it—how dangerous he could be if I were ever threatened again.

Yeah, it was definitely getting late. We needed to say good night before I found anything else attractive about him.

Arie pressed his lips to my forehead at the top of the stairs. "I'm so addicted to you," he said.

"Do you really think Jason and Sophie will try to fire you?" I asked.

"It's a definite possibility." Arie sighed.

"Well, if they do, I'll have to remind them that I'm an adult now, and that I won't be nearly as cooperative with this whole situation if they get rid of you."

"Well, when you put it like that, I'm not sure what they'll do. But I think, deep down, they'll be happy for us. They've seen how crazy I've been, trying to keep our relationship professional. I think they knew I'd eventually cave and give in to the temptation that was with me every day."

"Am I really a temptation to you?" It was so nice being able to talk to him about this and to have everything out in the open.

"Absolutely." He leaned against the wall by my bedroom door and smiled, showing his dimples. "I can't even tell you how many times I wanted to pull you into a corner and kiss you."

"You're telling me," I mused. "We should have had this conversation months ago."

Arie took hold of my hand and pulled me closer to him so my body was aligned with his. "Does it bother you that I'm four years older than you?" he asked, letting his hands clasp behind my waist.

"Of course not!" I smiled, happy to have him be so affectionate with me after so many long months of wishing. "That just makes it, like, ten times better." I combed through his soft hair with my fingers. "You know, me dating an older man is quite exciting." I laughed.

"Good." He moved his hands behind my neck and pulled me in for one more kiss. After a moment, Arie pulled his head away from mine with a sigh. "I think you better go to bed," he said. "If you don't leave me now, I may never let you go."

That sounded just fine to me. I didn't want to go to bed. I wanted to stay up all night, talking to him, cuddling with him, kissing him.

But he was right—I needed to get to sleep. We'd have all day together tomorrow. "I don't want to go, but I will because I know how cranky you get when you don't get enough sleep," I said, patting him on the chest.

He arched his eyebrows and grabbed my wrist. "*I'm* cranky when *I* don't get enough sleep?" He was smiling. "I'm *pretty* sure it's the other way around."

"Whatever," I said, swatting his hand away. "I'm as sweet as honey early in the morning."

"Maybe, if that honey happens to have a bee's stinger stuck inside of it and it stings your throat on the way down."

"Okay, okay. I get it. I need my beauty sleep or I'm a real beast in the morning."

He smiled and touched my cheek with his thumb. "Good night, Emma. Sleep well." He gave me one final kiss.

When he pulled himself away, his body went tense. His eyes locked on something behind me, and the feeling in the air changed. I wound my head around to see what had startled him but didn't see anything. Before I could ask what was wrong, he clamped a hand over my mouth.

"Did you close your bedroom door before we left?" he asked in a tone I could barely hear.

Had I? The hair on the back of my neck stood up as I tried to remember. I couldn't. But I didn't usually close it.

I shook my head, feeling my pulse throb in my temples.

"Someone's here." He pulled his gun out and rushed me past our bedrooms and down the stairs. A shot fired before we made it through the living room.

"Run! Take the car," Arie yelled.

I glanced back as he darted behind the couch. Adrenaline pumped through me as I searched the room for the car keys. They were on a hook by the back door.

Jason and Sophie clamored out of their bedroom, weapons drawn.

More shots rang.

Arie.

I couldn't leave him behind to die. I hesitated by the door, my hand shaking on the knob.

"Leave!" Arie shouted as he shot around the couch. "Get out of here now!"

My shoes were glued to the floor.

Footsteps retreated above.

Were they leaving the way they came?

Jason bolted up the stairs after whoever was trying to escape. Sophie followed behind him.

In a second, Arie was by my side, yanking open the door and pulling me around the back of the house just as I heard what sounded like a shot, and then a scream followed by someone crashing down the stairs.

"Hand me the keys!" Arie held out his hand.

I fumbled with them, and they slipped out of my numb fingers, landing in the damp grass. Arie swiped them off the ground, unlocking the car as we ran to where it was parked on the street.

I yanked open the door and climbed in. I tried to catch my breath as I waited for Arie to get in.

What was happening? Had I just heard someone die in there?

The driver's door opened. Arie climbed in and stabbed me in the chest with a needle.

I twisted in disbelief and saw someone I had never seen before: a middle-aged man with dark hair and dark eyes.

I screamed. But before I could do anything, the man put a gun to my head.

"Don't even think about moving," he said, his accent much like Sophie's.

I froze with fear. My head started to feel fuzzy as the man put the key in the ignition and drove away. I looked in the rearview mirror and saw Arie lying in the road just as everything went black.

46

EMMA

I WAS GAGGED and tied to a metal chair. I was so exhausted, both emotionally and physically. I'd been up most of the night, after waking from my drug-induced sleep, and the ever-present fear and anguish had drained me. My body ached everywhere, and my head was fogged over like I was waking up from a bad cold. Three men were talking in the corner of what appeared to be some sort of office space.

The large room was dark, with a single lamp giving off light from a desk about twenty feet from me. There was no light streaming through the windows since they were covered in black butcher paper. Because of the darkness, I wasn't certain whether the sun was up yet. I figured it had to be morning by now because of how much time had seemed to pass. I also knew we were a few stories above the ground, because I'd felt every single step as Damian, Mr. Lund's friend, had carried me on his shoulder up the stairs.

After we had arrived, I soon figured out that the man with the dark hair and dark eyes was actually Fenris—my long-lost uncle who wanted my money, then wanted me dead. Just a few minutes ago, I'd overheard Fenris say something about taking me to a bank and wiring money to his accounts.

It was only a matter of time before I would be killed.

Fenris walked across the room toward me, his shoes clicking on the cement floor.

"It is nice to finally meet you, Emma, after all these years," he said in a low, accented voice. "It's a pity there isn't much time to get to know each other better. You do look so much like your mother, Adelle. She was beautiful." He sighed. "It was such a disappointment when I heard she had found a way to get herself killed in that house fire before I had the chance to marry her myself. We could have been a happy family. With my father's fortune, I could have given you a glorious child-hood." He smiled smugly, which told me just how much he thought of himself. In another time and place, I may have thrown up in my mouth. But as it was, I only thought about how badly I wanted out of there. How I needed to figure out a way to escape.

"But there's no use in wishing for what might have been. I'm just thankful to have finally retrieved you from those irri-tating bodyguards of yours." He paused and looked at me with a calculating smile. "You must be happy to be rid of them. Locked up in that little condo for months. I did you a service in killing them. They were much too overprotective."

What? Had I heard him right? Did he just say he'd killed all my bodyguards?

I turned my head to the side and vomited on the cement floor, feeling so sick.

Not Arie. Tears surged to my eyes as the image of Arie slumped in the road flashed through my mind. Fenris had killed him. I fought to break out of my restraints. If I could just get free, I'd strangle Fenris with my own hands. I'd kill him. I would kill him and smile as I did it.

But the only thing my struggle did was exhaust my muscles further.

Fenris took a step back from my vomit. But his smile grew wider when he noticed the hateful glint in my eyes. "Yes. Three bodyguards are dead, all because of you. But don't worry. Your conscience will be cleared, too, by the end of the day."

Meaning I would be dead, too.

Fenris spoke again. "We live in a different world than we did twenty years ago. You really should have been more careful with those social-media sites." He laughed. "To think, just hitting some guy at a party was all I needed you to do." Fenris walked closer to me, patting my head with his hand. I attempted to jerk away from his touch, but he gripped my chin with his fingers. His face was inches from mine. "I've waited for this moment for eighteen years. And don't worry, I'll make this as painless as possible. It's the least I could do for my only niece." He patted my cheek twice and then let his hand drop. He walked away.

After he joined Mr. Lund and Damian, I surveyed the room for possible exits. There was one door that led to the stair-case we'd come up, and another door behind me that might lead to a balcony or outside exit. I was close to the balcony exit, but the other door was clear across the room from me, and I would have to get past my captors to escape.

I didn't have a chance.

47

ARIE

I DON'T KNOW how long I was lying in the street unconscious, but when I awoke my head was pounding. I ran a hand along the back of my head. It was wet with blood and had a huge bump on it.

Emma!

The car was gone. Emma was gone!

I stumbled back into the house and found Sophie crying over Jason's body.

*Oh no...oh no...don't let him be...*My heart constricted in my chest.

"Is he...?" I asked Sophie, my insides throbbing.

Sophie nodded and sobbed into Jason's chest.

"I'm so sorry." And I really was. But as sorry as I was, I needed to find Emma. Every minute I stayed here was another minute Emma was in danger. I looked around the main level and peeked up the stairs, but I didn't see a sign of anyone else in the condo. "I hate to leave you like this, Sophie, but I have to find Emma."

She nodded her understanding as more hard sobs escaped. "Go. Find her."

I grabbed the keys to Jason's car off his dresser, almost feeling like I was desecrating the space by running in there disrespectfully, but I had to hurry. They could be anywhere in this big city, if they were even in Philadelphia at all.

As I backed the car out of the garage, all I could think about was how hopeless this situation was. It was going to be like trying to find a needle in a haystack. I was alone. I had no leads, and this city was huge.

If only I had some way to track them.

My mind perked up at that thought. *Emma's tracking bracelet.* I rubbed my forehead. I was pretty sure she'd been wearing it on the date tonight. Hopefully she still had it.

And as long as her captors hadn't thought to destroy it yet, I might have a way to track her.

48

EMMA

"HOW MUCH LONGER UNTIL the banks are open, Shane?" Fenris asked from the other side of the room.

Mr. Lund glanced at his watch. "Thirty minutes."

"Very good." Fenris nodded. "Let's head to the car now. I'd like to get the money transferred first thing, and then you can take care of her before my flight leaves." He grabbed his cane and walked out the door.

Mr. Lund began untying me from the chair.

"I didn't know this was his plan," he said, his low voice behind me as his knife cut through the rope on my right leg. "Damian convinced me it would be a quick job—grab you in Maplebridge, hand you over, get paid. I didn't sign up for murder."

I couldn't tell whether he was telling the truth. But either way, he was not a good guy.

He moved in front of me and cut the rope around my other foot. "Fenris threatened to kill my fiancée if I didn't finish the job." When I looked into his eyes, I couldn't ignore the touch of fear that was there. *Was he telling the truth?* I took in his physique. He was tall and lean, not particularly muscular. He had the build of a school teacher, not a hardened criminal. Had he really just gotten mixed up with the wrong roommate?

I shook the thoughts away. He was just playing with my mind.

He glanced toward Damian, who was stacking some papers together in a blue file. Mr. Lund moved behind me, cut the rest of the ropes except the one tying my hands, and then helped me to stand. He pushed something small into my fingers. I felt around the object. It was made of metal, smooth and warm. His pocketknife?

"Use this when you can," he whispered in my ear before taking the object back and sliding it into my back pocket. "Arie's not dead."

My muscles went weak, and I would have collapsed if he hadn't grabbed me roughly and started yanking me toward Damian.

We were about halfway down the stairs when we heard someone coming toward us. "It's the police," Fenris gasped as he came into view around the corner. "Take the other exit."

Damian tossed me over his shoulder and bolted back up the stairs, darting into the room we'd been in a moment before. We were almost to the other exit when the door banged open.

"Where is she?"

I jerked my head up. Three policemen had burst the door open, two men and one woman, and were now blocking Mr. Lund and Damian. Fenris was nowhere to be seen. Each of the policemen was heavily armed.

"Put your hands where we can see them, and we won't shoot," the stockier of the male officers hissed in a menacing voice. He had his gun aimed right at Mr. Lund's chest. The woman trained her gun on Damian. They all looked so dangerous.

"I'm not here to make deals," Damian growled as he dropped me to the ground. He pulled his gun from its holster and aimed it in the officer's direction.

A shot rang out, reverberating off the cement walls surrounding me. I flinched and forced my eyes shut, expecting the officer to be hit.

When I opened my eyes, I saw Mr. Lund writhing on the floor. There was a mess of blood spilling all over his hand as he clutched it with his other hand.

Damian didn't miss a beat and shot at the woman, who darted behind a pillar. The bullet narrowly missed her. The last officer took a few steps to take cover behind a desk. I screamed as I struggled to get to my feet and find somewhere to hide. With all these shots being fired, it was only a matter of time before I was hit!

I ducked behind a desk. If I just stayed there, maybe I would be safe until the fight was over.

One of the officers had just fired at Damian again when someone snuck up behind me. Fenris. I darted my eyes round the room, but no one had noticed his appearance.

He hooked both arms under my armpits and yanked me back. I shifted from side to side, to make dragging me from the room more difficult, but he was stronger than I'd thought.

I remembered the knife in my pocket. If I could just get my hands in my back pocket, I might be able to get to it. I stretched my arms as Fenris pulled me back, but they weren't long enough. Then Fenris stopped, and I felt cool metal at my temple.

His gun.

"Come with me nicely, and I'll leave your family alone after I'm finished with you," Fenris said in a low voice.

I nodded.

My struggling stopped, but then I went like dead weight in his arms.

He'd said come nicely, not easily.

Before long, though, Fenris had me out the back exit and on a staircase, several stories above the ground. A brisk morning breeze whipped at my face, and I could hear the busy traffic below.

"I'm not about to let you slip through my fingers again." Fenris leaned against the railing to rest, wheezing from the exertion of pulling me outside.

More shots fired inside the building.

The sound of police sirens drifted up from the street, sounding only a few blocks away. Backup was coming. Hopefully, it wouldn't be too late.

Fenris swore. His gun clicked as a warning.

What was I supposed to do? Die now or die later? Was it even possible to escape once Fenris had the money transferred? What good would that little knife be, anyway?

But I had to try. I might not be able to use the knife now, but he had to untie my hands before taking me into the bank. And when he did that, I would use the knife on him.

We made it down one flight of stairs when a stampede of footsteps sounded on the steps below. I looked up, expecting to see a police officer. But instead, I spotted a man with dark hair and a familiar gray shirt rushing toward us. He looked over the railing, and our eyes locked.

Arie?

Arie!

He was alive!

Mr. Lund had told the truth.

Ferris yanked on my arm to get me to move, nearly tripping on one of the steps. Seconds later, Arie was standing only five steps above me, his eyes wild.

"Let her go!" Arie pointed his gun at Fenris as he took a step closer.

Fenris pulled me to his chest.

When I noticed his gun was pointed upward, with his hand on my shoulder, I stomped on Fenris's foot, slammed a fist to his groin, and shoved him off my back with all my strength.

Fenris's gun shot toward the clouds as he groaned and stumbled on the stairs. His hands searched for something to keep him from falling—they found my arm, and soon we were both falling over the railing.

A strong hand clamped around my frantic hand, yanking me upright. Arie's foot kicked past me, connecting with Fenris's chest.

And I was folded into Arie's arms.

Fenris's screaming stopped at the same time a loud thud sounded below. I did not need to look down to know that he was dead. Numbness poured over my body and tears streamed down my face as I shook.

"It's all over now, Em," Arie said, his cheek against mine. "It's okay," he repeated over and over again. He was trembling, too, as he pulled back and inspected me, as if to assure himself that I was really okay. Then he hugged me again and murmured as more police arrived down below, "You're safe. Fenris will never bother you again."

I wrapped my arms around his neck and sobbed into his chest. It wasn't until Arie leaned heavily against the side of the building that I actually looked at him. Blood was seeping through his shirt.

Arie had been shot.

49

EMMA

I GROUND a path into the carpet of the hospital waiting room as I waited for someone to tell me what was happening with Arie. Last I'd heard, they were taking him into emergency surgery. Was he going to be okay? No one would tell me anything. I had no idea how serious his gunshot wound was—whether it had hit any major organs or anything. I also didn't know what had happened to Jason or Sophie, and why Arie had shown up alone. Had they both been killed in the condo?

While I didn't know where my friends were, I did know that I was safe. Fenris was dead, I knew that for sure—the image of his crumpled body on the cement with blood seeping from his head would be burned into my mind forever. Damian was also dead. He'd received a bullet wound to his chest that had killed him almost instantly. And Mr. Lund, the good-bad guy, was seriously injured and had also been taken to the hospital.

But I still didn't know what had happened to my friends.

"Are you Emma?" A nurse walked up to me, breaking me away from my thoughts.

"Yes." I nodded, bracing myself for the worst. *Please let him be okay. Please don't let him die.* I'd already spent the last few hours thinking he was dead. I could not live in that reality.

"I have instructions to bring you to Mr. Blackwell's room."

I followed the nurse down the hall, my heart pounding like an angry hammer the whole way.

"He's waiting for you in there." The nurse smiled and gestured for me to walk inside.

I opened the door and stepped in, not sure what condition I would find Arie in. But I took the nurse's smile as a good sign.

I walked into the dimly lit room and found Arie lying in bed with a big bandage covering his abdomen. He was propped up on several pillows, with machines beeping all around. A smile spread slowly over his tired face when he saw me.

"Are you okay?" I rushed to the seat beside his bed, noting he wasn't nearly as pale as he'd been earlier. "No one would tell me anything. I thought I'd lost you again."

He held an arm out. That was all the encouragement I needed to hug him—gently, of course. "I'm going to be fine," he mumbled into my hair. "You can't get rid of me that easily."

A sob I'd suppressed for hours escaped my throat. "Did this happen at the condo when you were slumped in the street?"

"No." A faint smile lifted his lip. "If that were the case, I never would have made it to you."

Of course.

"Then when did you get it?"

"When I got to the building where Fenris was holding you, I had just snuck through the door as Fenris pulled you onto the stairs. I tried to make it to you without his men seeing me, but one of them shot at me before I made it through the door."

"I'm so sorry," I said. "This is all my fault."

"No," Arie said, his voice firm. When I looked him in the

eyes, they were soft and understanding. "This is Fenris's fault. He's the reason for all this."

I nodded. My throat tightened as I thought about my next question. I didn't know whether I wanted to know the answer. But I needed to know.

"Where are Jason and Sophie?"

Pain formed behind Arie's eyes, and it took him a while to answer me. "Jason was shot at the condo. When I came to, I ran in and found Sophie crying over him at the bottom of the stairs."

"Oh, Arie," I said, hugging him tighter with my head against his chest, crying for the kind man who had secretly watched out for me for most of my life. It wasn't fair that a good man had died today all because of Fenris's greed.

"I felt horrible leaving Sophie there alone. Leaving my dead friend there." His voice quavered. "But I had to find you."

I lifted my head off his chest. Moisture filled his selfless blue eyes. He was in so much pain. Physical and emotional. And he felt guilty for leaving our friends, when it was that action that had saved my life. I stroked my thumb along his cheekbone. "Thank you," I whispered as I leaned my forehead against his. "Thank you for saving my life."

He nodded and touched the bracelet on my left arm. "If it wasn't for your tracking device, we never would have found you in time."

I covered his hand with my other hand. "This small piece of metal around my wrist may have helped save my life, but the real heroes are Jason, Sophie, the police, and *you*."

"Mom! Dad!" I called as I ran across the airport toward my parents. I threw my arms around them. "I missed you so much!"

"We missed you, too." My mom squeezed me.

"We're so glad you're okay and that this is finally over." My dad kissed my head.

"Me too," I said, hugging them a little longer. I needed this. I had needed my parents so badly the last few months. I didn't want to be apart from them like that ever again.

My brother and sister, Carter and Lily, joined in on the hug, too, once they realized my parents weren't letting go anytime soon.

Arie was standing behind me when the family hug ended.

"Mom. Dad. You remember Arie."

"Of course we remember him." Dad held a hand out, which Arie shook. "Last time we talked, I recall advising him not to date my daughter."

Arie's mouth went slack.

"Dad!" Lily gasped. "You didn't."

My mom gave my dad a dirty look before wrapping Arie in a hug. "Thank you so much for saving our girl."

Arie awkwardly bent over to return her embrace. "You're welcome. I'm glad I was able to find her again."

The whole ride home, my parents kept glancing back at Arie and me, as if worried I might disappear on them again. I guess I couldn't really blame them after everything we'd gone through.

We had a quiet family dinner that night, which my parents were kind enough to include Arie in, since he was on his own now. After Jason's funeral, Sophie had packed her things and flown to France where her family now lived. It broke my heart to see her life ripped apart. Her husband had sacrificed his life for me, and there was nothing I could do to make her pain go away.

The doorbell rang. I looked to Arie with wary eyes, still not used to the fact that I was safe now and that I didn't have to worry whether the person ringing the doorbell was just waiting to kill me.

"I'll get that." My dad got up from the table. As he opened the door, we heard squeals.

Maya and Kathryn burst into the dining room a moment later.

"Emma!" Maya wrapped her arms around me before I could even stand. "You're back!"

I stood clumsily and hugged her. "Yes, I'm finally back," I said, and then I gave Kathryn a hug, too.

"Did you guys elope or something?" Maya peeked at Arie once our giggling and hugging calmed down. Then she eyed my stomach as if expecting to learn something from it. "You don't *look* pregnant or anything."

"Maya!" I gasped, feeling my cheeks flush. "Of course I'm not pregnant! I can't believe you thought I went away because of *that*."

"See, I told you she wouldn't do that," Kathryn whispered to Maya.

Arie chuckled behind me.

"Well, Arie *is* irresistible." Maya grinned. When she saw me shake my head, she said, "What else was I supposed to think when you both mysteriously disappeared the same weekend? Then we thought for sure the rest of the family went to save you from an imprudent marriage. Kind of like a whole Lydia and Mr. Wickham thing."

I had to laugh. Though I really did not like being compared with my least favorite characters in *Pride and Prejudice*.

"So if you're not married, then where in the world have you been?" Maya asked.

I glanced at Arie for a second, then back to Maya and Kathryn's waiting faces. "Where do I start..."

50

EMMA

I WALKED into the crowded arena where the commencement ceremony was to be held in less than thirty minutes. The floor below was cluttered with several of my classmates wearing the silver caps and gowns they'd waited so long to wear.

"Emma, get your butt over here," Maya called when she spotted me, waving me over to where she stood with Kathryn and the rest of our friends.

"I'm coming," I hollered back, squeezing past a group of proud parents snapping pictures of the soon-to-be graduates.

"You may be a rich heiress, but graduation in Maplebridge waits for no one." Maya giggled as I stood beside her, smiling as cameras and phones flashed at us.

"It should. I *am* pretty amazing," I whispered, placing my hands on my hips. I was joking, of course. I was more than happy that only my friends knew the truth about why I disappeared for a few months this school year.

Just a few months ago, I'd been sure I'd celebrate my graduation from high school miles away from here, with no loved ones close by to support me. I was so thankful that things had turned out quite the opposite.

The graduation ceremony lasted about two hours, full of speeches from fellow classmates—some reminiscing on the past four years of high school, others speaking about the future. I received the diploma I had worked so hard for years to earn, amazed at how one little piece of paper could be so valuable.

With diploma in hand, I beamed as I strode toward the most important people in my life.

"We're so proud of you!" My mom had tears in her eyes as she pulled me into a tight hug.

"Yes, we are," Dad said, embracing me after my mom let me go. "You looked beautiful up there."

"Thanks, Mom and Dad." I smiled at them. "I never could have done it without you guys." I pulled away from my parents and gave my sister and brother each a hug before coming to stand in front of Arie. He held a bouquet of roses, which he offered to me with a wide grin.

"Aw, they're beautiful! Thank you," I said, taking the flowers and sniffing them. I hadn't been expecting him to get me anything. It was just like him, though, always thoughtful.

"You're welcome." Arie leaned over to give me a hug. Then he whispered in my ear so no one else could hear. "Now that you've officially graduated, I can stop feeling like I'm breaking the law dating you."

I giggled and tapped his chest. "You know, I was eighteen before you even kissed me."

"Yes, but it feels like you're a little more legal now."

Later that night, after all the graduation festivities, Arie and I sat on the porch swing, moving back and forth. It was a peaceful spring evening, and the moon was full. I nestled into Arie's side, resting my head on his chest, enjoying the comfort of having his arms around me as we gazed at the stars. I didn't think I could ever get tired of cuddling up next to the amazing man I was lucky enough to call my boyfriend.

"So," Arie said, breaking the silence. "I finally told my mom what I've been up to for the past nine months."

"You mean she doesn't think you're an intern for some senator anymore?" I laughed. "How'd she take it?"

"She sorta freaked out." He shook his head. "She said she was catching the next flight over here so she could inspect my wound herself and make sure I was really okay." He sighed. "I had to tell her all about us visiting her next week, to keep her from running to the airport. So much for our big surprise. "

"Do you think she'll ever be okay with the idea of you working in such a dangerous field?"

"Probably not. That's why I'm waiting to tell her about my training in person. Then at least I'll be able to help revive her if she hyperventilates."

Arie had heard back from the Federal Law Enforcement Training Center and had been accepted for the ten-week training program that started in the fall. If he did well, then he would move on to the Special Agent training course near Washington, DC. I didn't like the idea of being separated from him once summer was over. But I didn't want to hold him back from his dreams, either. And honestly, if he would ask, I'd follow him to Washington, DC, in a heartbeat. I didn't care where I was or where I went to school, as long as I was near him. Some people might think I'm a lovesick teenager with her head in the sand, but sometimes you just know. And I knew Arie was the right guy for me. The only one.

But he hadn't asked me to come.

"And you're still okay with my backup plan, right?" he asked, interrupting my thoughts.

"Backup plan?" My chest contracted against my heart. What was his backup plan?

"Yeah, I always like to have a plan B. I figured if this whole Secret Service thing doesn't pan out, I could always have you be my sugar mama." He winked.

So he was just playing around right now. I drew in a breath and got myself into the headspace where I could play along with his light mood.

"Is that what I am to you?" I poked him in the chest. "A paycheck?"

He covered my hand with his. "Of course not. Though I have to say, you are the best boss I've ever had. I mean, my boss at the landscaping company was nice and all, but you kiss way better than him."

"Ack. I hope you don't actually know from experience."

Arie shifted me in his arms so I faced him. "Okay, so you're the only boss I've kissed."

"And let's keep it that way."

"Sounds good to me," he whispered before pulling my lips to his. Even though he'd kissed me like this more times than I could count in the past couple of months, his lips still had the same effect on me as they had the first time. My stomach muscles still tightened, and I felt like the luckiest girl in the world.

But when Arie pulled away, there was a hint of anxiety slipping into his expression. "Emma, I know you're excited to attend Maplebridge University in the fall and be roommates with Maya." He hesitated. "But I've been thinking a lot about that."

His serious tone made it hard for me to breathe. "Yeah?"

"And, well..." He leaned away and rubbed the back of his neck. "I..." He looked away and shook his head as if deciding not to continue with what he'd been trying to say.

"What is it?" I took his hand between mine. "Arie?"

His eyes searched mine, asking questions I couldn't hear. "This is going to sound really selfish of me," he finally said. "But I hate the idea of us being apart for so long."

I nodded, sparks of hope flitting around my heart.

"I just wanted to know if you'd ever consider going to school somewhere else?" He looked down at our hands and cleared his throat before looking back up at me. "What I mean is, would you consider coming to Washington, DC, with me?"

My heart leaped. "Do you really mean it?"

"Of course." He ran his thumb down my temple as his fingers slipped through my hair. "I love you. I don't ever want to go more than a few hours without seeing you."

I wrapped my arms around him. I didn't even have to think about it. "I'll move there in a heartbeat. I love you, too." I sighed as the last puzzle piece of my life fit into place. Everything was finally right with my world.

The back door opened a few minutes later. My mom stepped onto the deck, looking somewhat alarmed.

"Emma, there's someone here to see you."

I pulled myself out of Arie's arms and got up. "Who is it?"

"Just come." My mom waved me over. "Quickly."

Arie stood on high alert. Why was my mom acting so weird?

We walked into the house, and a moment later, we were standing in the living room with my parents and a woman I'd never seen before. She appeared to be in her early forties and had wavy nut-brown hair and light-blue eyes.

"Sorry to show up like this," the woman said in an accented voice, much like Sophie's. "But it was finally safe for me to come." She smiled at me nervously, her eyes moist. "I'm Adelle."

Join Judy's VIP Reader's Club for a Bonus Epilogue from Adelle's point of view. https://dl.bookfunnel.com/wo1vihwtu2

Don't miss the Eden Falls Academy series.

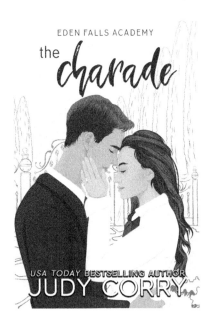

My math tutor has one rule: he doesn't date the girls he tutors at our private school.
But a fake relationship that's beneficial to us both?

That's another story.

Grab your copy! http://mybook.to/TheCharade

STAY CONNECTED

Join my Newsletter: https://subscribepage.com/judycorry

Join the Corry Crew on Facebook: https://www.facebook.com/groups/judycorrycrew/

Follow me on Instagram: @judycorry

DEAR READER

First off, THANK YOU for reading my book! It has been great to finally see this book get published.

Do you wanna know why I started writing YA Romance? It's because my marriage is the product of a high school romance that actually worked out (eventually anyway...we did have a couple years apart...but hey, we've been married for fifteen years now). So, I write YA Romance because I'm a total believer in being able to find your future spouse when you are that young.

Fun fact: Did you know that the first scene where Arie and Emma meet in the grocery store is loosely based on my embarrassing real life experience? (They say you write what you know, right?) Anyway, the backstory: My husband (Jared) and I dated when I was a junior and he was a senior in high school. The summer after he graduated, our relationship kind of fizzled out. We weren't quite ready for forever yet, haha. So we were "friends" that summer, though I was pining for him like crazy when he started dating someone else. (You want what you can't have, right?) Summer ended and I started my senior year of high school. Then Jared moved to Italy for a couple years.

Life went on. I crushed on more guys, graduated high school then went to college. But Jared was always at the back of my mind. In the winter of my freshman year of college, I met a guy who looked so much like Jared that I could not help myself from crushing hard. It was ridiculous.

One day when I was walking out of the grocery store with my cart, I saw him. Jared's-Look-Alike. I tried to act cool, not stare and make it obvious that I liked him. We passed each other as he came in (he totally didn't even notice me) and I was almost out the big sliding glass doors when I turned my head for one last, longing look. Then BAM, I crashed my cart right into a glass door and knocked it out of its guides.

As you can imagine, I was horrified. How had I done something so stupid? Luckily for me, the guy didn't seem to notice, though all the other shoppers chuckled as I tried to fix the dang door. I wanted to die! Tell me I'm not the only one who has done something like this because they were distracted by a good looking guy. It can't just be Emma and me, right?

Word-of-mouth is crucial for any author to succeed. If you enjoyed Protect My Heart, please review it on Amazon—even if it's just a sentence or two. It makes a huge difference and is very much appreciated.

Wondering what to read next? See more of Emma and Arie in Maya's story: Stolen Kisses from a Rock Star. Or read the first book in my Ridgewater High series: Meet Me There.

Happy reading!

Judy

ACKNOWLEDGEMENTS

Though my name sits on the cover, I can't take credit for everything that went into this book. There are so many people who helped bring it from a pretty terrible first draft of a first-time writer, to what it is today.

Thank you so much to Jared for supporting me in this crazy adventure, letting me bounce ideas off of you, reading an early draft, and holding down the fort so I could sneak away and write.

Thanks to James, Janelle, Jonah, and Jade for being excited about my books and bragging to all your friends about how your mom is a writer. Having your support means the world to me!

To my critique group—Kristina Starmer, Mike Kelly, and Wendy Jessen—thank you for helping me find the parts I was missing and making this story so much better.

To my beta-readers who took a chance on a first time writer and encouraged me all along the way: Jeff Corry, Arlene Ball, Amanda Wilcox, Jami Lyn Niles, Melissa Francisco, Victorine E. Lieske, Julie L. Spencer, Lindsey Corry, Laura Francis, Julia Corry, Tamara Robinson, Jamie Robinson, Michelle Robinson,

Jenna Corry, Janet Lott, Skye Longhurst, Cathy Woolsey, Ambri Cunningham, Amy Wright and David Baker.

To my editors, Precy Larkins and Karen B, for making me look better than I really am. You are seriously amazing!

To my parents for always believing in me and making me feel like I could do anything growing up. I realize more and more how lucky I am to have parents like you!

Thank you to all my family and friends for your love and support through the years. I couldn't do it without you.

Thank you to everyone who nominated this book on Kindle Scout. Your belief in this story has been amazing! My career wouldn't be where it is now if I didn't have the opportunity to work with Kindle Press for the first few years of my career.

Last of all, to my readers: thank you for giving me the confidence to finally take this step. You are like magic for my soul!

ENJOY THIS SNEAK PEEK AT THE CHARADE

"I'm going to miss you girls so much," my mom said, gathering my twin sister, Elyse, and I into her arms for one last hug before she left us at the entrance of our new private boarding school.

My sister and I hugged our petite mother, our five-foot-nine inch frames towering over her barely five-foot one.

"Sure you can't just take us with you?" Elyse asked our mother when we pulled away from the hug, the look of apprehension in her expression mirroring how I felt.

"Yeah," I said. "I mean, isn't online schooling all the rage these days?"

My mom shook her head as she gazed at my sister and then me. "I won't have you miss the last opportunity to be kids." But even as she said that, the tears at the corners of her dark brown eyes told me she hated saying goodbye as much as we did. "You're going to love it here. Some of my best memories were made at this school when I was your age."

I looked behind us again, feeling so small next to the hundred-year-old castle-like building that would be my home for the next nine months.

I'd been so on board with the dream of my mom finally making it big in the fashion world since I loved fashion and couture almost as much as she did. But if I'd known that her getting her own fashion show in New York this past year would soon lead to her traveling the world—necessitating that Elyse and I attend a boarding school to finish our senior year—I would have told her to hold off on that dream a little longer. Because I wasn't ready for the three amigos to be separated.

But ready or not, my mom's dreams had finally come true and now we were starting our last year of high school on the outskirts of Eden Falls, Connecticut—a world away from the tiny house we'd grown up in in Ridgewater, New York.

My mom had attended Eden Falls Academy when she was our age—her family being wealthy property developers in Israel and wanting to give her the study abroad experience.

So now that she could afford to send us here, there were apparently no other options worth considering. After all, if her strict Jewish parents had felt safe sending their only daughter half a world away to school here, then it was most certainly good enough for us.

So here we were with our suitcases already delivered to our room, ready to start our last year of high school at a school who's tuition and board for a year cost more than my mom used to make annually.

I was thankful my mom cared about us so much that she would do anything to give us all the things she felt we'd lacked the first seventeen years of our lives. But as a rabble of butterflies fluttered around in my ribcage when I looked up at the huge iron doors surrounded by vines with pink flowers before us, I couldn't help but think that staying at my grandma Cohen's home in Israel would have been a lot less daunting. I'd at least been there before, so it was somewhat familiar.

What if no one liked me here?

What if all the social groups were already so tightly knit that there wasn't extra room for new faces?

But since I knew this was already a hard enough goodbye, I forced myself to stand up straighter, pulled my shoulders back and said, "I'm sure once we're settled we'll like it." I looked at my sister, whose golden-brown eyes were the same color and shape as mine. "Elyse and I will watch out for each other."

"Yes, I'll make sure Ava gets at least some of her homework done in-between flirting with all the guys." Elyse said, shooting me a smirk.

"And I'll make sure Elyse has a little fun as she's maintaining her 4.0 GPA." I countered back with a wink.

"Just look out for each other and everything will be fine." My mom glanced to Elyse and then me. "And remember, I'm only a phone call away if you need me."

She gave us each one last hug and before we could shed too many more tears, she waved goodbye and climbed into the black car she had waiting for her on the cobblestone drive.

And there she went, the great Miriam Cohen, the woman who had clawed her way back up to the top after her father had disinherited her when she had Elyse and I out of wedlock.

I hoped I could be half as strong of a woman as my mom was someday.

Which meant that I needed to practice being strong now, even though I was afraid.

Elyse and I linked arms and waved as we watched the car holding our mother drive away, a cool fall breeze causing the leaves of the towering trees nearby to rustle.

Once the black car disappeared down the tree shrouded path and through the tall iron gates, Elyse turned to me, and asked, "Ready to go back inside for our tour?"

"I guess." My shoulders slumped.

And so instead of putting off the inevitable, we walked side by side up the few steps that led to the entrance of our new school.

———

A girl wearing one of the school's blue blazers and plaid skirts was waiting for Elyse and me when we made it back into the school's lobby. She had long, dark auburn hair and looked so much like a younger Lily Collins that I couldn't help but wonder if they were related.

"Ready for the grand tour?" she asked us when we got closer.

"I, um..." I glanced over to Elyse briefly, then returned my attention to the girl ahead of us. "Sure. That would be great."

"Perfect." She beamed. "My name is Scarlett, by the way." Scarlett held her hand out for me to shake. "I'm one of the captains for our house."

"I'm Ava," I shook her hand.

"And I'm Elyse." Elyse shook her hand next.

Scarlett narrowed her brown eyes for a moment, looking us up and down and side to side.

"Trying to figure out how you're going to tell us apart?" I guessed, knowing the look in her eyes well enough.

Scarlett pursed her deep pink lips. "Usually when I meet twins I can tell them apart because they do their hair or makeup differently from one another. But you two are obviously the kind of twins who like keeping people on their toes."

"Why have an identical twin if you can't have a little fun tricking your friends and family every once in a while?" I said, proud of the certain mystique Elyse and I took with us wherever we went.

"Just give me a few days." Scarlett's lips curved up into a

slow smile, like she thrived on the idea of a challenge. "I'll figure it out."

I shrugged. "We'll see."

Elyse and I *had* cultivated our own looks through the years with our own fashion styles and beauty preferences—me taking after our mother more when it came to dressing up and Elyse going for the more natural and casual look. But if we wanted to do the twin switch here and there, even our own mother had a hard time discerning who was who.

So if we could still trick our mom on a weekly basis, I didn't see this new acquaintance deciphering the tiny differences that made us unique anytime soon.

Scarlett guided us around the main section of the school first, showing us the various classrooms, the auditorium, and the gym. And despite the actual school building being over a hundred years old, everything inside was state-of-the art—the school and it's grounds breathtaking, actually. According to Scarlett, the school sat on ten acres. It had the usual football, baseball, and other sports fields which she pointed out from the doors near the swimming pool. But it also had lush gardens with a walking/running/bike path that reminded me of the beautiful gardens from the rich estates in the regency romance movies my mom sometimes watched.

It actually kind of felt like a real castle. Just instead of royalty living within the walls with servants helping to run the place, there were teachers and students milling around, chatting among their peers about their plans and hopes for the new school year.

"Do either of you play sports?" Scarlett asked Elyse and me after we'd walked around the girl's locker room, the school colors of maroon and silver everywhere.

"Definitely not," Elyse said, a hint of amusement in her voice, like the thought of anyone even asking if she was athletic was comical. "I think all the athletic genes went to Ava when the egg split. But I'll be first in line for this year's theater production."

"Oh cool. I'll have to introduce you to Nash and Cambrielle then. They're in our house too and know all about that." Scarlett turned to me next, an expectant look on her face. "So if you're the sporty one, does that mean you're going out for any of the girls' teams this year?"

"I'm hoping to try out for the girls' basketball team this winter," I said with a shrug, trying to seem like I didn't care too much if I made the team.

"Nice!" Scarlett said. "I'm on the girls' volleyball team right now, but basketball is my first love."

"Oh fun." My cheeks warmed at the prospect of already getting to know someone who had similar interests as me. "What position do you play?"

"I was the forward last year, so I'm hoping coach will put me there again," Scarlett said. "What about you?"

"I was the point guard at our last school, but I know that with coming in when there's already an established team that I'll be lucky just to get a spot on the roster."

"Our point guard actually graduated last spring," Scarlett said. "So I'm sure Coach Jenkins will be excited to have you try out."

"That would be awesome."

You know, as long as I earned grades high enough to even try out in the first place.

When my mom had applied for us to come to her alma mater, I almost didn't get accepted because my GPA was lower than they liked for such a prestigious school.

Eden Falls Academy was serious about their students education and only wanted to accept students who would fit into their high academic standards—they wanted to make sure they could continue to boast a ninety percent acceptance rate to all the Ivy League schools in the New England area.

But after a lot of back and forth between my mom and the headmistress, they came to the agreement that if I put extra effort into my math class this year—meaning I met with a tutor twice a week to keep my grade up—then I could join Elyse at the academy.

It was embarrassing that I hadn't even started the school year and was already set up for extra help with math, but I guess if Elyse could say that I got the athletic genes when our egg split, I could also say that Elyse had gotten the math genes.

So humiliating or not, I was already set up to meet with my new math tutor in the library after school tomorrow.

I just hoped it wasn't some hoity-toity rich snob that made me feel dumber than I already did.

Scarlett led us out of the girls' locker room, through the gym and across the hall to a long room with weight lifting machines and free weights lined up along the walls. When we stepped on to the padded black floor, I saw there were already a few guys who looked about our age at the other end of the room lifting weights.

"This is the weight room, obviously," Scarlett gestured to the various black and white machines beside us. "We have PE every day, but if you want to get some strength training in during your free time, this is open from six in the morning until nine at night for you to use."

I looked around at the various machines, not having the slightest idea of what I would even begin to do in here. I had never taken a weights class at my old school and had definitely never had a pass to a gym before, but I was intrigued and would probably try to find a time to sneak down here when there weren't other people to watch me fumble my way around the machines.

"Scarlett Caldwell?" A deep voice sounded from across the room, taking my attention. "Is that you?"

"Mack!" Scarlett turned her gaze to the owner of the voice, a huge grin lifting her cheeks. And in the next moment she was bounding toward a tall guy with rich brown skin, wearing a maroon stringer tank top that showed off his well-defined biceps.

"Do you think that's her boyfriend?" I whispered to Elyse as Scarlett enthusiastically hugged the guy she'd called Mack.

"I don't know," Elyse said, seeming to eye Mack's toned arms. "But if that's what all the guys at this school look like, I don't think I'll be complaining too much about transferring here."

"Me neither." I looked Mack over again. He was so tall, at least six-foot five from the looks of how he towered over Scarlett. And yes, he was super cute.

"Ava and Elyse," Scarlett said, turning back to my sister and me after pulling away from the giant beside her. "This is Mack."

I stepped forward, holding my hand out to him. "Hi Mack, I'm Ava."

"Ava?" He shook my hand, his large one engulfing mine. "Nice to meet you."

Elyse introduced herself next, and then Mack narrowed his dark brown eyes at us both. "So do you two always dress alike?"

"Not all the time," I said, looking down at the pink t-shirt with the graphic of a blue whale on it that matched Elyse's. "Just whenever we want to make a statement."

"I like it." Mack's big lips lifted into a crooked grin. "Though, hate to break it to you, but everyone at this school dresses alike. So you might need to find a new way to make a statement." He winked, and I knew immediately that I was going to like this Mack guy. He seemed like he was the kind of guy who could joke around with anybody.

"I guess we'll just have to find another way to stand out then," Elyse said, and I didn't miss the sparkle in her eyes as she looked up at the handsome stranger.

Mack turned his gaze to my sister, looking her over from head to toe. "Somehow I don't think you standing out is going to be a problem."

And in that moment I really hoped, for my sister's sake, that Scarlett and Mack were just friends because I really didn't want Scarlett to hate us after seeing the sparks between him and my twin.

When I glanced over to Scarlett to make sure she wasn't staring daggers at us, I was relieved to see that she had instead turned her focus to the two guys just racking their weights behind Mack.

"Carter. Hunter," she called, waving her hand. "Come meet my new friends before you start your next set."

A guy with dirty blond hair turned to look at us over his shoulder, and when our gazes met, my heart did a little flip-flop because...wow. He was gorgeous. Totally my type: Tall. Aqua blue eyes. Square jawline. An athletic build. Warm tan skin.

Yeah, he might even be cuter than the male model I'd been crushing on since my mom's fashion show.

I drew in a quick breath, hoping no one had noticed how I'd stopped breathing for a second and then made my gaze move to the other guy with chestnut colored hair approaching us.

But as the two guys moved closer, all I could think about was how maybe Elyse was right after all. Maybe transferring to a school full of extremely good-looking guys might just be the best thing that ever happened to us.

The guy with short chestnut hair held his hand out to Elyse

first. "Hi, I'm Hunter," he said in a deep voice. "Welcome to Eden Falls."

She shook his hand and told him her name, and then he shook my hand next.

"I'm Ava," I said. "It's great to meet you."

"Likewise." He nodded. "It's been a while since we've gotten new seniors to our house, so I'm sure everyone will be excited to meet you when school starts tomorrow."

I smiled, grateful for the positive comments. "I'm excited to get to know everyone."

Especially the tall, deliciously handsome guy behind you.

As if reading my mind, Hunter turned and gestured to Mr. Hottie McHot-Hot behind him. "And this is Carter. He's a senior too."

"Nice to meet you, Carter," I said, feeling all jittery with nerves.

But instead of offering his hand to shake in greeting like the other guys had, Carter simply folded his arms across his defined chest and gave us a quick nod. "Good to meet you." Then turning to look back at his friends he said, "Ready for the next set?"

Okaaaay, I thought, rocking back on my heels at his immediate dismissal.

So maybe not all the people at this school would be as welcoming as Scarlett, Mack and Hunter.

Mack must have noticed my discomfort because when Carter and Hunter went back to their weights and Scarlett and Ava walked over to look at the dance studio, he put a hand on my shoulder and said, "Don't take Carter's one track mind personally. He's just the kind of person who likes to focus on one thing at a time."

I furrowed my brow, not understanding. "What do you mean?"

Mack lifted one of his broad shoulders. "Let me just put it this way. If he's marked a workout in his planner from 3:30 to 4:15, you can bet that he will work out from exactly 3:30 to 4:15 with only thirty seconds to a minute break between each set."

"So he's very regimented and likes to stick to a specific routine?" I asked.

"Precisely," Mack said, his big lips forming into a smile. "But he makes time for socializing too."

"As in he probably wrote, 'Work out with Mack and Hunter' into this planner of his and considered it bro bonding time?"

Mack lifted his ball cap from his head, rubbed his hand across his short, curly hair and said, "I mean, I didn't look at his schedule for today `or anything, but yeah, knowing him, that's probably what he wrote."

"Well, maybe we'll have to teach him to add a few minutes of wiggle room into his calendar here and there so he can make a better first impression when he's meeting new strangers."

Mack looked back to where Hunter was spotting Carter as he started a rep using the bench press. "I'll make sure to tell him that one of the cute new girls says he needs to be more flexible." And when he shot me a flirtatious wink, my cheeks heated.

Had this tall, dark and handsome hottie just said I was cute?

And then winked at me?

I was just trying to think of a witty response to his comments when Scarlett and Elyse returned.

"Ready to see the girls' dormitory?" Scarlett asked.

"Um, sure." I tucked a lock of my light brown hair behind my ear. "That would be great."

"Great," Scarlett said before turning to head out of the door we'd come through with Elyse trailing behind.

Before I followed them I turned back to Mack who still hadn't returned to his friends and said, "It was great to meet you, Mack. I'm sure I'll be seeing you around."

"I'll make sure to save a spot for you and your sister at my table tonight." He winked again.

"Thanks." My cheeks flushed even deeper at his offer. "I guess I'll see you later."

Deciding to end on that high note, I made myself walk away from probably one of the most welcoming and cutest guys I'd ever met before, and went to find Scarlett and Elyse.

Read more of The Charade at: http://mybook.to/TheCharade

Also By Judy Corry

Eden Falls Academy Series:

The Charade (Ava and Carter)

The Facade (Cambrielle and Mack)

The Ruse — (Elyse and Asher)

The Confidant — (Scarlett and Hunter)

The Confession — (Kiara and Nash)

Ridgewater High Series:

When We Began (Cassie and Liam)

Meet Me There (Ashlyn and Luke)

Don't Forget Me (Eliana and Jess)

It Was Always You (Lexi and Noah)

My Second Chance (Juliette and Easton)

My Mistletoe Mix-Up (Raven and Logan)

Forever Yours (Alyssa and Jace)

Standalone YA

Protect My Heart (Emma and Arie)

Kissing The Boy Next Door (Lauren and Wes)

Rich and Famous Series:

Assisting My Brother's Best Friend (Kate and Drew)

Hollywood and Ivy (Ivy and Justin)

Her Football Star Ex (Emerson and Vincent)

Friend Zone to End Zone (Arianna and Cole)

Stolen Kisses from a Rock Star (Maya and Landon)

ABOUT THE AUTHOR

Judy Corry is the USA Today Bestselling Author of YA and Contemporary Romance. She writes romance because she can't get enough of the feeling of falling in love. She's known for writing heart-pounding kisses, endearing characters, and hard-won happily ever afters.

She lives in Southern Utah with the boy who took her to Prom, their four rambunctious children, two dogs and a cat. She's addicted to love stories, dark chocolate and chai lattes.

Printed in Great Britain
by Amazon

13297230R00181